RUBY, Laura

The boy who could fly

Also by Laura Ruby

In the Wall and the Wing stories:
The Invisible Girl

For older readers:
Good Girls

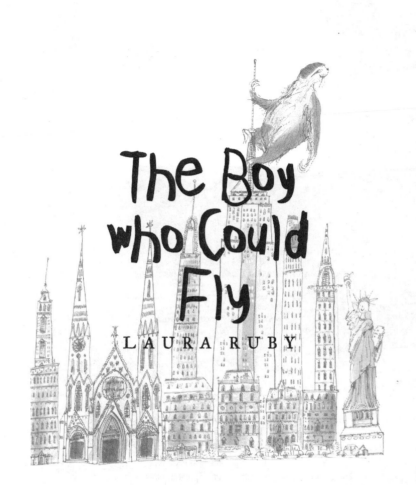

The Boy who Could Fly

LAURA RUBY

HarperCollins *Children's Books*

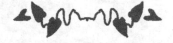

First published in paperback in Great Britain by HarperCollins *Children's Books* 2007
HarperCollins *Children's Books* is a division of HarperCollins*Publishers* Ltd
77-85 Fulham Palace Road, Hammersmith, London W6 8JB

The HarperCollins Children's Books website address is:

www.harpercollinschildrensbooks.co.uk

1

Copyright © Laura Ruby 2007

ISBN-13: 978-0-00-721010-7
ISBN-10: 0-00-721010-8

Laura Ruby reserves the right to be identified as the author of the work.

Printed and bound in England by Clays Ltd, St Ives plc

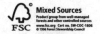

Mixed Sources
Product group from well-managed
forests and other controlled sources
www.fsc.org Cert no. SW-COC-1806
© 1996 Forest Stewardship Council

FSC is a non-profit international organisation established to promote the
responsible management of the world's forests. Products carrying the FSC
label are independently certified to assure consumers that they come
from forests that are managed to meet the social, economic and
ecological needs of present and future generations.

Find out more about HarperCollins and the environment at
www.harpercollins.co.uk/green

For Steve, for making order out of chaos.

- Laura

"I am always at a loss to know how much to believe of my own stories."

Washington Irving,
from Tales of a Traveller, 1824

The Chapter Before the First

Mr Fuss Makes a Fuss

He was too old for this, far too old. The storm drain was cold and damp and smelled of mildew. A thin trickle of water that wended its way down the concrete tunnel splashed each time he planted one of his feet. At first, he'd tried flying, but found it too exhausting to do for very long. Instead, he'd settled for this ungainly shuffle-run. The floor was slippery and he'd already fallen once, his knee bleeding through a tear in one trouser leg. (Lord, how he hated wearing trousers.)

Still, he struggled on. In one arm, he held what looked like a human hand mounted on a black marble base; in the other, a tiny gilded birdcage in which a blue budgie twittered and sang. Various other items bulged in the pockets of his jacket. A white kitten popped her head from his breast pocket, saw where she was, squeaked, and pulled her head back in.

Where are we going? The Answer Hand said, using sign language.

The Professor grunted. "I hate it when you ask questions you know the answers to."

The cats aren't happy.

Behind The Professor, more than a hundred cats hopped daintily around the trickle of water and wrinkled their noses at the mouldy smell.

"Are cats ever happy?"

You'd be surprised, said The Answer Hand. *Sun spots on carpets make them happy. A good long nap. Chewing on the houseplants. Sitting on the laps of people who can't stand them.* The Answer Hand pointed accusingly with its index finger before beginning again: *Cats don't like wet things. They don't like stinky things. The cats*, The Hand said, *are very annoyed.*

The Professor glanced back and had to agree, though he would never say so. "I thought you weren't supposed to give any answers unless I asked you a specific question?"

You asked if cats were ever happy and I told you. As for the rest, maybe I'm getting tired of waiting to be asked.

"Perfect," The Professor replied. "That's just what I need."

What you need is to move faster.

"You are so helpful. Where's the man now?"

He's still a few kilometres back, The Answer Hand signed. *But gaining. He dislikes you intensely.*

"I figured that out myself."

Amazing! Well, that's something to celebrate. Which we could do if we were back at home instead of running through the bowels of the city because we lost the most powerful object we'd ever invented.

"Who's this 'we' that you're talking about? *I* invented the pen."

And then you lost it. And that's not the only thing you lost. I wouldn't be so proud of myself if I were you.

"I'm not proud of myself," The Professor snapped.

Also something to celebrate, signed The Answer Hand. The Professor was astonished that something that didn't even have its own face could achieve such magnificent sarcasm.

"At least we know the crows have the pen," said The Professor.

I told you who had the pen. But that's not going to help much if we can't get to them before they do something stupid. You know how they are about shiny things. I think you need to reconsider my plan.

"It's too complicated. It will never work. Besides, you also told me that the book is in the library. It's safe."

Is it? said The Hand.

"Of course it is," The Professor huffed. "Nobody can awaken the book unless they use the pen, and then only if they write precisely the correct thing. Only if the pen wants it to happen. And the odds of that are—"

Fifteen trillion to one, The Hand said.

"See? Impossible."

For once, The Answer Hand didn't answer. Thoughtfully, it rubbed its thumb and middle finger together. Then: *In this city, nothing is impossible. For example, take a look behind you.* The Professor turned to see a large dark figure moving obscenely fast through the tunnel. The figure wasn't flying. He was walking briskly on the *side* of the tunnel, his body perfectly parallel to the wet floor. As The Professor watched, the figure strode around to the top of the tunnel, so that he was walking upside down.

How does he keep his trench coat from flopping around his ears? The Answer Hand asked.

"I thought you knew the answer to everything," The Professor said.

I don't know the answer to that.

"You're scaring me," said The Professor.

It's about time.

The budgie stopped twittering. Some of the cats began to growl.

"Is he afraid of cats?" The Professor asked hopefully.

No, signed The Answer Hand. *Not even a little.*

"Darn," whispered The Professor.

Things were getting out of control, thought Mr Fuss. And Mr Fuss didn't like when things were out of control. What made Mr Fuss fussy: messes, troubles, unruliness, vexation or chaos.

In short, Mr Fuss didn't like fuss.

Odd, then, that he had chosen to live and work in this vast and sparkling city, this city at the centre of the universe, the city that was the very definition of messes, troubles, unruliness, vexation, and chaos. Odder still that it was *his* job to tidy things up.

What we do for money, thought Mr Fuss.

He could see the little man with his ridiculous green hair and his pathetic army of felines up ahead. Good. One thing he could cross off his list for the day. As Mr Fuss walked, he pulled his day planner and a tiny pencil from his pocket. He read through his list:

1. Bull in china shop.
2. Runaway carousel horses.
3. "Magic" pretzels for sale on the corner of Sixth and Thirty-third (if you ate one, you could understand any language spoken to you, though effects were temporary).

4. Fortune-teller on Upper East Side telling actual fortunes.

5. The Professor.

Mr Fuss put a check mark next to this last line and tucked the day planner and pencil back in his pocket.

The Professor started to run, if you could call the awkward hobbling of an ancient man *running*. Really. Such a waste of time and effort. Where was the man going to go? This storm drain went on for kilometres. Plus, high tide was coming. Any minute now The Professor and his nasty little menagerie would be washed out to sea. If it had been up to Mr Fuss, that's exactly what he'd want to happen, too, a tidy ending to an untidy person. But his employer had other ideas.

Mr Fuss's phone rang. Sighing, Mr Fuss flipped it open. "Fuss here," he said. "Yes, I have him. Well, nearly. He's about fifty metres ahead of me. I won't lose him." There was a pause and Mr Fuss rolled his queer, amber-coloured eyes. "Of course I won't *hurt* the man. Why would I hurt the man?" Another pause. "But that was an accident." More eye rolling. "And that was an accident too. Well, perhaps that wasn't *entirely* an accident, but... Yes, yes. I promise, no more accidents. Yes, sir, we are clear. Clear as glass. Clear as water. Clear as air. Clear as...." He looked at the phone, frowning. His employer had hung up.

That was another thing about this city that Mr Fuss couldn't stand: everyone was so unspeakably rude.

The Professor had sped up a bit, the awkward hobbling now a sort of crazed shambling.

Funny that he still gets reception even seventy floors below ground, signed The Answer Hand.

"Yes," said The Professor. "Funny."

Almost high tide, said The Answer Hand. *What are you going to do?*

"You know the answer to that." The Professor looked to his right, where a rusted grate sealed off another tunnel. "Can you open it?"

No, The Hand replied. *But the budgie can get through the openings in the grate. And so can the cats. The tunnel goes all the way to the surface. They'll be fine.*

The Professor nodded. He heard the distant roar of water rushing. He unlatched the door on the gilded birdcage. The budgie flew in circles around The Professor's head. "Go," he told the bird. "Find Gurl. Find Bug. Do what you can."

The budgie, who spoke English, French, Italian, German, Polish, pig Latin, and could request a cab in Croatian, said, "Ood-gay uck-lay!" before darting through the grate. The army of cats followed suit, shrinking their seemingly boneless bodies through the slats, mcwling their farewells as they did. Last to leave was the tiny white kitten, who licked The Professor's face before disappearing.

The Professor watched them go. "Well," he said to The Answer Hand. "It looks like it's just you and me."

Yep, signed The Answer Hand.

"That guy's going to be really mad," said The Professor mildly. Mr Fuss was still upside down in the tunnel, but now he was the one running. Underneath the man, a frothing wall of water surged towards The Professor.

He's mad all right, signed The Answer Hand, just before the water hit them.

Mr Fuss punched open the manhole cover and climbed up on to the street, ignoring the cars that swerved to avoid him. As The Professor had predicted, Mr Fuss was mad. More than mad. He was irked, vexed, and most definitely put out. He had never thought that the crazy old man would just allow the tide to sweep him out to sea, and with him The Answer Hand, the location of the pen, and certain other items of interest. His employer would not be happy, that was certain. Even if it was an accident. (And it absolutely was an accident.)

Pushing through the crowds of would-be flyers – fools! – he strode across the street and found a bench. He sat, pulled his phone from his pocket and hit speed dial. "It's me," he said. "He's gone." Pause. "No! High tide rolled in and took The

Professor with it." Another long pause. "What do you mean, forget about it?" Mr Fuss's eyes widened. "What about the pen?" His fingers scratched at the wood of the bench, dragging up paint and slivers of wood. "Yes, sir, but what if the pen isn't at The Professor's apartment? What if he gave it to someone else to hold for him? What if he's invented other things? There's no telling how much chaos—" The splinters of wood bit into the tips of Mr Fuss's fingers, but he didn't seem to notice. "I *know* there are plenty of other things to do, but-"

He rifled through his pockets with his free hand and found his day planner, in which several newspaper articles were clipped. These he unfolded. "There were two children he spent some time with several months ago. Maybe he told them something. Maybe—" He made a fist and pounded the seat of the bench, but didn't change his tone. "Yes, I understand. I won't approach the children." He shook his head no while saying, "Yes, I will move on to the next item on my list. I will not jeopardise my employment. I won't—" He looked at the phone. His employer had hung up. Again.

Mr Fuss squeezed the phone so hard that he crushed the metal. Then he tossed the phone over his shoulder. His employer was losing his touch. How were they supposed to keep control of this city if there was no follow-up? No follow through?

No, thought Mr Fuss. This would not do at all. If his

employer was not willing to step up to the plate, then Mr Fuss would have to take matters into his own hands. And he wouldn't have to jeopardise his employment, either. As a matter of fact, if Mr Fuss were to find the pen on his own, he was certain that he would be compensated handsomely. Perhaps he'd even take his employer's job.

A small, unpleasant smile played at Mr Fuss's lips as he consulted his notes and the newspaper clippings. The girl was living with her ludicrously wealthy parents now, and the boy was starring in television adverts. Wasn't that special? There was a chance that one or the other had information about The Professor and his various inventions and could be convinced to give that information up. It was a small chance, but it was one that must be taken.

But the children would be difficult to get to. Freelancers, unfortunately, would have to be hired. Mr Fuss could not afford to be associated with the plan until the mission was completed.

Mr Fuss refolded the articles and clipped them into the planner. The planner then went back into the coat pocket. Suddenly, Mr Fuss was very tired. And in addition to formulating some sort of plan to find the pen, he still had four other unfinished tasks on his list for today. Ah well. He could go get himself a "magic" pretzel first. And he would take the subway uptown. Unlike most people who lived in the city, Mr Fuss enjoyed the subway. It was quiet and gloomy and most of the idiots who thought they could fly didn't bother with it. He didn't even mind the alligators. Sweet, really, when you got to know them. Mr Fuss took a moment to admire his own alligator-skin boots.

Mr Fuss stood up from the bench, walked over to the Bleecker Street subway station and trudged down the steps.

There, at the bottom of the steps, was a leather-clad, Mohawk-haired, combat boot–wearing Punk spray-painting a message on the wall: SID WAS HERE. Next to this, the Punk had painted something that looked like a beetle or maybe a happy face with a birthday hat. It was difficult to tell. Still, the Punk was concentrating on this bit of nonsense as if it were the finest work of art that had ever been painted.

Hmmm, thought Mr Fuss. *This could work.*

After about ten minutes, the Punk noticed Mr Fuss. "Whatcha lookin' at?" he snarled, his wolfish eyes black as, er, black.

Mr Fuss smiled politely. "You're quite the artist."

The Punk blinked. "Not that anyone appreciates it."

"Oh," said Mr Fuss, "I am a great appreciator of art like yours. Outsider art – art produced by those people outside the traditional art establishment."

"I'm not in any *tradition*," the Punk barked. "I'm not in any *establishment*."

"Of course you're not," said Mr Fuss smoothly. "You

know, I believe you could make a lot of money. If you knew the right people."

"I could?"

"Oh, absolutely."

The Punk set his spray can on the ground. "Are you the right people?"

Mr Fuss smiled. "I am exactly the right people."

Chapter 1

The Saddest Little Rich Girl in the Universe

Her given name was Georgetta Rose Aster Bloomington, and she was, literally, The Richest Girl in the Universe. Most people would find this to be a pleasant situation involving lots of shopping and diamonds and yachting around the Mediterranean, but not Georgetta Rose Aster Bloomington. She didn't care much about having more money than everyone else.

But other people cared.

A lot.

People like Roma Radisson.

Roma Radisson was officially The Second-richest Girl in the Universe. And she was *not* happy about it. Roma was doing her very best to make sure that everybody, especially Georgetta Rose Aster Bloomington, knew it.

"I hope you all found the dinosaurs as fascinating as I did! Next up is the Hall of Primitive Mammals," said Ms Storia as she led the girls of the Prince School through the American Museum of Natural History.

"*Primitive* Mammals," Roma repeated. "Well, Georgetta Bloomington should be right at home."

As the other girls snickered, Georgetta, or Georgie, as her parents called her, flushed angrily and looked down at the floor. She had been at the Prince School for just three weeks, but she had already spent many days flushing angrily and staring at the floors. And now here she was, on her very first school trip, counting dots in the tiles while she tried to follow her parents' advice. *Just ignore it.* But *just ignoring it* wasn't going so well.

"I hear that those ancient mammals were giants, too," Roma said. "Maybe there's a giant monkey in there. Maybe it's your long-lost aunt."

You're the monkey, thought Georgie. Except that was too stupid to say. Also, an insult to monkeys. *Dunkleosteus*, a vicious sea predator with jaws so sharp they could cut through bone – now that was more like Roma. Georgie almost said so, but she knew that just saying the word *Dunkleosteus* would get her labelled the worst sort of egghead-nerd-freak. At the Prince School, it was not cool to know things.

"That's enough, Roma," said Ms Storia, as if that was going to stop Roma. Roma had been keeping up a steady stream of insults since they came to the museum. Georgie was related to the walrus. Georgie was related to the squid (which Roma had wrongly called an octopus. Georgie made the mistake of pointing out the obvious differences between a squid and an octopus, something that Roma said only proved her point).

But this time Roma shrugged and flounced into the Hall of Primitive Mammals, her fire-red hair a beacon for the others. Wherever Roma went, the other girls of the Prince School quickly followed. The only one who didn't was the senior girl acting as a chaperone, who seemed to prefer the long-dead animals on display to the pack of princesses she was supposed to be chaperoning.

Georgie tried to hide in the middle of the pack, tuning out Ms Storia's talk about how the platypus had so many primitive features it was called a "living fossil" and wasn't that just fascinating? Georgie wished she were back at home with her parents, discussing their plans for the day, the way they had all winter and into the spring. Some days, they went to one of the city's many museums. Most days, they went to the library and picked out books for Georgie to read. Even though The Richest Girl in the Universe could have purchased every book in the city and still have enough left over to buy a few planets, Georgie thought it was lovely to be able to borrow any book you wanted, and then bring it back and exchange it for another.

Before you think Georgie a skull short of a full skeleton, you must understand that there were very good reasons for Georgie's lack of interest in the truly mind-boggling amount of money she had. You see, Georgetta Rose Aster Bloomington wasn't always The Richest Girl in the Universe. As a matter of fact, she wasn't always known as Georgetta Rose Aster Bloomington. Just six months before, Georgetta Rose Aster Bloomington was a girl named Gurl who lived in a miserable orphanage. There, she spent much of her time daydreaming about a happy life, a real life, without ever expecting to live one. But reality turned out to be more mind-boggling than any daydream. Half a year ago, she learned a lot of things about her life, among them:

a) That she had been kidnapped by the gangster Sweetcheeks Grabowski when she was just a baby.

b) That she was subsequently *lost* by the gangster Sweetcheeks Grabowski because of a special power she had, the power to turn herself invisible.

c) That she was found by a homeless woman and

given to an orphanage called Hope House for the Homeless and Hopeless.

d) That Georgie escaped Hope House for the Homeless and Hopeless with the help of her good friend Bug, who turned out to be none other than the son of the gangster Sweetcheeks Grabowski.

e) That her real parents were The Richest Couple in the Universe.

And finally:

f) That this was an awful lot for a person to take in and still remain sane.

But Georgie was doing her best to adjust to her new life as well as she could, and that included trying to ignore the snotty second-, third- and fourth-richest girls in the universe and paying attention on school trips. Up ahead, Ms Storia was yammering enthusiastically about the development of marsupials. At least that was better than the teachers at Hope House for the Homeless and Hopeless. The only animals they ever wanted to talk about were the ones that could fly.

"Next up," Ms Storia said, "is the Hall of Flight! We'll see birds, of course, but also flying squirrels and insects! And we'll see how scientists are studying the evolution of human flight! Isn't that fascinating?"

Sigh.

"We are going to learn so many important things!"

Uh-huh, thought Georgie. The most important thing that Georgie had learned in the last six months was the fact that money does not buy happiness. Because as happy as Georgie was with her parents, there were many other things that made Georgie unhappy.

"Ow!" said Bethany Tiffany when Georgie accidentally crashed into her.

"Sorry," Georgie muttered.

"That is the third time you've bumped into me!" Bethany said, rubbing her elbow as if Georgie had hit it with a hammer.

"I said sorry."

"You're *always* bumping into people and you're *always* sorry."

Georgie clenched her teeth to refrain from saying something rude about Bethany's tiara. Georgie'd had a growth spurt that had happened overnight and her body wasn't her own any more. The doctor said it was from good nutrition and seemed pleased by this turn of events. Georgie, whose joints ached and whose feet grew so fast that her parents couldn't keep her in shoes, wasn't as pleased. She felt like a marionette, all arms and legs jangling and none of them ever under her control.

This wouldn't be so bad if she wasn't a leadfoot – a person who couldn't fly at all. Apparently, you can have more money than everyone in the universe put together, but if you can't fly even a smidge, well, then you might as well be living in Hope House for the Homeless and Hopeless, eating lard on toast and getting pounded by a girl called Digger (who got her name because she picked her nose). And it didn't matter that Georgie had a special power all her own. The fact that she could turn herself invisible – that she was the first person in more than a century who could – was the reason she had been kidnapped by Sweetcheeks Grabowski in the first place. Her parents didn't want to take the risk ever again. They had made her promise that she wouldn't use the power or even mention it. They had told her to trust no one with her secrets. And that meant that it was impossible to make a real friend.

"Fly, I mean, *walk* with us, Georgetta."

The red-haired goddess herself, Roma Radisson, appeared next to Bethany Tiffany and London England. Georgie was immediately suspicious.

"Georgie," Roma simpered. "We were just kidding before. We didn't mean anything by it."

Right, thought Georgie. Roma meant every spiteful word she said. But then, even with everything Georgie had been through, she was a deeply curious girl, the kind of girl who watches the world and misses nothing; she wanted to know why Roma was talking to her. And though she would never have admitted it, Georgie was also a hopeful girl. In the back of her mind, a little voice told her that maybe, *maybe*, if she were nice to Roma, if she could joke and laugh like the rest of the girls, Roma might be nice to her.

"Tell us," Roma said. "Were you really kidnapped when you were a baby?"

Even though the story had been in the papers for months and months, everyone always asked the same questions over and over again, as if Georgie would suddenly answer them differently. "I was kidnapped by Sweetcheeks Grabowski. He's in jail."

"Amazing!" said London. "And is it true that no one could find you for years and years, and you lived in an orphanage practically your whole life?"

Georgie nodded. "I didn't even know my real name."

"Speaking of real," London said, eyeing Georgie's thick silver ponytail and fluffing her own blond curls with her fingers, "is that your real hair?"

"Whose hair would it be?" Georgie joked.

The other girls gave each other funny looks, and not the kind that indicated they thought Georgie's joke was amusing. "Well, anyway," said Roma, fanning the air. "I bet that orphanage was just so grimy and horrible. I did a TV special once where I had to meet some poor people. They sent me to a farm. I had to pick tomatoes. Awful! I had dirt under my fingernails and everything!"

"At least you could have eaten the tomatoes," Georgie said. "At the orphanage, I was always hungry." The girls gaped at her. So much for joking. Since Georgie was always trying not to reveal too much, she was prone to saying strange and unfunny things. (When you've spent years in an orphanage shunned by everyone but a cat, you're prone to saying strange and unfunny things.) Georgie cleared her throat. "So, you were on TV? Was it, uh, cool?"

"She's been on TV thousands of times," Bethany said, eyes so green that Georgie wondered if Bethany had ordered them from a boutique. "You haven't seen Roma's advert for Cherry Bomb lip balm?"

"Or the video from her new CD, *Don't Get Up, Get Down?*" said London.

"Or the ads for Jump Jeans?" said Roma.

"No," said Georgie. "I don't watch much TV."

"What do you do?" Roma demanded.

"Well," Georgie said. "I've been reading a lot."

"Reading!" London said, her sky-blue eyes wide. "Why would you do that?"

Roma admired her French manicure, glancing askance at London. "Have you ever thought, London, that she's been reading my memoir, *Fabulousity?*"

"Oh!" said London. "Right. That's a different story."

Georgie didn't believe that *fabulousity* was an actual

word, but she decided not to say so. Instead, she said another wrong thing. "I've been reading *From the Mixed-up Files of Mrs Basil E Frankweiler*."

"The mixed up *what*?" London said.

"That's a kid's book!" said Bethany in horror.

Georgie was tempted to point out that, technically, they were still considered kids, at least by adults too dim to know better, so a "kid" reading a kid's book wasn't so surprising, but somehow knew that wasn't the right thing to say. She was also tempted to tell the girls how thrilling it was to pore over all the books she'd missed reading as a child, but then she knew that wasn't the right thing to say either. Georgie lumbered along, trying to figure out something fabulous and witty to talk about. *Mechanical monkeys stole my memory?* No, too crazy. *My cat Noodle is really unusual, even for a cat. She's what they call a Riddle, see, and she can put you in a trance if she wants to...* no, too childish. Um, *there are giant rats with filed teeth living underground that call themselves The Sewer Rats of Satan. They're obsessed with kittens.* No, too bizarre.

"So tell us about Bug Grabowski," Roma said, stopping to stare at yet another mounted skeleton of something or another. "Is he really Sweetcheeks's son?"

"Yes."

"Oooh! A gangster's boy! How dangerous!" said London.

"Well," said Georgie. "It was until they threw Sweetcheeks in jail. Now he's just a regular boy."

"Not such a regular boy," said Bethany. "Is he your boyfriend?"

Georgie felt herself flush. "No, he's not my boyfriend."

"Did you see that advert he did for Rocket Boards?" Bethany said. "Those muscles!"

Ever since Bug was declared the youngest winner of the citywide Flyfest competition, he'd been spending hours and hours every day working out with his personal trainer. Like Georgie, Bug had also grown some centimetres... wider. His biceps bulged and his stomach now looked as if someone had carved furrows in it. Georgie still hadn't decided whether she liked it or not, but it was clear that Roma, London and Bethany did.

"He's got the most interesting face," Roma said, which, to Georgie, was a polite way of saying that Bug looked a lot like a bug. "If he's not your boyfriend," said Roma, "you won't mind setting me up."

"Setting you up?" said Georgie. "But..." She trailed off. She wanted to say that she never saw Bug herself, now that he was so famous. And then she wanted to say that Bug was just another reason she knew money couldn't buy happiness. That the last time she did see him, months ago, things hadn't gone so well. He couldn't seem to remember her real name and kept calling her Gurl, and she didn't know what to say about his father being... well, his father. She asked him if he wanted to go flying and he bragged about a late-night photo shoot he'd been on and how that had made him too tired to do anything. He asked her if she wanted to turn them both invisible and wander around the city, but she told him that her parents didn't want her to do that any more. They'd sat at the Bloomingtons' huge dining room table and pushed the chef's food around their plates in silence.

But Georgie wouldn't talk about any of this with Roma, London, and Bethany. And even if Georgie wanted to talk to them, they wouldn't have given her the chance.

"What?" said Roma. "You don't think I'm good enough for him?"

You're not, Georgie thought. "No!" Georgie said. "It's just..."

"It's just what?" Roma snapped.

"Nothing," Georgie said. "I meant—"

"Just because you're rich doesn't mean that you're all that, OK?" Roma said, her voice icy. "Anyway, you don't have *that* much money."

A hot flash of annoyance made Georgie blurt, "I'm The Richest Girl in the Universe."

"Oh!" said Roma, lavender eyes blazing. "Well. You might have more money than most people, but you've never actually done anything."

Georgie, who had rescued her cat from an army of giant rat men, unwillingly stolen for a matron with a plastic surgery obsession, endured a makeover by a magical Personal Assistant named Jules, defeated a cabal of Punks, escaped a narcissistic gangster (twice) who just happened to be a former child model, evaded a zipper-faced pterodactyl, and befriended a genius Professor with grass for hair, said, "I've done a lot of things!"

Roma put her hands on her hips. "Have you made your own CD? Written a book? Had your own line of deodorants?"

Georgie, who didn't think that having your own line of deodorants was anything to boast about, said, "No, but—"

"You can't even fly!" exclaimed Roma. "You're a leadfoot! And I *know* you haven't trademarked your own slogan. Have you ever heard anyone say: 'That's so fab'? Well, I own that."

"Own what?"

"The words! I made up that phrase all by myself!"

"But anyone can say that!" Georgie protested. Oops. Roma got so red in the face that she resembled a Roma tomato.

"Fine," she said, glaring at Georgie with her lavender eyes. "I only invited you to walk with us because I was trying to be nice. I won't bother any more!" She and the three girls sped ahead of Georgie, Roma announcing: "Georgetta Bloomington in is love. With *herself*. So *not* fab™." The three girls flew off as if Georgie was just another dead thing the museum had mounted on a stick.

Georgie looked down at the floor and resisted the urge to call them all a bunch of *Dunkleosteuses*. Of course, Roma and her friends had only wanted to grill her about Bug because Roma wanted a new boyfriend. Who knew that the Prince School would turn out to be so much like Hope House for the Homeless and Hopeless?

Georgie paused in front of the skeleton of a spiny anteater. *Oh, get a grip, Gurl*, she told herself. So the other girls at the Prince School didn't like her. And so what that Bug was running around the city, starring in adverts for Foot Fetish foot powder and Cheeky Monkey shaving cream, even though he didn't shave yet? So what that he hadn't called her in weeks and that was only for five minutes to tell her about the film roles he'd been offered? So what that the only time she got to see him was in magazine pictures? He was busy, that's all. That didn't mean they weren't friends any more.

Did it?

Georgie realised that she'd got pretty far behind the group and had to run quickly to catch up. And that, you see, was her biggest mistake. When one has experienced a serious and dramatic growth spurt that has caused one's feet and limbs to lengthen far beyond one's brain's ability to compensate, doing *anything* quickly is unwise. Georgie tripped over someone's outstretched leg and crashed into an unfinished exhibit entitled "Mega Marsupials". Georgie's own mega-sized limbs took out the partially-assembled bones of a giant wombat, which then landed in a painful, thunderous heap on top of her. Georgie was dazed, but not nearly dazed enough to block out the loud, mocking laughter of the Prince Girls, Roma Radisson's loudest of all.

Yes, her name was Georgetta Rose Aster Bloomington, and she was, literally, The Richest Girl in the Universe.

But all she wanted to do was disappear.

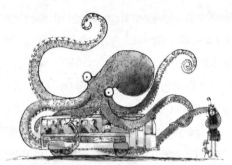

Chapter 2

Eight Arms to Hold You

"Good, good," said the photographer. "Now hold that pose. Hold it, hold it, hooooooold it, just another minute." The camera whirred and clicked.

Bug had been holding his arms over his head in a V – for victory! – for what seemed like hours now. Every muscle in his body ached, the tip of his nose itched, his feet were killing him, and he had spots burned into his retinas from the camera flashes. He never knew standing still could be such hard work.

It was a gorgeous April day – the sky a rich, robin's-egg blue, the sea beyond the docks sparkling as if the surface were sprinkled with gems. A day perfect for flying. Bug was sure that Central Park was packed with people doing just that. The thought made him so wistful that he forgot to stand still; he looked up at the sky and sighed. Not because he wanted to fly, but because he didn't want to. He didn't know people could be this tired and *live*.

"That's gorgeous," said the photographer. "I love it! Now look towards the water; I need a profile shot. Come on, I need you to think regal, OK, Bug? You're a duke! No, you're a king! You're the king of flyers!"

Bug rolled his over-large, buglike eyes, wondering how he could look like the king of flyers with both feet flat on the ground, but he turned his face to the sea anyway. He was being paid a lot of money to do this ad for Skreechers trainers, money that his agent, Harvey "Juju" Fink, said Bug could use. "What about all the money from all those other ads and posters and everything else?" Bug had asked. "What about the Cheeky Monkey campaign?" For that one, Bug had spent hours stuck in a hot bathroom with bitter-tasting shaving cream melting into his mouth. Ugh.

"What other adverts? Those little things? Pennies! Nickels! Dimes!" said Juju, who got his nickname because of his magical ability to promote athletes, and because all of his hair – including lashes and brows – had fallen out all at once on his twenty-fifth birthday. (There are two kinds of juju, superstitious people say. Good *and* bad. Juju seemed to have a little of both.)

"Skreechers trainer company is offering you your biggest contract yet," Juju informed his youngest and most valuable client. "The biggest you could *ever* get, if you never win the Flyfest again."

"What are you talking about?" Bug told him. "I'll win Flyfest again. Wait and see. I'm going to win a whole bunch of Flyfests."

"Of course you will, of course you will," Juju said, his bald wrinkly head and naked eyelids making Bug think of a turtle in a suit. "But don't you want to have another ten million in the bank for a rainy day? Just in case?"

So Bug had signed the papers. Here he was, posing on a dock at South Street Seaport in a pair of gold trainers called "Buggy Gs", trainers the Skreechers people expected to sell all over the world. About thirty metres away, executives from the company watched the photo shoot, relaxing over lobster rolls and late afternoon cocktails, while Bug stood as still as possible and tried to look regal. Juju gave Bug the thumbs-up as he paced back and forth, barking into his mobile phone, and the photographer snapped, snapped, snapped his pictures, darting around Bug like a dragonfly.

It was all deeply boring.

Bug wondered what Gurl was doing. Probably hanging out with her rich friends from the rich school she went to. What was it called? The Princess Academy? Everyone that went there was loaded. Technically, Bug was loaded too, but he didn't enjoy it the way other people seemed to. The only reason he was doing this whole endorsement thing was so that he didn't have to touch his father's money. He didn't want to use a cent of that money – gangster money, hate money, blood money. Bug was not like his father at all. And he was going to prove it to the whole world. He would even prove it to Gurl and her parents, if he ever got a chance to see them. But Gurl was probably having a ball with all the rich girls. She wasn't even calling herself Gurl any more; she was calling herself Georgie, a name that Bug still hadn't got used to. He hadn't seen Gurl – um, Georgie – in months, which made him feel guilty, but not too guilty, because *Georgie* didn't seem to be trying too hard to see Bug. At first, it was because she finally found out who her parents were and she wanted to take the time to get to know them. (Bug understood *that*. He wasn't an *insect*.) But then weeks went by, and then a month, and then the whole winter was gone. What was up with that? What was a person supposed to think?

Exactly what I am thinking, Bug thought. That *Georgie* had better things to do than hang out with the son of Sweetcheeks Grabowski, no matter how many stupid adverts that son had been in.

Bug heaved another sigh, trying to ignore the bright blue sky stretched overhead, trying to ignore his aching arms, trying to pretend he was back home in his apartment (but then, he didn't want to be there either, because no one was there, and who wants to hang out all by yourself with no one to talk to, even if you don't really want to talk, you just want to sleep).

Oh great, thought Bug, *now my ankle itches.* But this itch wasn't really an itch. It was more like a gentle pressure, like a finger poking him. Bug looked down. There was something grey and slimy lying limply across his foot.

"What the..." said Bug. Was it a rope? Where did the rope come from? He tried to shake it off.

"Bug! What are you doing!" shrieked the photographer. "Stand still!"

"There's a rope—" Bug began.

"Who cares?" the photographer shrieked again. "I'm shooting your face now. So stop frowning!"

Bug frowned even more deeply when the grey, slimy rope began to writhe, began to pluck at his shoelaces. He shook his foot again, this time more frantically.

"You're ruining my shots!" the photographer wailed, turning round to look at Juju. "Juju! Tell your boy he's ruining the shots!"

"Bug, baby!" Juju called. "Don't ruin the man's shots." He gave the Skreechers execs a bright, toothy smile, waggling the skin where his brows would normally be.

"These athletes. So twitchy. Can't get 'em to stand still."

One of the executives eyed him with eyes the colour and warmth of polar icecaps. "You better get this one to stand still. We're paying you enough."

But Bug was not standing still. He was staring down at the grey, slimy thing; he was trying to pull away from it.

It looked like a tentacle. Yes, it looked *exactly* like a tentacle. Suckers and everything.

And it was doing more than playing with his laces, it was curling around his foot, it was *grabbing* him by the foot, and it was dragging him towards the edge of the dock.

The photographer threw up his hands and whirled in a dramatic circle. "How am I supposed to work like this? I'm a *professional*! I want to work with *professionals*!"

Juju covered the mouthpiece of his phone, not even looking in Bug's direction. "Bug!" he yelled. "Quit fooling around!"

Bug looked up, a wild and not very regal expression on his face. "I'm not fooling around. Something's got me, something—"

His last words were cut off as the rope that was truly a tentacle jerked Bug right off the dock. He barely had a second to register that he was *in* the water before the tentacle was pulling him *under* the water, into the greyish murk, deeper and deeper. Bug flailed wildly and his lungs burned. His mind screamed silent, hysterical things like *WHAT IS IT?* and *WHAT'S GOT ME?* and *I'M IN THE WATER!! I CAN'T FLY AWAY IN THE WATER!!!* Whatever held his ankle had him in an iron grip as it dragged him down, down, down.

And then, suddenly, it stopped.

Bug had the sensation of dozens of questing fingers running over his face, but he didn't dare open his eyes for fear that he'd see a monster there, a monster with arms for legs and teeth for eyes and hooks for teeth and razors where its lips should be. His mind screamed more hysterical things, but these things weren't words, they were just sounds, just bright bursts in his head, as the arms or legs or suckers of the razor-lipped, hook-toothed thing prodded him like a doctor feeling for swollen glands.

And then, just like that, the thing let him go.

His lungs close to popping, Bug kicked away from the monster and swam up towards the surface of the water. When he got his first lungful of oxygen, he launched his body from the murk like a rocket. Bug hovered in the air a moment before collapsing face-down on to the dock.

"Ow," he said, and coughed.

"Bug," said a stern voice.

Bug flipped to his back, still coughing.

"Bug!"

"What?" Bug managed to say. He opened his eyes, which

had been squeezed shut, to see a great many very angry people glaring down at him.

Juju's wrinkled turtle head was even more wrinkled. "What do you think you're doing?"

"What?" Bug gasped. "What do you mean?"

"What do you mean what do I mean?" Juju said. "If you wanted to go swimming, we could have gone after the photo shoot."

"Something pulled me into the water!"

The Skreecher execs shook their heads. "Mr Fink," said the one with the polar-ice eyes, "we don't appreciate these sorts of displays."

"Well, neither do I," bellowed Juju. "And I assure you it will never happen again. Will it, Bug?"

Bug was astonished. "Didn't you see?" he said, coughing up more brackish water. "Didn't you see the tentacle grab me?"

"What are you talking about?" said Juju. "What tentacle? You tripped over a rope."

Bug squinted, focused in on the photographer. "Didn't you catch it with the camera?"

"Catch what?" shrieked the photographer. "Who could catch anything with you shaking and dancing around like that?"

Another of the Skreecher execs shook his head. "Maybe we made a mistake hiring someone so young. They can never control themselves."

"We could still cancel the contract, remember? We've got that 'bad behaviour' clause," said Polar Ice Eyes. "I'll talk to the boss." He whipped around. "Darn it! Paparazzi!"

Everyone turned to see a small army of new photographers buzzing around like mosquitoes. "Hey, Bug! Look over here!"

"Don't look!" screeched the Skreecher execs. But it was too late. Bug looked, the photographers snapped, and the execs freaked.

But Juju managed to work his juju. He convinced the Skreecher execs that Bug's bad boy persona would only bring more street cred to the Skreecher brand.

"What do you mean, bad boy persona?" said Bug. "I don't have a bad boy persona. I don't even know what a persona is!"

"Sure you do," said Juju, giving Bug a wink.

Mr Ice Eyes nodded. "I see what you mean. Skreechers are hip. They're tough. They're gritty. They're mad hot."

Mad hot? Bug wondered if the guy had eaten some bad clams.

Juju and the Skreecher execs were so excited about their trainers' new street cred that they forgot all about Bug. He was left to dry alone on the dock like a fish at a seafood market. Even the paparazzi had got bored and moved off in search of other famous people doing humiliating things.

No one else had seen a tentacle; no one believed that there was a tentacle. After all that shrieking and lecturing, Bug was beginning to wonder if he hadn't got his foot tangled in some rope and fallen into the water. It was possible. The photo shoot had gone on for hours; he was exhausted and distracted; he'd been holding his arms over his head for so long that perhaps not enough blood was going to his brain. Maybe he had got confused.

He should have taken the Bloomingtons' offer, he realised. Right after Flyfest, they'd asked him to move in with them for a while, just till he got on his feet. But he'd said no. He'd said he wanted to do things on his own. He'd just got Juju appointed his agent and legal guardian, and he said he'd be fine.

Sure. Right. Fine. He was so fine he was conjuring up imaginary tentacles and flinging himself off docks. He could hear his father laughing now. *You're less than nothing, Sylvester. You're just less, how about that?*

Bug sat up. The water lapped gently, laughing at him. Nope. No razor-lipped monsters lurking there.

Geez, what a spaz he was. He made a fist and punched the dock.

Wham!

A strange sucking noise and a briny sort of smell made him glance towards the water.

A tentacle was patting the dock. Patting the dock as if it were looking for something.

Looking for him?

Bug scrambled backwards on all fours as another tentacle flopped on to the dock, then another, and another. As Bug watched in horror, two huge, dark eyes peeked over the surface of the dock. Then the tentacles curled themselves around the wooden columns all around the dock, and the biggest octopus Bug had ever seen – the biggest octopus Bug had ever *imagined* – hauled itself out of the water. Its skin was a mottled bluish-grey, with a craggy, rocklike texture that was all bumps and gnarls and knobs. So terrified that he forgot he could walk, run or fly, Bug scrabbled off the dock as fast as he could, not able to tear his eyes from the approaching monster. The octopus's arms were at least six metres long and lined with rows of suckers the colour of teeth, while its weird, balloon-like mantle hung limply behind its eyes like an empty hood. The octopus used its insanely long tentacles to shimmy and curl and twirl itself across the surface of the dock to the street beyond. It paused as it passed Bug, blinking its large, unfathomable eyes.

Fish food, thought Bug. *I'm fish food.*

But the octopus wasn't interested in Bug; it cycloned its rubbery limbs over to the table where the Skreecher execs had been enjoying a late lunch. The octopus snatched up big tentaclefuls of lobster rolls and shrimp cocktail and clams casino and shoved them underneath its head, where Bug knew its mouth was hidden, where its able-to-crush-shells-and-bone *beak* was neatly tucked. Bug glanced around, frantic to find a person, any other person, but this area had been closed off for the shoot and there was no one else to see what he was seeing.

The octopus ate all the food left on the table, right down to the lemon garnishes and the daffodil centrepieces. When it was satisfied, it turned on its coiling, muscular limbs and snaked its way back towards the dock. As it passed Bug, it paused again. The octopus reached out a single tentacle and, like a fond aunt, ruffled Bug's hair. Then it was moving quickly past Bug, over the wooden dock. It slipped into the waves with the barest of splashes. When Bug could finally bring himself to the edge of the dock to look, the water murmured secretly to itself – as if there had never been anything there at all, and if there had, the sea wasn't telling.

Chapter 3

Pinkwater's Momentary Lapse of Concentration

"Are all you brats just going to stand there? Aren't any of you going to see if she's alive? Oh, never mind. Hello! Are you all right?"

Georgie opened one eye and peeked out through the pile of bones. It wasn't Ms Storia. A stunningly beautiful girl with olive skin and white wrap on her head stood looking at her. Hewitt Elder, the senior chaperone.

Georgie tried to climb out of the pile. The tibia of the giant wombat rolled off her shoulder and landed on Hewitt's foot.

"Sorry!" Georgie said.

A muscle in the girl's cheek twitched, but otherwise she made no other movement. "Are you injured?" she said stiffly.

"Um..." Georgie flexed her arms and legs. "I don't think so."

"So nothing's broken?"

Bethany Tiffany snickered. "Nothing except the entire exhibit," she said.

Hewitt Elder ignored Bethany. "Next time, watch where you put your feet." She glanced at Roma Radisson. "There are people in this world who enjoy tripping you up."

"I'll remember that," Georgie said. The beautiful girl turned and walked away, moving so gracefully that she appeared to be flying, but she wasn't. Georgie wished she could move like that. She wished she were small and graceful and beautiful enough to wear a wrap on her head instead of being huge and pale and clumsy enough to take out a mega marsupial.

Roma put her hands on her hips as she watched the beautiful girl walk away. "Who does she think she is?" But she didn't say anything directly to Hewitt. Something about Hewitt cowed even Roma Radisson.

Ms Storia, who had been busy apologising to the museum employees because of her destructive student, marched to Georgie's side. "Girls, the excitement is over now. Let's get moving." She hissed in Georgie's ear, "*Please* be more careful next time!"

Georgie said nothing, the shame overwhelming her vocal cords. She waited till the last giggling, snickering, laughing Prince School girl passed her. Then, after ducking behind the nearest skeleton, she vanished.

Literally.

As soon as Georgie was invisible, relief flooded through her body. This way she could visit any exhibit she wanted without having Roma calling her a monkey or a marsupial or whatever else came into her vicious *Dunkleosteus* brain. And Ms Storia would be so busy being fascinated by all the sights in the Hall of Flight and so busy sharing that fascination with the girls of the Prince School, she'd never notice that Georgie was missing.

As she strolled the near-empty Advanced Mammals gallery, she did feel the merest, slightest twinge of guilt. Her parents had let her attend school on one condition: that she never use her power of invisibility in public. But, she told herself, this was an emergency. Her parents couldn't expect that she wouldn't use her power in an *emergency*. They wouldn't want her to be humiliated by Roma Radisson, Walking *Dunkleosteus*. They wanted Georgie to be normal. They wanted Georgie to be happy.

And, looking at a skeleton of a sabre-toothed tiger, she

was happy. There was something soothing about literally fading into the woodwork. No one to stare at her ridiculous mop of silver hair. No one to see her trip over her own feet. No one to ask her "How's the weather up there?" and giggle as if that was the funniest thing anyone ever said. Nobody taking pictures of her when they thought she wasn't looking because her parents happen to be The Richest Couple in the Universe. No one gaping—

—a little boy was gaping. But he couldn't possibly be gaping at her, because she was invisible. And there was nothing else close but the sabre-toothed tiger. *It's OK*, she thought, *he's just afraid of the tiger.*

"Mummy?" said the boy in a quivering voice.

His mother, a largish woman in stretchy green trousers who was examining the skeleton of an ancient horse, said, "What, honey?"

"Mummy, look!" He tugged on her trouser leg. He had large brown eyes that seemed to grow larger by the second.

"What is it?"

"There's a nose!"

"What did you say?" said his mother.

"There's a nose floating in the air. Right there!"

"Oh my!" said the woman, clapping her own hand over her mouth in shock.

Oh no! thought Georgie, clapping a hand over her face.

Georgie fled the Advanced Mammals gallery, the woman's shouts following her all the way down the stairs and through the Hall of North American Birds. She didn't stop running until she reached the State Mammals gallery. Breathing heavily but trying not to, she lifted her hand and peered at her reflection in the glass of a display. There it was, as clear as the poor, sad stuffed bobcats behind the glass.

Quickly, she focused all her energies: *I am the wall and the ground and the air I am the wall and the ground and the air I am the wall and the ground and the air...* She looked into the glass again. Her nose was gone, just the way it was supposed to be.

What was that *about?* she wondered. Then again, she hadn't disappeared in more than five months. And it's not like anyone had ever explained invisibility. It's not like there was anyone who could, except maybe The Professor, and she hadn't seen him since Flyfest in November. She never understood how it worked, why her clothes disappeared with her, why objects or people she touched did too, but not, say, whole houses when she touched the walls. She'd brought these things up with her parents, but they never wanted to talk about it. They warned her against experimenting with it, as if the power of invisibility was some sort of weird itch one had to try not to scratch, like eczema or chicken pox.

She sighed and poked around the State Mammals Hall,

which displayed the state's most common mammals in dioramas. She studied the porcupines, hares, and shrews but swept right by the bats. (She heard enough about flying without having to see the bats.) She turned the corner to the next hall, where she caught her foot on a metal radiator, which might not have been a problem except that she was wearing open-toed sandals.

"OW!" she shrieked.

A family of four who had been waiting for their turn at the water fountain looked in her direction, then all around the hall. "Did you hear something?" the father said to the mother. "I thought I heard something."

Georgie staggered away on her mangled foot, making it all the way down the stairs and out the front door of the museum before realising that perhaps this wasn't the best idea. It was one thing to defy her parents about the invisibility thing – even though this was clearly an exception to the rule, being an emergency and everything – but it was another thing to skip out on a school trip. *You have to go back*, she told herself. *You have to find some private place to reappear and then you have to go back to Ms Storia's group and be appropriately fascinated by all the fascinating things at the museum. Just like any normal girl on any normal day.*

Except she wasn't a normal girl. And nothing was going to make her one.

So, instead of rejoining the girls of the Prince School, Georgie limped home. She'd forgotten how much she liked wandering (er, hobbling) the city streets unnoticed. It was spring, and people were springing: some hopping, some floating, some zipping along on flycycles, a few walking. And of course the birds were out in force along with their owners – mynahs, parrots, budgies, cockatoos – all flying lazily on thin rope leashes.

She approached her building and saw the tall and grave-looking new doorman standing at the door – Dexter or Deter or something. Georgie crept by him and slipped into the building after crazy old blue-haired Mrs Hingis. She waited until Mrs Hingis had been swallowed up by one of the lifts before catching the other one up to the penthouse. When she was safely on the top floor, Georgie reappeared, making sure to account for every single body part – even turning around to check to see that her bum wasn't missing. Then she opened the door and walked inside. The Bloomingtons' penthouse had windows that served as walls and high cathedral ceilings that made a person feel as if they weren't living in a house as much as living on top of a mountain. Even now, even after coming to this penthouse for months, she was shocked that it was her home.

"Hello?" Georgie said. "Anyone here?"

"Hello!" Agnes the cook boomed. "Who is there?"

"The President of Moscow!" Georgie hobbled into the kitchen.

Agnes was cutting potatoes while watching the tiny portable TV she kept on the counter. "Russia is country. Moscow is city. Moscow can't have president."

"I know that, Agnes. I was just kidding."

"Kidding?" said Agnes, as if such a thing was a foreign concept. The Polish cook put down her knife, scooped up a dish towel and snapped it at the open window, where a crow sat staring. "Shoo!" she said. "Go home!" She returned to her chopping block, muttering, "Nosy." She frowned at Georgie. "What's wrong with you?"

"What do you mean?"

"You look very bad."

"Thanks," said Georgie. "I work at it."

"What's that? More kidding?" said Agnes. She wiped her hands on a towel and opened the refrigerator. She pulled a plate full of Polish sausage and a jar of purple horseradish out of the fridge. Then she cut several slices of sausage and arranged them on the plate with a spoonful of the horseradish. "You eat. Horseradish clean out your head."

"My head is fine," Georgie said.

Agnes shook her own head. "Your head is not good. You do funny things."

"What do you mean?"

"I have to say?" Agnes said. She pursed her bow lips. Agnes was very small and pretty, with fluffy blond hair down to her shoulders. She would look much younger, Georgie was sure, if she didn't wear baggy men's jeans and oversized football jerseys. But no matter how weird her outfits or sense of humour, Georgie would never think of making fun of Agnes because Agnes knew things. She knew when Georgie was hungry and when she was full. She knew when Georgie wanted company and when she wanted to be left alone. Georgie thought that if she were to turn herself invisible, Agnes would be able to see her anyway.

"Agnes?"

"Hmmm?"

"Are you my Personal Assistant?"

Agnes frowned. "I am cook."

"Well, yeah, but are you my Personal Assistant, too? You know, kind of like a fairy godmother? Or father? I had one named Jules once, and I thought he'd come back. But maybe you were sent..." Georgie trailed off, realising as she spoke that she sounded completely nuts.

"Never mind," said Georgie. "What's on TV?"

Agnes shrugged. "News," she said. "Not much news on news."

Georgie turned up the TV. An overly tanned man with blinding white teeth and what looked like plastic snap-on hair said: *"And in other news, the American Museum of Natural History reported the theft of the remains of a colossal cephalopod. Try to say that ten times fast. Heh. Ahem. Apparently, a scientist was working on them in his lab, turned his back, and the remains disappeared. The cephalopod, a giant octopus, was the largest specimen scientists had ever discovered. It is estimated that the octopus might have weighed more than a hundred kilos when alive and had limbs more than six metres long. Whoa! Wouldn't want to meet that in a dark alley, ay, Bob? Heh."*

"This guy is stupid," said Georgie.

Agnes grunted. "He should eat horseradish."

"Here's our entertainment reporter, Katie Kepley. Katie?"

"Thanks, Mojo. Well, here's the question that's on everyone's mind: Is Bug Grabowski bugging out?'"

"Bug?" said Georgie. "What's wrong with Bug?"

"It appears that Sylvester 'Bug' Grabowski had a mental breakdown and threw himself into the East River at a photo shoot this morning. Though he claims some sort of sea monster pulled him into the water, renowned fashion and advertising photographer Raphael Tatou disputes the story. 'There was no sea monster,' said Mr Tatou. 'Only a very difficult child playing games and wasting everyone's time. Or maybe he was having an attack of nerves, I don't know. All I know is that I'm a professional, and I want to work with professionals.'"

Pictures of a wet and dishevelled Bug flashed on the

screen. *"Hey!"* said Mojo the news reporter. *"Maybe it's the giant octopus."* Katie Kepley giggled her signature giggle.

Agnes *tsk*ed and waved her knife. "Too much funny stuff for horseradish. Need something else."

"What? Like pierogi?"

"No," Agnes said. She thrust the handle of the knife at Georgie. "Chop. I be back."

Agnes swept out of the kitchen. Georgie sliced potatoes until Agnes returned. Carrying a birdcage. With a bird in it. Noodle stopped batting the bit of sausage around the floor and stared at the cage.

"What's that?" Georgie asked.

"Elephant," said Agnes. "See? You not only kidding person."

"What am I going to do with a bird? Noodle will eat him."

"Bird is not for cat or for you," Agnes said. "Bird is for Bug. You bring."

Georgie looked at the TV screen, at the pictures of Bug, drenched and bedraggled and sad. She thought of the last time she saw Bug, how awkward she felt. "I don't want to see Bug," she said.

"Too bad," said Agnes. "He wants to see you."

"He does?" Georgie peered in at the bird. "Does it have a name?"

Agnes reached into her pocket and pulled out some sort of official-looking certificate. She handed this to Georgie.

"'Pinkwater's Momentary Lapse of Concentration, CD, Number Fourteen,'" Georgie read.

Agnes nodded. "Purebred for bird show." Deftly, she sliced the last potato and put the slices in a pot. "But bird not blue enough for show. Or something stupid like that. What I know?"

Footsteps echoed in the huge penthouse and Georgie's mother, Bunny Bloomington came into the kitchen laden with bags. "Georgie! I thought I heard your voice," she said. "What are you doing home so early? And when did we get a bird?"

"Wombat!" chirped Pinkwater's Momentary Lapse of Concentration.

"What?" said Bunny.

"The wombat exhibit was, um, broken, so the tour was a little short. They sent us home. The bird must have heard me and Agnes talking about it. He's for Bug. I'm going to bring it to him later."

"That's so thoughtful," Bunny Bloomington said. "Well. It's too bad that your very first school trip was cut short, honey."

"Oh no. I wanted to come home."

"Why?" said Bunny, instantly concerned. "Is anything wrong? Aren't you feeling well?" When Georgie first came back to live with her parents, Bunny got more and more terrified she might lose Georgie again, that someone might kidnap her and take her away. After a while, she didn't want to let Georgie out of her sight. Now it seemed that Bunny was calming down again, but she was still more nervous than the average parent of a thirteen-year-old. Which meant she was still very, very nervous.

"Nothing's wrong, Mum," said Georgie. "Everything's great."

Bunny unconsciously clutched at her heart. "Oh, I'm so glad. You know, I wasn't sure about sending you to school. I would have been much more comfortable with a private tutor. I still would. But it does seem as if you're having a wonderful time." She studied Georgie's face. "You are, aren't you?"

Georgie forced herself to smile. "I am, Mum, I swear. If it was any more wonderful I would probably have to be hospitalised for over-joy." She kept her lips peeled away from her teeth till her mum beamed back at her.

"I knew everyone would just love you. How could they not?"

After Bunny swept out of the room, Agnes shook her head. "Stop with that fake smiling. You're giving me creeps."

"You mean I'm giving you *the* creeps, Agnes."

"Yes," Agnes said. "Those too." She thrust the cage at Georgie. "You bring Bug. He need friend." Those sharp eyes appraised Georgie. "And so do you."

Chapter 4

Bad

A few hours later, Georgie found herself nodding at Deter or Dexter or Derek the doorman and schlumping down the street carrying Pinkwater's Momentary Whatever His Name Was in his tiny gold cage. Other people with birds stopped her every few metres to admire the budgie, ask his name, when she got it, etc. It was only after they'd been chatting for a few minutes that they noticed who they were talking to.

"My Lulabella is just four months old," one man told her, holding out his arm so that Georgie could admire the scruffy little parrot perched there.

"She's very pretty," said Georgie.

"Don't you just love birds?" the man said.

"Well, actually, this isn't my bird. I'm bringing it to a friend. I have a cat."

The man pulled his arm back in and stared at Georgie as if she'd just said, "I have a komodo dragon."

"What in the world would you want a *cat* for?" he said. "Cats are the enemies of birds!"

"Cats are cute," Georgie told him.

"Cute!" the man said. "Say, aren't you Georgetta Bloomington?"

"Yes," she said.

"And you like *cats*?"

"Yes, I do."

He hurried away, his bird cawing, "Bad, bad, *bad*."

"You hear that, Pinkwater?" Georgie said. "I'm bad."

"Bad," Pinkwater agreed.

Georgie switched the cage to the other hand. "And people want to know why I like cats."

She kept walking, wishing that she was invisible again. But then, who knows if she would be able to do it right? Who knows if she'd leave something showing – a hand, a foot, or something totally bizarre like her rib cage or an eyeball? In the beginning, turning invisible was an accident, nothing she had to think about. And later, it always seemed to be something that she did when it was necessary to do, when her life or someone else's might depend on it. When you're being chased by a giant rat man with filed teeth or attacked by a bunch of Punks in the subway, you don't have time to think, *Hey, wow, I'm invisible, it feels so weird, I can't see my hands and how will I reach that door handle, blah blah blah*. When you're being chased, there is no thinking, there is only doing.

But now when she was perfectly safe, when she had time to think and consider, she messed up. And the fact that every limb was about thirty centimetres longer than it used to be made it worse. A good day was a day she didn't fall flat on her face.

It only took ten minutes for Georgie to reach Bug's building. She followed a Mrs Hingis look-alike into the building. This old lady was juggling a pile of books and wearing a funny pink hat. Once inside the lift, the woman turned to Georgie.

"Do you like books? Or are you one of those young women who prefers to watch that insufferable celebrity nonsense on television? Or destroy your hearing by stuffing those little contraptions in your ears?"

"I like books," Georgie said.

"Well," said the woman. "Then you are an unusual young person. Perhaps you'd like to join our book group." She handed the books back to Georgie so that she could open the suitcase-sized pocketbook again. She pulled out a flyer. "We meet on the third Thursday of every month."

"Thanks," Georgie said.

"But if you come, don't expect to be reading any mysteries or romances or nonsense for babies."

"OK."

The woman grabbed for the pile in Georgie's arms. "Books aren't supposed to be fun."

Georgie frowned. "They aren't?"

The old woman sniffed and got off on the fifth floor.

As Georgie waited for the lift to get to the top floor, she got more and more nervous, though she wasn't sure why. She was visiting a friend; people visited friends every day. But she didn't feel right. She felt like disappearing. She told herself that she shouldn't, that she would just get it wrong again, but she couldn't seem to help it. By the time the doors opened, Georgie and the birdcage she held were invisible. She stepped out into the hallway and tripped as her foot caught the lip of the lift.

"Big feet!" chirped Pinkwater.

"Oh, shut up."

From what Georgie remembered of their last conversation, Bug owned the whole floor. She wondered why he needed a whole floor. He was just one person. But maybe he had lots of friends now. Athlete friends, model friends, dancer friends, friends who all came to hang out at Bug's enormous apartment. At the thought of this, she nearly turned around and left. But then the budgie chirped, "Agnes!"

Georgie scowled, but then walked to the end of the hallway towards a set of enormous double doors. She was about to set the cage down by the door when it flew open and Bug stomped out, carrying an armful of T-shirts and jeans.

"Ow!" Georgie yelled as he trod on her foot. Pinkwater zoomed around his cage, chirping furiously.

"What the heck?" said Bug. For a second, she just stared at him, knowing he couldn't see her (at least, she hoped he couldn't). He looked exactly the same but completely different. Bigger, a little taller, a lot stronger probably, but so worn around the edges that it could have been thirteen years rather than three months since they last saw each other.

"Gurl? Is that you?"

"Georgie," she said, popping into view. "Who else would it be?"

"You got taller," he said.

Georgie blushed, unconsciously slouching her shoulders. "So did you."

Bug scowled as the bird raced around his cage. Georgie was surprised how much she missed that old scowl.

"Your bird's a little hyper."

"He's not mine," Georgie said. "He's yours."

"What do you mean?" said Bug.

"I mean, he's a present. For you."

"Oh. Well." He looked at the budgie as if it were the last thing in the universe he needed. Georgie couldn't believe Agnes had made her come here.

Bug shifted the pile of T-shirts in his arms. "Thanks. Um. You want to come in?"

"Sure," said Georgie, certain she'd rather have gum surgery.

Bug led the way through the huge double doors into his apartment. Huge, with wide windows on two sides, it should have been bright and cheerful. Instead, the place had the look of a charity shop, packed with odd, unrelated items and not nearly enough actual furniture. A fine tapestry hung on a wall next to random posters of athletes. A giant stuffed gorilla sat in the corner of the living room. A suit of armour stood by the doors to the apartment. Georgie had heard that living alone made people weird, and this apartment was proof. She wondered where his agent, who was now his legal guardian, was. Bug always made it sound as if the guy was like a father to him.

"Sorry about the mess," Bug said. "I was just going to do some laundry." He dropped the clothes he'd been holding on to the ones strewn all over the floor. "There's a chair around here somewhere." He kicked through piles of junk to a lone chair set in front of a television the size of a cinema screen. "Here," he said. "Sit down."

"Thanks," Georgie said.

Bug eyed Pinkwater's cage. "I guess we can put that on

the floor." He set Pinkwater's cage down. "Do you want something to drink? I'm not sure what I've got."

"Anything is OK," Georgie said.

He left, and Georgie could hear him banging around in the kitchen. "All I have is Kangaroo Kola."

"That's good," said Georgie.

He came back with two cans, one for her and one for himself. "I did an ad for them," he said. "They sent me a year's supply."

"Great," said Georgie. She sipped her Kangaroo Kola. If you could fly, Kangaroo Kola could make you fly just a teeny bit higher (or so the advertisements claimed). Georgie supposed that was the only reason why people drank the stuff. It tasted like cough syrup.

"So," Bug said. "Thanks again for the bird."

"What's a Wing without a pet bird, right?" She almost winced as she said this, it was so lame.

"Right," said Bug. "Maybe I should let him out?"

Georgie shrugged. Bug crouched and opened the door to the cage. The budgie whirled around the room.

Bug said, "Does he have a name?"

"Pinkwater's Momentary Lapse of Concentration, CD, Number Fourteen," Georgie told him. "He's a show bird. They all have names like that." Abruptly, Pinkwater dive-bombed Georgie's head, startling her so much that she spilled her

Kangaroo Kola. She scrambled to her feet. "Oh no! I hope I didn't get anything on your chair."

"Nope. All over yourself, though."

Plucking at the cold, wet patches on her thighs, she wanted to disappear again. She picked up one foot and shook it, spraying droplets of soda everywhere. "Sorry," she said.

"Don't worry about it. All these companies are always sending me T-shirts and stuff that I never use. I'll get you some." His eyes brightened. "And you know I'm doing this big ad campaign for Skreechers, right? I've got a million pairs of Skreechers trainers. I'm sure I'll have something that fits you." He eyed her feet. "You look about the same size as me."

He turned and walked to the bedroom while Georgie sat, blushing furiously. *Great,* she thought. She had feet the same size as a *guy.* Just what every girl dreams of. Maybe she'd grow a moustache, too. Yeah. That would be really cool.

She folded her arms and waited. It was so strange to be here, to see Bug in this big and messy place, like he was some little kid playing house. Which, she thought, he was. So many things here seemed familiar. Like the monkey in the corner. The suit of armour. The tapestry on the wall, just like Bug's father had in his lair. She hugged herself even tighter.

Bug came out of the bedroom carrying jeans, a T-shirt, and a pair of trainers. "Here," he said. "You can put these on in the bathroom." He pointed. "Over there."

"Thanks," she said. She went to the bathroom and shut the door. She dropped the wet clothes to the floor and pulled on the dry ones. Thankfully, they were big enough to fit her. (It would have been horrible if the stuff had been too small.) Then she looked at herself in the mirror and sighed. The T-shirt said HOT STUFF in orange flames. She was hot stuff, all right. Her hair was in its customary thick ponytail, but random wisps stuck out all over, spraying sideways and tumbling down her shoulders and back. "Hi!" she said to the mirror. "I'm HOT STUFF!"

"What?" Bug called from outside the door. "Did you say something?"

"No!" Georgie said. And then, under her breath, "Just talking to myself like a complete lunatic." She pulled out the ponytail and tried to comb her hair with her fingers as best she could, but it was no use. Her hair, like her body, was apparently intent on taking over the city.

Georgie threw open the bathroom door. "I have world domination hair," she said irritably.

Bug frowned. "What?"

"Never mind," Georgie said. She was going to sit in the chair, but Bug was sitting in it. She searched the room for another chair, but she didn't see one. She settled for a coffee table shaped like a tree stump. Or maybe it *was* a tree stump, she didn't know. Perching on the stump, she said, "Thanks for the stuff. I'll give it back to you."

"Don't worry about it," Bug said.

Georgie frantically searched her feeble brain for something to say. "Do you know that pen that your... um... that Sweetcheeks wanted me to steal from my dad?"

"Yeah?"

"You won't believe what it does."

"Let me guess: writes?"

Georgie glanced up sharply, a little hurt that Bug sounded so sarcastic. "Yes, it writes. But it makes anything you write with it come true."

Bug raised an eyebrow. "You're kidding, right?"

"Nope. But things come true only the way the pen wants them to come true."

"No way."

"That's what The Professor told my dad. And that's what my dad told me. That people wouldn't even be able to fly if someone hadn't written something about flying a long time ago."

"I think I remember The Professor hinting around about that the first time we met him. Something about how people weren't supposed to fly."

"Yes," Georgie said. "But whoever started it didn't write, 'I wish all people could fly' or whatever, he wrote something else, something that had nothing to do with flying at all. The pen did whatever it wanted to do. And now, well... you know the rest."

"Wow," said Bug.

"Wow is right," said Georgie. She waited for Bug to say something else, but he didn't. "So, um, if you had that pen, what would you want to write with it?"

"What?" said Bug. "I don't know."

"Come on. You must want something. It's a pen that makes dreams come true." Yikes, she thought. She sounded like one of those chain e-mails people send to all their relatives. She was now giving herself the creeps.

"My dreams did come true," Bug said, fidgeting. "I mean, I'm a Wing now, right? And in all these adverts. Did I tell you about the Skreecher campaign?"

So much for conversation. "Yeah, you did. Just before."

"Oh." He pulled the sleeves of his jumper over his hands. He tipped his head, as if he was considering something. "So, how do you like school?"

"OK," said Georgie, too embarrassed to tell him about Roma Radisson. Too embarrassed to tell him that even though she might be The Richest Girl in the Universe, no one liked her any better for it.

"I've got tutors," said Bug. "Too much work to do to go to school."

"I don't know that falling into the East River counts as work." She hadn't meant to say that, but out it popped. When your arms and legs and feet and hair are threatening to take over the world and you're wearing a T-shirt that says HOT STUFF in orange flames, things that you don't intend pop out.

"I didn't *fall*," Bug said. "Something pulled me into the water."

"OK," said Georgie. "Whatever you say."

Bug's cheeks got noticeably redder. "What's that supposed to mean?"

"Nothing," Georgie said, backtracking. "I don't know what happened. I heard about it on TV. I wasn't there."

"No, you weren't there." He muttered something under his breath, something that sounded like "You're never there."

"What?" Georgie said.

Bug shook his head, a lock of sandy-brown hair falling into his eyes. "Forget it."

More silence. Pinkwater's Momentary Lapse of Concentration seemed to feel the tension, seemed to want to fix it. He darted back and forth between Bug and Georgie, as if he were trying to stitch them together. "Hello!" he squeaked. "Hello, you person!" He alighted on Bug's shoulder, and proceeded to bonk Bug in the cheek with the top of his little blue head. *Bonk, bonk.*

"I think he wants you to pet him," said Georgie.

Bonk.

"Oh," Bug said. He reached up and petted the bird.

"Purr," the bird said.

"Once he stops dive-bombing, he's OK," Bug said.

"Purr," said the bird.

Georgie watched Bug pet the bird. "I think he likes you."

"I think he does too," Bug said. "So where's Noodle?"

"Home," Georgie said. "Which is probably where I should be going." She felt tired and she felt stupid and she missed Noodle and she missed Agnes and the edge of the tree stump was making her bum ache. Maybe, she thought, she was outgrowing more than clothes and shoes. Maybe she was outgrowing her friend, too. That thought made her achy right in the middle of her chest.

Bug looked down at the clothes spread across the floor like wads of seaweed left by a storm surge. "It's OK. I've got lots to do anyway."

He seemed so lonely that for a second Georgie almost changed her mind, almost said something crazy like "Hey, maybe we could go flying in the park. Maybe we could make ourselves invisible and sneak into the cinema." But she didn't say these things. What she said was: "I like your suit of armour."

"Thanks," Bug said. "I found it. Well, that's not exactly true. There were these guys moving out a couple of floors down. I think they meant to take it with them, but they forgot it in the hallway."

"So you stole it," Georgie said.

"I didn't steal it. They *forgot* it," Bug said.

"You could have found them," said Georgie.

"How would I do that?"

"You could have asked around for their new address." She had no idea why she was saying this stuff. She didn't care about the suit of armour. And for all she knew, those guys didn't want it any more and left it on purpose. But she couldn't seem to help herself. "You could have shipped it to them."

"I said, they forgot it."

"Fine," said Georgie.

"Anyway, you should talk."

"What?"

"You've stolen things before," Bug said. "A lot of things."

"That wasn't my fault," said Georgie, getting angry.

"No? There was Noodle. She was just wandering around, and you kept her. And you don't seem to feel too bad about it. What's so different?"

Georgie felt the rush of blood through her veins, as if all of sudden she had too much blood and not nearly enough vein. "You sound just like your father."

Bug sounded like a robot when he said: "Get out."

"Bug, I just meant—"

Bug flew forwards so fast that he blurred before her eyes, and Pinkwater exploded into the air in a burst of feathers. "*Get out*!"

Georgie jumped back, whipped round and charged

towards the door. As she ran, she misjudged her footing, slamming into the suit of armour. It fell over like a stack of pots and pans. She opened the door, Pinkwater's disapproving chirp following her out:

"Bad!"

Chapter 5

Punk Rock

Georgie sprinted nearly all the way home from Bug's apartment, slowing only to catch her breath before she reached her building. She didn't want anyone to think she'd been running from something. Because she wasn't running. She'd just been in a hurry to get home, that's all. Bug? Who's Bug? Oh, that weird-looking guy in the Cheeky Monkey ads.

"Ha!"

Georgie focused in on the crow perched in a nearby tree. "What are *you* looking at?"

"Ha! Ha!" said the crow.

"Keep laughing, beak-face. I'm going upstairs to get my kitty."

"Ha!"

Dexter the doorman was waiting at the entrance of the building. "Good afternoon, Miss Bloomington," he said gravely. He said everything gravely. His grave manner went with the grey hair, the grey beard and the grey uniform.

"Good afternoon, Dexter."

"It's Deitrich, Miss."

"Oh, sorry," said Georgie. "Deitrich."

"Are you all right?" Deitrich said. (Gravely.)

"Yes, why?"

Georgie was tall, but Deitrich was one of the few people who was much, much taller. He looked down at her, gravely, but kindly. "You seem sad."

"Sad? No, I'm not sad. I'm absolutely fine. Great, even," Georgie told him.

"Of course," said Deitrich, opening the door so that she could enter the building, discreetly slipping her a tissue so that she could wipe her eyes and blow her nose before going up to the penthouse.

"Georgie? Is that you?" Bunny Bloomington drifted into the foyer. "You're a little late."

Georgie couldn't imagine she'd been more than an hour, but she knew her mother. "I hope you didn't worry."

Bunny pressed a kiss to Georgie's cheek. "I didn't. At least, not that much. Well, a little bit. Some." She looked at

Georgie critically, as if seeing her for the first time. "Where did you get those clothes?"

Georgie had forgotten about the clothes. How could she forget about the clothes? And, duh! She'd left her own clothes at Bug's! "I spilled some Kangaroo Kola on myself, so Bug gave me this stuff to wear."

Georgie could see her mother working to take this information in. "Oh," Bunny said. "Next time you're on a long visit, could you give me a call, please? I'm not saying that I don't trust you, please don't think I don't trust you, I know you're thirteen, and—"

"I know, Mum," Georgie said. "You're right. I should have called."

Bunny bit her lip. "You and Bug didn't decide to go on any, um, outings, did you?" That was her mother's word for invisible exploration. *Outings*. "Because I'm just not comfortable with that. That's the very thing that got you kidnapped in the first place, and I'm so afraid that someone will see you popping in and out of sight and get ideas."

"Mum, we didn't go on any outings. We sat in his apartment for a while and I left."

"His apartment," Bunny said. "Was that man there? His guardian? What's his name? Foo Foo?"

"Juju?"

"Yes, Voodoo. Was he there?"

Georgie got the idea that her mother would not be pleased to hear that she had spent some time with a boy alone in his bachelor pad. "Juju was there. He looks like a turtle."

"Yes, well, it's not his fault, is it?" Bunny said.

"Guess not."

"So," Bunny said. "How is Bug doing these days? I see him all over the television and in every magazine."

"Bug's a jerk," said Georgie.

"What? Did you two have an argument?"

Georgie sighed. "Sort of. I don't know."

"Well, you are getting older. You're changing. Becoming a beautiful young woman. Maybe," Bunny said, "that's confusing to your friend."

Georgie sighed again. There was nothing beautiful about what she was becoming, she was sure of it. In the short time she had known her parents, she had grown to love them with all her heart. That didn't mean she always understood everything they said to her. And it didn't mean that they always understood everything she said to them.

"Maybe he's confused because he didn't know that a girl could actually get to be twenty metres tall," Georgie said.

"Oh, honey," Bunny told her, "there's nothing wrong with being tall. It doesn't mean boys won't like you. Your Aunt Tallulah on your father's side was very tall, and she had five husbands! Or was it six?"

"That's something to look forward to," said Georgie.

Bunny laughed. "Noodle missed you, you know. She's been yelling at me for the last half hour. Sometimes I swear she's trying to tell me something and if I listened hard enough, I'd understand."

"Where is she?" Georgie said.

"In your room. The last time I checked, she was playing solitaire on the computer, but she might be napping. If people knew what that cat could do, everyone would want one."

"I'm going to say hi to her," said Georgie.

"Sure," Bunny said. "I didn't even ask you. How was the museum?"

"Filled with lots of stuffed dead things," Georgie said.

"Just the way a museum should be," her mother said. "Anyway, you can relax for a while. Maybe we can all watch a film after dinner. How does that sound?"

Her parents preferred films in black-and-white with people tap-dancing and twirling around in fedoras saying things like "swell" and "you don't say?" but Georgie didn't have the heart to tell her mum that the films all made her bored and sleepy. "That sounds great, Mum."

Georgie went to her room, where she found Noodle sprawled across her bed. As soon as she walked in the door, the cat opened her eyes and began berating her with fierce yowls.

"I know, I know," Georgie said. "Where was I all day long?"

"Yowl," said Noodle.

"What was so important that I had to leave my favourite cat?"

"Yowl," said Noodle.

"What's my problem?"

"Yowl," said Noodle.

"Why am I so boring? Why is Bug such a rock head? Why is my hair so weird? How come I'm built like a daddy longlegs?"

Noodle was silent, choosing to jump down from the bed and wind herself around Georgie's legs until Georgie picked her up. "Why does everyone hate me, Noodle?" Georgie said again, her nose in Noodle's fur. As usual, when she held Noodle, when she petted Noodle, a strange riddle came into her head: *If a tree falls in a forest and no one is around, does it make a sound? If a tree falls, if a tree falls, if a tree falls...*

The next thing she knew, her mother was calling her for dinner. She put Noodle back on the bed. Her head felt empty and clean and light, and she wasn't quite so miserable.

"Thanks," she said. She could have sworn Noodle nodded before curling up for yet another nap.

"How's my best girl?" said Solomon Bloomington as Georgie came in to the dining room and kissed his cheek. It was what he always said.

"I'm your *only* girl," Georgie replied. It was what she always said.

"Not such a girl any more," he said. "A young woman!"

Georgie smiled, wishing that her parents would stop with the young woman thing. It made her tense. She'd barely had any time to be a girl with them. And now she had to hurry up and be a woman? No, thank you.

"Still a girl for a while," Georgie said, and her father beamed.

"How was the school trip?" he wanted to know.

"OK," she said.

"What did you learn?"

She shrugged.

Sol piled his plate with roast beef, mashed potatoes, gravy and fluffy biscuits that Agnes had prepared. (Agnes didn't believe in diets. Or cholesterol. Or vegetables.)

"You must have learned something," Sol said. "A word in another language? The name of a former president? A major scientific discovery?"

"Let's see," said Georgie. "I learned that Roma Radisson is about as deep a thinker as this." She held up one of Agnes's biscuits.

"Hmmm. That might be an insult to the biscuit," Sol said.

"Sol!" said Bunny.

"Well, you've met the girl," said Sol.

"Sol!"

"What?"

Bunny clucked her tongue at them both, but Georgie

could see that she was smiling. Georgie devoured many slices of meat, a pile of potatoes and four biscuits. She was about to reach for a fifth when she realised that perhaps it was Agnes's high-calorie food that had caused her freakish growth spurt. She decided to skip dessert, which was some sort of quadruple-chocolate, triple-fudge, double-butter, possibly deep-fried cake.

After dinner, the family retired to the media room, which was set up like a cinema, complete with stadium seating and a popcorn machine. Sol cued up one of his favourite black-and-white films, one about a guy who goes to Paris and meets some beautiful girl who doesn't talk that much but dances around a lot, and the two of them dance on the ground and dance in the air and the whole thing ends up in this long ballet sequence that Georgie didn't entirely understand, but didn't find entirely horrible. At least, she didn't fall asleep. But her parents did. By the end of the film, the two of them were slumped in their seats, their heads tipped together, as if one were about to turn and whisper something to the other. Georgie watched them for a while as the credits rolled. They were nice people, her parents. Nobody had a right to be miserable with parents like these. So what if Bug was a jerk face? So what if Roma was an idiot? So what if the Prince School was packed with spoiled princesses who'd never had to work for anything in their whole entire lives? She wouldn't be there for ever. As a matter of fact, she would only be going to the school for a few more months before she'd move on to high school. That would have to be better, wouldn't it? She would have to try harder to be happy.

Georgie kissed her parents good night, careful not to wake them. She wandered back to her bedroom where Noodle was looking at a website called catsinexile.com, which seemed to be some sort of blog with photos. Georgie was amazed to see so many pictures of so many different cats, considering how rare cats were. Maybe some cats had escaped The Professor's apartment. But then, she didn't want to think about The Professor, not really. Cats reminded her of stealing, which reminded her of Bug, which reminded her of the mean, mean thing she'd said to him in his apartment and the way he'd yelled at her and told her to get out, and she didn't want to think about that any more. She didn't want to think about it *ever*.

She changed into a pair of pajamas and crawled into bed. She considered the pile of books on her nightstand before pulling *Charlie and the Chocolate Factory* from the pile. She was nearly finished with the book; she was right near the end where the glass lift flies. Georgie knew a lot of things that flew, but none of them were lifts. She liked this book very much.

She settled back into her pillow, opening the book with a sigh. She had just read a single paragraph when an odd noise caught her attention. An odd, shuffling sort of noise, like a cat wearing slippers.

She looked at Noodle, but Noodle was downloading a photo of a white kitten sleeping in a sink and seemed absorbed in the work. *Probably the computer making the noise.* Sometimes the computer whirred and chuffed like an animal. Georgie shrugged, and went back to her book.

Shush, shush, shush.

Georgie glanced up sharply. A shadow lurked under door. As if someone stood behind it. Listening.

"Mum?" Georgie whispered.

No answer.

"Agnes?"

There was someone behind the door, Georgie was sure of it. But who? The Bloomingtons had the most advanced alarm system in the universe. People couldn't just walk into the building. And nobody could just walk into the Bloomingtons' penthouse. It was ridiculous. It was imposs—

The door creaked open. There, in the doorway, was a man wearing skinny plaid trousers, combat boots and a spiked collar. A white T-shirt, emblazoned with the logo GOD SAVE THE QUEEN, was splattered with paint and food stains. His blue hair stood up in a stiff Mohawk. Though it was dark, he wore sunglasses.

"Oi, oi, oi!" he said. "You must be Georgie!"

Noodle hissed, leaping from the desk chair to Georgie's bed. The fur along her back spiked in an imitation of the man's Mohawk.

"Who..." Georgie said. "How..."

The man held up a set of gold keys that dangled from a cheap Statue of Liberty key ring. "Keys to the City," he said. "Let you in anywhere."

"But the doorman..." said Georgie.

"Came in through the parking garage. Nobody keeps a decent eye on the parking garage. Easy after that." He removed his sunglasses so that Georgie could see his wolfish, pupil-less eyes. A Punk. A Punk was standing in her doorway. In her house. That would have been amazing enough, except that the Punk threw in a little dance, bopping his head to music only he could hear.

He stopped bopping as quickly as he'd begun. "Do you like art?"

"What?"

"Art," he said. "You know. Paintings. Sculpture."

"Uh," said Georgie, her eyes darting around. Where were her parents? Where was Agnes? What if he'd hurt them?

"Good," the Punk said. "You'll be seeing lots of it. You and your friends. Rich kid like you has to have a lot of rich friends."

Noodle growled loud in her throat – because there was a crazy Punk in the room or because he'd suggested that Georgie had lots of friends, Georgie wasn't sure.

"Speaking of friends," said the Punk. "Heard from The Professor lately?"

"What do you mean? Who are you?" Georgie demanded.

"Don't got to be so loud," the Punk said. "You want to wake the 'rents?"

"The what?" said Georgie.

"'Rents. Parents. Oi, you're not such a smart one, are you?"

Noodle's growling got louder. "Go away! Get out of my house!" said Georgie.

"Just having a friendly chat, is all," the Punk said. "No need to get your blankets in a twist. You can call me—"

"Sid," said Georgie, who knew that all male Punks were called Sid and all female ones called Nancy.

"No!" the Punk bellowed. "I'm not *Sid*. Never, ever call me *Sid*. Call me Mandelbrot. That's the name of a famous mathematician, you know. Studied chaos. And I'm the king of chaos, you know?"

"OK," said Georgie, who didn't know, but also didn't want to find out.

"So, like I was saying. You see this Professor lately? Maybe he rings you once in a while? Maybe gives you some things to hang on to?" The Punk's eyes fell on the cat. "Maybe this is his kitty and you're watching it for him, right? Something special about this kitty?"

The Punk reached out for Noodle and Noodle hissed a ferocious hiss, the most ferocious hiss that Georgie had ever heard, a hiss that was too piercing and too big and too much to come from so small a cat. The Punk was startled, then enraged. Remarkably, incredibly, *madly*, he hissed back. The two hissed and hissed and hissed until Georgie couldn't take it any more, until Georgie used the only part of her that didn't seem to be frozen, her voice. She screamed as loud as she could. She leaped out of bed, grabbed up her cat, and vanished.

"Crikey!" shouted the Punk.

Agnes burst into the room with a lasso of sausage links swinging overhead and a meat fork pointing at the Punk's heart. "Out!" she ordered. "Or not even queen can save you!"

The Punk hissed one last time before running across the room and flinging open the windows. He pressed a button on his metal belt. A parachute opened as he jumped out into the black night.

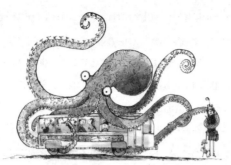

Chapter 6

Patience and Fortitude

Her parents were in the room a second later.

"Georgie!" Her mother grabbed her.

"What is it?" said her father. "Did something happen? Did you see someone? Was someone here?"

"What?" said Georgie. She was no longer frozen. She was no longer invisible. She looked around wildly. The window was open, the wind swinging the curtains, but there was no Punk in sight. Noodle mewled, tucking her head under Georgie's chin. Agnes tucked the meat fork in the pocket of her nightdress.

Solomon cupped Georgie's chin in her hand. "Georgie, tell me what you saw. I need to know."

Georgie took a deep breath, her mind scrambling for an answer. Georgie turned from her mother to her father, taking in their worried, anxious faces – terrified faces. She couldn't bring herself to scare them more then they'd been scared. She cared about them too much. "Sweetcheeks," she said. "I dreamed of Sweetcheeks." She stared at Agnes, pleading with her eyes. *Please don't say anything about the Punk. Please help me protect them.*

"Oh, honey," said her mother.

"I dreamed that he could fly, and that he was coming to take me away from you." Though this was not what she had seen at all, just thinking about it made her eyes tear up. She shivered.

The worry fell off the Bloomingtons' faces. "You worried me," said Bunny. "For a minute, I..." She trailed off.

"It's all right, Bunny," Solomon said, patting her shoulder. "She's here. With us. Everything's OK."

"I'm sorry, Mum," Georgie said.

"Don't be sorry," Bunny said. "It was just a bad dream. Sweetcheeks can't hurt you any more."

"That man is in jail for the rest of his life," added Solomon. "And not only is he in jail, he's in jail in Wyoming. He's so far from us he might as well be on Neptune." Muscles in Solomon's jaw clenched. "You have my word: you'll never see him again."

"That's enough talk about that evil man." Bunny kissed

her on both cheeks and hugged her again, tightly, tightly, tightly. "Would you like some warm milk? I can go make some. That will put you back to sleep. That will chase the bad dreams away."

Georgie hated warm milk, but Noodle didn't. And any kitty fierce enough to help drive off a Punk deserved a reward.

"Sure," Georgie said. "We, I mean *I*, would love some."

The Bloomingtons hurried off to fetch the milk. Agnes also turned to go, but Georgie stopped her. "Thank you, Agnes."

Agnes waved her meat fork. "For what?"

Georgie and Noodle split the warm milk. Perhaps because it was warm, perhaps because her mother was the one who had warmed it, the milk did manage to drive away all thoughts of gangsters, Punks, and every other thing that goes bump in the night. Georgie slept soundly, not thinking about anything awful until she was on her way to school the next day. And then everything came flooding back:

I hate the Prince School.

I hate Roma Radisson.

I hate Bug.

I hate Punks.

So many awful thoughts, so little time. The bell rang and Georgie ran to her first class. Unfortunately, she had to sit next to Roma, who cleared her throat loudly and announced, "I don't know what this school is coming to. Some students have to stay in boring museums packed with dead stuff all day long while *other* students" – here she looked pointedly at Georgie – "can cut whole afternoons and it doesn't seem to matter. I guess if you have enough money you can do whatever you want."

Ms Letturatura, the English teacher, floated over to Roma's desk and scooped up the bottle of polish Roma was using to paint her toe nails. "I guess you can," she said dryly, holding it out of Roma's reach. "Does everyone have their permission slips? If you don't have a permission slip, you won't be able to go to the library. And if you can't go to the library, you can't do research for your papers. And if you can't do the research for the paper, you can't do the paper. And if you can't do the paper, you get an F."

Everyone started searching for their permission slips. Ms Letturatura was the only teacher at the Prince School who was a stickler for such things. Georgie had forgotten to ask one of her parents to sign the slip, and her mum had left early that morning, so she'd asked Agnes. On the line that was meant for parent's signature, Agnes had scrawled "Georgetta's Mum."

Well, thought Georgie. *This ought to work very nicely.*

But it did. As Ms Letturatura collected the slips from the girls in the auditorium, she didn't seem to notice what was written on Georgie's. (Nor did she notice that Roma

Radisson had written "Whatever!" on hers.) And she didn't seem to notice that Roma half skipped, half floated behind Georgie down the streets and on the subway, deliberately kicking the backs of Georgie's knees so that Georgie's legs would collapse. Georgie yearned to disappear and stick out a huge invisible foot, sending Roma pinwheeling through the air. But of course, Georgie did not. She allowed herself to be kicked all the way to the public library. Not because she couldn't get out of Roma's way, but she couldn't muster up the energy. And maybe she deserved to be kicked in the backs of the knees. For defying her parents. For worrying her parents. For Bug. For generally being a spaz. A few crows perched high up in a tree agreed: "Ha, ha, ha!" they laughed.

But Georgie's dark mood was no match for the public library. As soon as she saw the grand white building, she felt herself cheering up. Ms Letturatura asked the students to gather around her. "The library itself is built in the Beaux-Arts style, characterised by high drama, huge columns, and freestanding statuary, like the world-renowned library lions behind me. These lions, originally sculpted by Edward Clark Potter, have seen everything. They almost seem to be looking at you, don't they? Their names have changed a few times since the library opened in 1911. First they were called Leo Astor and Leo Lenox, after library founders John Jacob Astor and James Lenox. Then, even though they're both male lions, they were later known as Lord and Lady Lenox. During the Great Depression, Mayor Fiorello LaGuardia observed that the qualities city-dwellers seemed to have in abundance were patience and fortitude. And that's what the lions are still called. Patience guards the south side of the Library's steps and Fortitude the north."

Georgie was the only one in her class – one of the few people in the whole world – who knew that Patience was really an actor named Henry Goldberg, and that Fortitude was a man whose stage name was Jean-Michel Renée Clouseau. The real pink marble statues were way too valuable to sit outside, and were stored somewhere in the bowels of the library. The trustees had used actors in lion suits posing on the steps for decades. Georgie knew all this because one night, while invisible, she observed the actors changing shifts and overheard them talking about rumours of the trustees' plans to stop using actors and install cheap stone animals outfitted with security cameras instead. "If they do that, I'll have to go back to dressing as a turkey sandwich and handing out flyers," Henry had complained.

"Now," continued Ms Letturatura. "I have a lot of fortitude, but I do not have a lot of patience. I want you all to act like young ladies while we're touring the library, do you understand? That means that you are to be polite, respectful and most of all, quiet."

At this, Roma Radisson kicked the back of Georgie's knee and Georgie fell forwards. The other girls giggled.

Ms Letturatura took a deep breath. "Georgetta. You seem to be having some trouble moving today. And standing still. Is something the matter? Do you need medical attention?"

"Yes!" said Roma.

"No," Georgie said, getting to her feet.

"Are you sure?"

"Yes, I'm sure."

"Good. Now remember what I said, ladies. Anyone making too much noise or generally acting out of turn will get a detention."

London England yawned widely and Bethany Tiffany varnished her lips with one of Roma's trademarked lip glosses. "The library. I'm already bored out of my mind," Roma whispered.

"Did you have a question, Ms Radisson?" Ms Letturatura said, pausing at the base of the stairs.

"Yeah," said Roma. "When's lunch?"

"Polite, respectful, and quiet, Ms Radisson."

Roma rolled her eyes. "Whatever."

"Thank you."

Ms Letturatura led the group past the lions, up the stairs and into the library. Despite the attitudes of Roma, Bethany and London, the other girls were quiet as they entered the big building. Footsteps echoed reverently and conversations stopped as the group took in the vaulted ceilings, the enormous columns, the arches and the windows that bent the sunlight into an ethereal haze. Ms Letturatura conferred with a petite girl wearing a bright scarf wrap on her head. It was Hewitt Elder, the Prince School senior who had chaperoned the museum school trip. Georgie smiled a greeting, but the girl didn't look as if she recognised anyone. Or just didn't want to.

"Ladies," Ms Letturatura said, "Hewitt Elder will be leading the tour today. She's a regular volunteer at the library, so she knows all about it. And if any of you are poetry buffs, you might already know that Hewitt published several volumes of poetry as a child. She's quite the prodigy."

"Hello," said Hewitt in the most unenthusiastic voice Georgie had ever heard. She might well have said, "Goodbye," or perhaps, "Get out," or even "Drop dead."

Bethany Tiffany sucked in her breath. "She looks like some sort of model. Or rock star. Or something. Have we seen her in a video? Do you think she's an actor?"

Roma glared at the slim, tiny girl with the chocolate eyes, olive skin and elaborate head scarf, and Georgie could tell she didn't like what she saw. People just weren't supposed to be more beautiful and more delicate and more exotic than Roma. Roma seemed to gather up her courage and spat,

"What kind of name is *Hewitt?*"

Hewitt Elder turned her dark eyes on Roma. "It's an English name meaning 'smart one'."

"Really. Well, I'm named after a—"

"City. Yes," Hewitt said. "You must be very proud."

Roma tossed her hair. "I am. I—"

"As you might already know," Hewitt Elder said in a louder voice, "the city library opened in 1911. The architectural style is considered Beaux-Arts. Notice the details such as..." She continued talking about the features of the building as if she didn't care about Roma at all. Which, it seemed, she didn't.

"Nice scarf!" said Roma.

Hewitt blinked, her eyes unreadable. "The main reading room on the top floor is nearly two city blocks in length. We'll be visiting that last. If you'll follow me, I'll be taking you through the various galleries. Try to stay close." She whipped round and started to walk away.

"Why are you *walking?*" Roma said contemptuously. "Are you a leadfoot? Can't you fly?"

Hewitt half turned, her lips twisted in amusement. "Yes. If that awkward bounce you and everyone else does could actually be called *flying.* I prefer to move with a little more grace."

London England murmured, "Um, I think she's making fun of you."

Roma tried again. "And why are you wearing that scarf? Don't you have any hair?"

This time, Hewitt didn't bother to turn. "Why are you wearing that wig? Don't *you* have any hair?"

The girls gasped, staring at Roma's signature red hair. "It's not a wig," Roma shouted. "It's not!"

Ms Letturatura tapped Roma on the shoulder. "What did I say, Roma? Polite. Respectful. Quiet."

Roma: "But she—"

"Shhh!" said Hewitt. "This is a library!"

Roma clamped her mouth shut, self-consciously smoothing her hair and muttering to herself. Georgie had never seen anyone put Roma in her place, and thought Hewitt was quite possibly the most fascinating person that she'd ever met. She wondered what kind of poetry she'd written, and whether she wanted to be friends. Especially that last part. If she made another friend, maybe she wouldn't be so upset about Bug. Maybe she could forget about him. Maybe Hewitt would have a way to scare off Punks and Georgie could be friend-full and Punk-free for ever. Maybe she could have a real life just like a normal person.

"Um, hi," Georgie ventured as the class was touring a gallery of maps. "I was wondering, um..."

"If that silly twit's hair is real or a wig," Hewitt said.

"No," Georgie said. "Well, yes. I mean, I guess I'm curious

about that. But I wanted to ask about your poetry."

"Really."

"Yes."

One eyebrow lifted slightly. "Do you read much poetry?"

"No, but—"

Hewitt sighed a this-conversation-is-more-boring-than-death sigh.

"But I'm interested in trying," Georgie continued doggedly. She had patience, she had fortitude, she would make this girl like her. "I'd love to see one of your books."

"Nobody reads real poetry," Hewitt said. "Nobody appreciates art any more. They just want greeting cards."

Georgie had no idea what Hewitt was talking about. "Yeah."

Hewitt gave Georgie a long look. Her face didn't soften, exactly, but it did seem less cold. "If you're really interested in my work, forget about my books. Go to my website. Hewittelder.com. My e-mail address is there too. Write me and tell me what you think."

"OK! I will. Thanks."

Hewitt nodded. Then she clapped her hands and motioned the class to follow her to the next gallery. For the first time in a month, Georgie felt like she had a little something to smile about.

Take *that*, Roma Radisson.

Chapter 7

The It Club

The two bouncers manning the door were the size and shape of refrigerators, if refrigerators came with tattoos, nose rings and extremely bad attitudes.

"Young man," said Mr Fuss to the refrigerator closest to him, "I think you need to let me by."

"Us," said the Punk skulking behind Mr Fuss. "You need to let *us* by."

Mr Fuss frowned at the Punk, who was now calling himself Mandelbrot, of all things.

"Did you two miss the velvet rope?" the fridge said. "Did you miss the line behind you?"

Mr Fuss turned and looked at the line of people waiting to get into the nightclub. "Goodness," he said. "How horrifying. Who is teaching them all to dress?"

One of the fridges scowled harder. "Look, dude, we've checked the list and you're not on it. Neither is your friend there. That means you'll have to move to the back of the line and wait like everyone else."

Mr Fuss smiled politely. "I don't wait like everyone else. I don't wait like anyone else. As a matter of fact, I simply don't wait, full stop." He reached up and pressed the tip of his finger to the nearest fridge's forehead. If it hadn't been so dark, perhaps someone would have noticed that the tip of that finger seemed to sink *into* the bouncer's head up to the first knuckle.

"That tickles," the bouncer said.

"Yes, I bet it does," replied Mr Fuss. He removed the finger and wiped it off on his handkerchief.

"I think he's on the list," said the bouncer, rubbing the spot where Mr Fuss's finger had been.

"What?" said the other bouncer. "I thought you said you checked it."

"I must have missed it," he said. He unhooked the red velvet rope and gestured Mr Fuss through. Mr Fuss was irritated to note that the bouncers also let Mandelbrot through.

"Thank you, young man."

As Mr Fuss entered the club, he heard one fridge say to the other, "Are you *sure* he's on the list?"

"Did you know that in certain areas of the tropics, it rains frogs?"

"What?

Mr Fuss smiled and kept walking, Mandelbrot right behind him.

"Oi, that was cool," Mandelbrot said. "What did you do to the bloke's head?"

"You don't want to know," Mr Fuss said.

The club was dark and cave-like, the only light coming from small red lava lamps pulsing in the gloom. All around the club, women in glittery dresses sipped candy-coloured drinks or made half-hearted attempts to dance while the men watched. Though the music was pumping at a volume that Mr Fuss found distinctly unnecessary, all of the clubbers looked bored. Particularly bored was the band of pale-skinned types that lurked around the edges of the room. As a rule, they seem to prefer clothes in black velvet and capes. On other people, these clothes might look a bit ridiculous, but the pale-skinned types wore them like they were second skins. Mr Fuss amused himself with the notion of telling the clubbers that they were hanging out with a bunch of vampires. But of course, he had no intention of telling anyone in the after-hours club about the vampires in their midst. After what the Punk had told him about his visit to the little girl, the fact that she was a Wall, Mr Fuss knew he needed more freelancers. Special kinds of freelancers. He had a proposition for the vampires. And a bit of a bribe.

Mr Fuss approached a thin man with blond hair and eyes that would probably have been described as "soulful" if vampires actually had souls. The man wore black velvet trousers and a shiny black shirt open at his white, white throat.

"You're still here," said Mr Fuss, shouting to be heard over the thumping music.

The man turned his soulful-soulless eyes on Mr Fuss. "What?"

Mr Fuss frowned and suddenly, the music instantly muted as if someone had pressed a button. No one else at the club seemed to notice.

"I have something for you," Mr Fuss said. "For all of you."

"For all of who?"

"Let's not play games, shall we?" replied Mr Fuss. "I know who you are, Phinneas. I know *what* you are."

The pale man shrugged, bored. Vampires were perpetually bored. (If you had "lived" for five hundred years and had heard the miniskirt hailed as the "newest thing in fashion" ten times in five decades, well, you'd be bored too.)

The other vampires at the club noticed Mr Fuss and

gathered around him. "What do you have for us?" one of them asked.

"Something dead?" said another.

"Something better," Mr Fuss told them. "Take a look." He pointed to the centre of the dance floor, where Mandelbrot had created his own mosh-pit and was stomping all over the rest of the club kids with his big combat boots. Every few seconds, he'd let out a giant "whoop-whoop!" Or an "Oi! Oi! Oi!" He yelled, "You have no future!" and "You want to be anarchy!" He laughed like a loon when he knocked over a group of party girls like a bunch of bowling pins.

One vampire said, "Well, he's not boring."

"I could watch him for a while," said another. "A little while."

"Can we have him?" still another said. "He can dance for us."

"Oh, I don't know," said Mr Fuss. "Punks are often more trouble then they're worth." After the debacle at the Bloomingtons', Mr Fuss had confiscated the Keys to the City and considered drowning Mandelbrot in one of the It Club toilets. Then again, if the vampires wanted to do a little trade...

Phinneas the vampire blinked. "What do you want in exchange for him?"

"I think I'd like a seltzer with lime," said Mr Fuss. "And I have a job that I need you to do."

Chapter 8
Good Dog

Georgie sat back in her chair, her forehead creased in puzzlement. She read the poem out loud for the twenty-second time:

My soul
Is a freckle
On the sun
My eyes are glass marbles
Shattered on stone
My bones are snapped
Branches on a dying tree

I wait
For a bus
That never comes.
Stupid.

"I don't get it," Georgie said. She looked at Noodle. "Do you get it?"

In response, Noodle mewled at the screen.

"Maybe it's too deep for us or something," Georgie said. Noodle batted the mouse, trying to click over to another website. "No, Noodle, I'm still reading."

Noodle sniffed audibly, jumped down from Georgie's lap, and loped out of the room.

"You don't appreciate real art," Georgie called after her. "You just want greeting cards!" But then, she had to admit that greeting cards were a lot easier to understand than any of the poems posted on Hewitt's website, all of them about broken bones and busses that never come and stupid people who are so stupid they don't know they're stupid. She'd been poring over them for days now. Still, she liked Hewitt. Even if she was the grumpiest teenager in the universe, Hewitt had shut Roma up, and that was hard to do. And though Georgie didn't admit this to herself, Hewitt seemed to be everything Georgie wanted to be, and that alone was reason to get to know her. Georgie clicked on Hewitt's e-mail address and wrote this message:

Dear Hewitt:

This is Georgetta Bloomington. I was with a group that toured the public library two weeks ago, the one with Roma Radisson? You told me that if I was interested in your poetry, I should check out your website, which I did. Your poems are really cool. My favourite is the one about the moon looking like a bloodshot eye winking at you.

Anyway, I have to go because there's a school trip to the Museum of Modern Art today and I don't want to miss it (even though Roma Radisson will be there – yuck). I hope you chaperone today. But if not, I'm at the library a lot. I hope I'll see you again sometime.

Sincerely,

Georgie Bloomington

She left the computer and started to gather her books for school. There was a photograph taped to her computer, and she stopped to look at it. Her father had taken it on New Year's Eve. It showed Bug and Georgie sitting together on the Bloomingtons' couch, both of them laughing. She remembered that night so clearly. She had only been with the Bloomingtons a little over a month and was still awed by the turn her life had taken. And Bug had had to absorb a lot of changes as well – his father jailed, Bug himself a star athlete. It was such a relief to get together and feel normal again. Like kids. They'd toasted the New Year with sparkling grape juice and stayed up with her new parents till midnight to watch the ball drop in Times Square. It was one of the best times of her life.

And now everything was different.

She said goodbye to her parents, assuring them that yes, she'd be careful, yes, she'd call if she was going to be late, no, she wouldn't talk to strangers, yes, she loved them too, and yes, she'd have a good day. Try, anyway. Ever since Hewitt had embarrassed her at the public library, Roma had been in a bad mood. And when Roma was in a bad mood, she liked to take it out on Georgie. Georgie wished that it were Roma that was being menaced by Punks, but then, as her parents always told her, the world wasn't a fair place. Georgie was thankful that there wasn't much more time before the school year would be over and she would be free of Roma Radisson for ever. Roma had already declared her intention to quit school and become a world-famous actor. Her first film, she said, was about a very rich heiress with a heart of gold and a really great boyfriend. She was penning the script herself. Also directing and producing. She was sure it would be a hit at Cannes. On the red carpet, she planned to wear a gown made entirely of hundred-dollar notes.

"Well, either it will be made of hundred-dollar notes or thousand-dollar notes. I haven't decided yet," Roma said on the way to the museum.

"You could make the dress out of credit cards," offered London.

"Tacky," said Roma.

"Yeah," Bethany said. "What are you thinking?"

"Stop thinking," said Roma.

What Georgie was thinking: the sequins that Roma had sewn all over her uniform skirt made her look like some sort of insane majorette. All she needed was a baton and one of those huge fuzzy hats with the chin strap and they could have their own Prince School parade.

Ms Letturatura herded the group to the E train. She was one of those teachers who thought that taking the subway was a gritty urban adventure that the girls of the Prince School would relate to their grandkids one day, something that had to be experienced at least once. She seemed to feel the same way about the hot dogs served at nearly every street corner and had once taken an entire English class for lunch at one. "Stay together, girls."

"I don't want to take the subway," London said as they barrelled towards midtown. "I'm afraid of the Punks."

Roma scoffed. "Don't be such a wimp. There are no such things as Punks."

Oh yes there are, thought Georgie.

"Oh yes there are!" said London. "My grandma saw one once. He was tagging a subway car. She said his eyes were the creepiest things. Like black holes or something."

"Your grandma thinks the FBI is following her," said Roma. "And the CIA. And the president."

"Well, they could be!" said London. "Ouch!" She turned and glared at Georgie, who had lost her footing and bumped into her.

"Sorry," Georgie muttered.

"You're *always* bumping into people and you're *always* saying you're sorry!" said London. Georgie could have mouthed it along with her, but didn't. She was too busy looking for Hewitt Elder in the crowd of girls, but didn't see her anywhere.

Ms Letturatura ushered the girls off the subway at Rockefeller Centre and the remaining blocks to the museum on Fifty-third Street. Georgie wished they hadn't taken the subway. Not just because of the Punks, but because she loved to walk through the city, loved to look up at the buildings scraping the sky, all of them different: some giant, smooth walls of glass, others as ornate as any wedding cake. She loved the smell of hot dogs and pretzels, the blaring horns of the taxicabs, the whoosh of the people flying – or trying to fly – by.

"Ladies, again, I want your best behaviour as we move through the galleries," Ms Letturatura announced before they went into the museum. "And I want to see you girls paying attention and taking notes. You'll be writing an essay on what you saw here today."

There was much groaning and complaining from the girls of the Prince School, most of whom thought writing essays was something that you paid someone else to do for you.

"What we're going to do is split up into small groups and explore. I want you to select two pieces of art and study them. In your essay, you will be comparing and contrasting those pieces of art. How are they the same? How are they different?"

The girls stopped groaning when they heard that they would be allowed to wander around the museum without a tour guide. Even though it was a boring museum filled with boring paintings and boring sculptures and boring people, it was still better than sitting in class listening to lectures about maths or science or literature or history. "Who needs to know what happened twenty years ago?" Roma said. "I wasn't even born yet!"

Georgie didn't tell anyone, but she already knew which paintings she would be writing about; she even knew where to find them. As soon as Ms Letturatura told them to meet back in the main lobby at noon and then let them loose, Georgie went to look for Van Gogh's *Starry Night*. She knew about Van Gogh, of course. Her parents had told her. During his lifetime, he'd only sold one painting. He also went totally bonkers and cut off his own ear (which sounded incredibly painful as well as strange). But here he'd painted this beautiful starry night. Maybe it was a crazy sort of painting, all brush strokes and swirls, but Georgie liked all the blue and gold, liked the enormous glow of the oversized stars and the big great blob of the moon. (Could you use the word "blob" in an essay? Georgie wasn't sure.)

After looking at the painting for a while, she went to find the other piece she'd had in mind, Matisse's *Icarus*, plate VIII. This was also blue with bright splashes of gold, but to Georgie, this was the sadder piece. Not because of the artist, who was brilliant and successful and really famous (and wasn't prone to chopping off any body parts), but because of Icarus, the guy in the artwork. In Greek mythology, Icarus was wearing this set of wings that his dad made him, but he was having so much fun flying that he flew too close to the sun god Helios. The wax holding his wings together melted, and he fell into the sea. Matisse had cut pieces of paper and arranged them to make a dark figure falling through a blue and starry sky. The thing that killed Georgie was the little red spot about where Icarus's heart would be. Icarus was falling, and his little heart was red. Did he know? Was he scared? Or was he happy to the very end? It reminded her of Bug, the first time he flew. He'd looked so full of joy, so thrilled to be alive, that his heart could have been visible from the outside had someone been looking for it.

But that was the old Bug. The good Bug. Not the new Bug, the changed Bug, the I'm-in-adverts-and-aren't-I-amazing Bug. His heart was probably a grey pebble. A lump of coal. A balled-up napkin with a blob of ketchup on it.

It was getting close to noon, so Georgie decided that she had time for one more gallery before she had to get back to the group. She ended up in a sculpture gallery. She stopped at a piece by a guy named Alberto Giacometti, a piece simply called *Dog*. "Dog" was small, lumpy, and funky-looking, like a pile of sticks that a creative kindergartner had decorated with globs of papier-mâché, but then it also really looked like a dog, tail down, nose close to the ground, sniffing for a scent trail. Georgie thought it was funny how not-dog and so-very-dog *Dog* was.

She moved on to a sculpture called *Standing Woman*. *Standing Woman* had been cast in the same way as *Dog*, the same, lumpish stick-figure way, but this felt different. "Standing Woman" seemed stretched entirely out of proportion, with a small head, super-long skinny legs, and enormous feet. Her face was cast downwards just a bit, as if someone had just told her to stand up straight but she couldn't quite make herself do it.

"Look at that!" said a voice behind her. "Someone made a sculpture of Georgetta Bloomington! That's so fab™!"

Georgie whirled around. Roma, Bethany and London were standing behind her. Roma was pointing to *Standing Woman*. Specifically, pointing at *Standing Woman*'s supersized feet.

"How long did you have to pose for it?" Roma said sweetly.

"Yeah, how long?" Bethany said.

London twirled a blond curl around her little finger. "I don't really think it's tall enough to be Georgie."

"What did I say about thinking, London?" Roma said.

"Oh, right," London said, dropping the curl.

Georgie racked her brains for something witty and cutting to say, tried to imagine Hewitt Elder in the same position – what would Hewitt do? Hewitt probably wouldn't hear a word Roma said, and if she did, she wouldn't care about any of it. But that was the problem. Georgie always heard. Georgie always cared. She remembered thinking something mean and maybe even a little funny about the sequins on Roma's skirt, but her thoughts refused to gel.

"Anyway," said Roma, turning away from Georgie as if she wasn't there, "Bug and I were talking about what we're doing on Saturday. He wants to take me to this new restaurant that's opening up downtown. It's called the Red Room. It's supposed to be amazing."

Georgie's brain buzzed. Bug? Roma and *Bug*? Impossible.

"And then later, he wants to take me flying."

"That's *so* fab," Bethany said.

Roma glared. "Hey, that's trademarked, you know."

Not fab, Georgie thought. Not. Fab. Flying was their thing, hers and Bug's. It was not possible he'd take someone like Roma. Someone who thought sewing sequins on a uniform skirt was a good idea, someone who wanted to wear a dress made out of thousand-dollar notes, someone who kicked other people in the backs of their knees to make them fall down.

"I can't believe you guys are going out," said London.

"What's so unbelievable about it?" Roma said. "He's famous, I'm famous. What could make more sense? Maybe we'll even get to do an advert together. Maybe I'll put him in my film."

"Oh, wow!" Bethany said. "That would be perfect!"

Perfect? Sure. Perfectly disgusting.

Georgie walked away from Roma and her friends, her stomach in knots. She gripped herself around the middle. So what? She and Bug weren't talking anyway. It wasn't as if they were actually friends any more. What did she care? No, she didn't care at all.

Not at all.

She marched towards *Dog* on her way out of the gallery, but some odd movement caught her eye. It was *Dog*. Or rather, the person standing next to *Dog*.

"Hewitt?" Georgie said. But the person turned and walked briskly from the gallery before Georgie could see her face. Georgie looked towards the statue and gasped. Instead of having his nose pointed towards the ground, *Dog*'s head was lifted, his ears pricked up, his tail wagging. As Georgie watched in astonishment, too surprised to move, *Dog* jumped down from his platform, ran up behind Roma, and bit her right in the sequins.

Chapter 9

How Much is That Demon in the Window?

"Ouch!" yelled Roma. She twirled around in a circle, but *Dog* had already scooted from the gallery, out of sight.

Roma's eyes narrowed when she saw Georgie standing there, staring. "You!" she said. "You did this!"

"Did what?" Georgie managed to squeak.

"I don't know," Roma said. "But you did something. I know you did!"

A security guard heard the commotion and floated over. "Is there something wrong, miss?"

Roma started to sob – big, heaving sobs that involved no actual tears. "She's always hated me. She's always been so mean to me!"

"Now, now," said the guard. "Why don't you tell me what's going on."

"Her!" Roma stuck a finger at Georgie. "Georgetta Bloomington. She thinks she's better than everyone else 'cause she's so rich. She must have kicked me or something!" She sobbed again.

The guard turned to Georgie. "Is this true, Ms Bloomington? Did you actually kick this young woman?"

"I'm Roma Radisson!" yelled Roma. "How could you not know my name! I'm in the ad for Jump Jeans! I have my own line of deodorants! I'm in a video!"

"It wasn't me," Georgie said quietly.

"What?" the guard said.

"I didn't do anything. It was the dog."

"What dog?" said the guard.

"The one that was over there," Georgie said.

The guard saw the now-empty display where *Dog* had been and gasped. "Ms Bloomington, did you do something with the statue?"

"No!" Georgie said. "It just jumped off that shelf thing and bit Roma in the... uh..."

"The statue jumped," said the guard.

"Yes," said Georgie. Roma, Bethany, and London were staring at her. Everyone in the gallery was staring at her.

"A *statue*," repeated the guard. "A statue made of bronze."

"Um, that's what it looked like," Georgie said, realising too late that she had, yet again, said a strange and unfunny thing, the type of thing that was bound to get her noticed for all the wrong reasons. "Actually, it probably just fell down and hit her. That's what happened."

"It fell down and hit her though she was standing nowhere near it."

Georgie said nothing.

"And then what?" the guard said.

"What do you mean?"

"Where's the statue now?"

Georgie opened her mouth, but no sound came out.

The guard took hold of Georgie's arm and pulled a walkie-talkie from his belt. "Darius," he said. "You better get over to the Giacomettis. We've got a problem."

"Yes, Mrs Radisson, I understand that," Bunny was saying into the phone. "Georgetta feels very sorry for Roma. But she says she had nothing to do with, er, whatever happened to Roma. And I trust my daughter."

Bunny winced and pulled the phone away from her ear as Roma's mother screeched and then hung up. Bunny replaced the handset in its cradle. "That went well," she said mildly. "I don't think I'll be invited to any more of her fundraisers."

"Big loss," said Solomon.

"Sol," warned Bunny. Both the Bloomingtons looked at Georgie, who was curled as tight as a wood louse in the leather chair in her father's office. Whenever the Bloomingtons had something important to discuss, they always discussed it in Sol's office. Usually, Georgie loved Sol's office, which was much more of a garden than an office, a garden that was always in bloom. Tulips and daffodils sprouted in colourful bunches around the chairs and waves of silvery wheat danced around the perimeter of the room, while a peach tree, heavy with fruit, loomed over the desk. Georgie reached down and plucked a ripe strawberry from one of the many strawberry bushes, but couldn't bring herself to eat it. She gave it to Noodle, who sat on her lap. Noodle didn't like to eat strawberries, but she did like to roll them with her nose.

"Georgie," Sol said. "Why don't you tell us again what happened?"

"I already told you, Dad. I was walking out of the gallery when one of the statues just... came to life. It bit Roma. Then it was gone. That's all I know."

"That's crazy," Bunny said.

Georgie picked at her fingernails. "So's a room with

vegetables growing out of the carpet," she muttered.

"The city is a strange place," said Sol. "Stranger things have happened."

Bunny sighed. "I know. I don't have to like it, though."

Georgie had to wonder if her parents knew how very strange the city was. So many things seemed to worry them. She didn't want to worry them. She didn't like the way they looked with their eyebrows all furrowed and their mouths curving down. She wanted them to be happy. "Maybe," she said, "the statue did fall. I mean, it looked like it bit Roma, but maybe it just sort of fell on her or something."

"That sounds more reasonable," said Bunny hopefully.

"It does," Sol said, even more hopefully. "If I didn't know better, I would think that the pen is causing all of this, but The Professor has it, so..." He trailed off.

Bunny cleared some climbing roses off the other chair and sat down. "How bad is this trouble with Roma Radisson?"

"Everyone has trouble with Roma, Mum," Georgie said. "She's not a very nice person."

"Sometimes," said Mrs Bloomington, "people aren't very nice for reasons that might seem surprising. Maybe she's having a hard time growing up."

Noodle dropped the strawberry on the floor and meowed a truly sarcastic meow.

"Don't start," Bunny said, eyeing the cat. "Maybe it's easy for kittens, but people do have a hard time growing up, you know. Roma's parents are always jetting off to Europe and Asia. They don't spend much time with her. She probably has low self-esteem," Bunny suggested.

Georgie thought that Roma had an overabundance of self-esteem. Roma had esteem poisoning.

"What if you tried to be more understanding?" Bunny said.

"Oh, nobody wants to understand Roma," said Sol.

"Sol!"

"It's true, Bunny. You're just too nice to say so. But," he added, "that doesn't mean that you don't have to try to get along with the other girls."

"I do!" Georgie said. "But because Roma doesn't like me, nobody does."

"I can't believe that," said Sol. "You're a wonderful person."

That was the problem with having fabulous parents: they were so busy loving you and supporting you and telling everyone that you were the best thing that ever happened to them that it was impossible for them to comprehend that other people might not think you were the cat's meow. The bee's knees. All that and a stick of gum. They tended to believe that any interpersonal problem was nothing more than a silly misunderstanding, that if you just smiled a little more, said "hi" a little more, got a good haircut once in a while, the world would fall at your feet.

Sure.

Georgie pulled Noodle close and stood. "OK," she said. "I'll try to get along."

Sol beamed. "That's my girl."

One a.m. and Georgie couldn't sleep. She was sitting up, *Harry Potter and the Goblet of Fire* open in her lap, but Harry reminded her of Bug, which reminded her of Roma, which reminded her of Bug and Roma, which reminded her that the idea of Bug and Roma going out or even occupying the same planet made her queasy. She closed the book, got out of bed, and checked her e-mail, but Hewitt still hadn't responded to her note, and the only other people who had written were people wanting to sell her real estate and watches and arthritis medication.

"It's official, Noodle," Georgie said. "Except for you, I'm friendless."

Noodle lifted her head and mewled, as if to say that having a cat for a friend more than made up for a lack of human ones. Which was mostly, but not completely true. How strange, Georgie thought, that she'd had no real friends at Hope House for the Homeless and Hopeless for all those years and yet she felt worse now than she ever had then. Before, she supposed, she hadn't known what she was missing. Now she did.

And it was horrible.

Noodle mewled again and Georgie sat on the edge of the bed to pet her, figuring Noodle would cast her kitty spell and clear Georgie's head. But the cat didn't turn on her hypnotic purr, and Georgie's thoughts kept coming. Bug. Roma. The Punk. The statue. Bug. Roma. The Punk. The statue. Over and over again, like a cyclone of wasps.

Georgie decided that snacks were called for. She left her bedroom and crept into the kitchen, almost shrieking with surprise when she found Agnes sitting at the table, the newspaper and a plateful of pierogi in front of her.

"Agnes!"

"What?"

"What are you doing?"

"I wait for you. You wake me up."

"How did I wake you up?"

"All that thinking. You think too much. You need pierogi."

"Not horseradish?"

"Pierogi," said Agnes, and pushed the plate over to Georgie.

Georgie sat down at the table. The pierogi were sweet, with a luscious blueberry filling.

When Georgie was finished, Agnes said, "Better?"

"Yes, thank you. Agnes?"

"What?"

"How did you know what to do with the Punk?

"What Punk?"

"You know what I'm talking about," said Georgie.

For a minute, Georgie didn't think Agnes would answer. But then she said, "I'm from Poland. Lots of Punks there. Vampires too."

Well. What do you say to that?

Agnes took Georgie's plate. "OK. You go talk to him tomorrow."

"Talk to who?"

"Talk to who. Boy, that's who."

Bug. Of course Agnes knew Georgie was thinking about Bug. "He doesn't want to talk to me."

"Sure he does."

"I can't."

Agnes shrugged and put the plate in the sink.

Irritated, Georgie picked up the paper and read through the headlines. PRESIDENT DECLARES CHICKENS NOT REAL BIRDS. AIRBOURNE INDUSTRIES INTRODUCES NEW FUEL-EFFICIENT MOTORISED FLYCYCLE. MUSEUM OF NATURAL HISTORY UNVEILS *MEGATHERIUM* EXHIBIT. ROMA RADISSON PLANS TO SUE MUSEUM OF MODERN ART FOR PAIN AND SUFFERING. SYLVESTER "BUG" GRABOWSKI FILMING ADVERT AT THE EMPIRE STATE BUILDING; CITY PREPARES FOR TRAFFIC NIGHTMARE.

Georgie read the entire article. Apparently Bug would be filming an advert for Hero® brand sportswear at the Empire State Building the next day.

With her back still to Georgie, Agnes said, "So don't talk. Go see him."

"He doesn't want to see me."

"He not see you."

Agnes wanted her to turn herself invisible and go see Bug. Why did she want her to go see Bug so badly? "My parents don't want me to do that any more. And besides, I don't want to see him either. I don't like him."

"Hokay," said Agnes. She put the washed plate in the drain. Then she opened up a jar. She scooped a few tablespoons of whatever was in the jar into a plastic bag. Then she handed this to Georgie.

"What's this?"

"Birdseed for budgie," said Agnes. "Just in case."

"I'm going to bed," Georgie announced.

Georgie went back into her room. She could go to Bug's shoot. Tomorrow was Saturday, so she wouldn't miss any school. And she wouldn't have to talk to Bug, either. She'd sneak over, check into that Roma thing. She just needed to know that it wasn't true. And then everything would be OK. Sort of. So, since Georgie was feeling sort of better, or at least anticipating feeling sort of better, she turned off the light and crawled back into bed. She pulled the covers all the way up to her chin and Noodle rearranged herself so that she was warming Georgie's feet. Georgie's breathing had just begun to slow, her eyelids had just begun to flutter, when she glanced at the window, nearly falling out of the bed when she saw someone hovering outside, scratching a fingernail down the length of the glass.

"Bug?" she whispered. She yanked back the covers and crept over to the window, waving eagerly. Maybe he had come to apologise.

But her hand flagged when she saw that the boy outside her window wasn't Bug. This boy was much older than Bug, nearly a man, pale and thin, dressed in a very shiny black shirt and skinny black velvet trousers. His hair was blond and gelled and spiked, and she thought he might be wearing makeup. He didn't seem to care that Georgie had stopped waving; he waved at her, two fingers snapping from the forehead in a salute.

She approached the window warily. She didn't know any people besides Bug who could fly this high. She couldn't imagine who he was or what he thought he was doing. Was he just trying to show off? Was he some sort of freak? Was he here to kidnap her?

He gestured again with his fingers, this time crooking them, telling her to come closer. She took one step forwards, and then another. The eyeliner was a little much, but he didn't look scary. Actually, he didn't seem that scary at all. And the outfit was very nice. Stylish. Like you'd see in a magazine. *Bug should get some trousers like that*, Georgie thought, so close to the window that she could almost kiss it. *I really really like those trousers*. And his big black wings were so pretty.

The man mouthed something and Georgie shifted her face even closer to read his red, red lips. *Can I come in?*

She thought about it for a second, thought about how not scary he was and how nice his outfit was and how pretty his wings were, and would a person wearing such a fabulous outfit be anything but fabulous? It seemed impossible.

Georgie nodded.

And that's when the man smiled a sad smile, his white fangs gleaming in the moonlight.

Chapter 10

Mega Megatherium

Juju Fink sat across from Bug in the limo, working the phone. "I don't care what you have to do," he said. "I want M&M'S, huge bowls of them all over the place. Little snack bags of M&M'S, too. And I want all the brown ones removed. Bug doesn't like brown M&M'S, he never eats them, and if he sees one, well, I don't even want to say." Juju snapped his phone shut.

"I don't have a problem with brown M&M'S," Bug said.

"Doesn't matter," said Juju. "We're just keeping everyone on their toes."

Bug didn't understand how making people pluck out all the brown M&M'S was going to do much but make them hate Bug. Then again, Bug also knew that arguing with Juju was pointless. Bug sighed and looked out the window, trying to ignore the paparazzi who half ran, half flew alongside the car snapping pictures.

"Remember," said Juju, "wait until the job is finished before you decide to act up like you did at the Skreecher shoot."

"I wasn't acting up," Bug muttered.

Pinkwater, who was sitting on Bug's shoulder, chirped, "Calamari!"

Juju scowled. "Do you really have to take the bird everywhere with you?"

"What difference does it make?" said Bug.

"OK," Juju began, rubbing his browless forehead, thinking. "Say, you rescued a bird from a shelter. A sick and dying bird that you nursed back to health yourself. You fed it with an eyedropper. Chicken soup."

Pinkwater erupted in a flurry of squawks and flapping wings.

"OK, OK. No chicken soup. You fed it with an eyedropper, though. Medicine. Water. That's good stuff. We need a little something to balance out your bad boy persona." He flipped open his phone. "Yeah, Delores? Get me Frankie's number. He's at the *Times*. I got a story for him."

"Rubbish!" said Pinkwater, and bonked Bug in the jaw with his head.

Bug absently petted the bird with a fingertip. It was rubbish, of course. But then most of what Juju told the press about Bug was rubbish. Sometimes Bug had trouble understanding how all this rubbish was helpful. When he first won the Golden Eagle back in November, it seemed as if the whole city was his friend. But then, feelings began to change. People started to doubt that he'd really flown as high or as well as he had. People said that the Golden Eagle should be revoked because he was never officially entered in the race and so therefore had no right to the trophy. Reporters wrote article after article about how Sweetcheeks Grabowski had also started out as a child model and look where he ended up. They seemed to go out of their way to print photographs that made him look crazy or tired or just plain ugly, and paired with captions like "Bug Grabowski Parties Too Hardy?"

Juju said all press was good press, but Bug thought it was unfair. Like the world was just looking for a reason to hate him. The only reason he was doing this advertising stuff was so he could make enough money to live on his own and be his own person and fly like no one in his whole family ever had. So people could never say that he was like his dad. And they all said it anyway.

After Juju finished his call, he snapped his mobile phone shut. "You know what you need?"

"No," said Bug, "what?"

"A girlfriend."

Bug blushed. "Why?"

"What do you mean, why? Because it would be news, that's why. Publicity. Has to be the right girl, though. An athlete could work. Maybe one of those cute little ice dancers. Do you like ice dancing?"

"I—"

"Forget the ice dancers. A film star or a singer would be better. A TV personality. Someone really famous."

For some totally strange reason, Gurl – Georgie – popped into his head. Technically, she was famous, being the daughter of The Richest Couple in the Universe. But then, Gurl – Georgie – was just like everyone else. She had told him that he was like like his stupid, cheating, thieving father. How could she say that? Why would she say that? He had been tempted to give Pinkwater back. Almost did it too. Flew over to the Bloomingtons one day with every intention of handing Gu—uh, Georgie that bird and telling her that he didn't *want* her gifts and didn't *need* her gifts. And it was hard, really hard, because Pinkwater was a talker and Bug had forgotten how nice it was to talk to somebody that wasn't trying get him to sell something, even if that somebody was small and blue and prone to insane exclamations. Anyway, the chef – Agnes? – opened the door and told him that Gurl—duh! Georgie! wasn't home, and no, he couldn't give the bird to Agnes to hold, because Agnes didn't want the bird to be eaten by the "fat kitty" and he would just have to keep the thing until he saw Gurl—Georgie, Georgie, Georgie again. Which, of course, was never happening.

So technically, it wasn't his choice to keep the bird. And if Juju wanted a newspaper to print up a bunch of rubbish about where he got it, and *Georgie* happened to see it, well then, technically, there wasn't a thing that he could do about it.

Another thing he could do nothing about: traffic. It took half an hour for the limo to get Bug to the Empire State Building, and another twenty minutes for security to manoeuvre Bug through the waiting crowd to his trailer. Bug was exhausted. He had slept little the night before; he kept hearing this strange knocking at his window, kept dreaming of a voice whispering *let me in, let me in*. He was so tired that he told Juju he wanted a few minutes to himself before they had to do his hair and his makeup, and then he spent a few minutes wondering how in the world he'd got used to saying things like "I'd like a few minutes before they do my hair and makeup." Juju pushed him inside the trailer and slammed the door shut.

"Company!" chirped Pinkwater.

Bug turned to see someone sitting on the couch. A very pretty someone with red hair and purplish eyes.

"Hi!" she said.

He knew her. At least, he knew who she was. Roma Radisson. An heiress. Probably one of the richest girls in the universe, besides Georgie (who he was *not* thinking about).

"Hi," he said back.

"I bribed one of the guards to let me in here. I hope you don't mind."

He hunted his brain for words, but the only word he could think of was "pretty". And "wow". Could he say that? No. That would be dumb. What wouldn't be dumb? "Uh..." he said.

"I didn't think you'd mind," she said. "Did you get my messages?"

"What?" he said. Wow. Wow. Wow.

"Messages. I left three of them with your agent. Well, my assistant left three messages."

"Assistant?" She'd turned him into a parrot. A dumb parrot.

"You mean she didn't leave messages? That girl is so fired. Anyway, I thought it would be nice if you and I went out tonight. The Red Room would be perfect. What do you think?"

"What?" he said again.

"The Red Room. It just opened. Supposed to be fab. Dutch-Asian-South African fusion."

"Uh..."

"And maybe a film after that? Peter Paul Allen has a good one out about something. I forget. Oooh, look! M&M'S!"

She reached into a bowl and pulled out a yellow one, held it up, and then put it back.

Bug made some sort of gargling noise. He couldn't seem to understand anything she was saying. Her hair was distracting. He'd never seen hair so red. And shiny.

"I was thinking of wearing this pink dress that I have? Hot pink, you know, like bubble gum? With a ruffle around the neckline? So fab™. But then I have this other dress, it's green with a black ribbon that goes down the side, like all the way down to my ankles. And then a blue velvet dress with a handkerchief hem, but I suppose I can't wear that one now. Wrong season. Of course, I *am* Roma Radisson; maybe I'll start a new trend. Velvet in the springtime! I could call *Vogue*. They could do a whole spread."

"OK," he said. He had no idea what she was talking about. There was something in there about handkerchiefs, that much he knew.

Her brows crinkled. "We'll have to do something about your hair."

"Hair," he said, still staring at hers.

"And your clothes. You need a different outfit."

"Outfit?"

"You can't wear jeans to the Red Room. You must have a suit, right?"

"A suit? Like for a funeral?"

"No! Like for a restaurant!" Roma said. "Have you been listening to me at all?"

"Sure," he said. Her hair was shiny, her eyes were shiny, even her teeth were shiny. Her skin seemed to have some sort of sparkly powder all over it.

"Shiny!" chirped Pinkwater.

"Well, that's good. Because I expect you to listen to everything I say."

"Uh-huh," he said, still mesmerised.

The door to the trailer opened and Madge the makeup artist and Bruce the wardrobe man came in, laughing and talking. They stopped, shocked when they saw who was in the trailer.

"Oh!" said Madge.

"Oh!" said Bruce.

"Yes, it *is* me," Roma said. "But I was just leaving. Bye, Bug. See you later." She turned to go, then turned back. "Oh, and Bug?"

"Yeah?"

Roma smiled a magnificent, shiny smile. "Lose the bird."

Bug walked out of his trailer, makeup done, hair done, Hero® brand socks, T-shirt, and warm-up trousers on. Pinkwater sat on his shoulder, bonking him in the face.

Lose the bird? *Lose the bird?*

No one was that shiny.

Bug walked faster. And what was all that stuff about his

hair? What was wrong with his hair? His eyes, maybe – having them so huge and buglike was kind of weird – but he always thought his hair was OK. And a suit? Was she crazy? He pulled a snack bag of M&M'S from his pocket, but shoved them back in when he realised that they might mess him up (he was messed up enough by genetics, thank you. He didn't need to have chocolate stuck in his teeth like a five-year-old).

As he headed towards the set, he saw Roma standing behind one of the barricades. She blew him a kiss. The paparazzi went nuts, snapping, snapping, snapping photos of Roma, photos of Bug walking by.

"Roma!" yelled one of the photographers. "How long have you and Bug been an item?"

"Practically for ever," Roma said.

"And how are things going?" yelled another photographer.

"You know what I always say? That's so fab™. And it is." She winked, and the photographers burst into another explosion of photos.

In Bug's ear, Pinkwater chirped, "Fabulousity!"

Great.

Bug tried to forget about Roma, forget about the paparazzi and focus on the job at hand, which was the advert for Hero®. He only had one line, which was "I'm a hero for Hero®". He was supposed to say this line, flex a bicep and then launch himself in the air. Simple enough, and yet it would probably take all day to shoot and he would feel like he'd flown four hundred races afterwards. How did he get himself into this? Why did everything feel so hard?

Roma was still chattering at the photographers when Bug took his place in front of the cameramen filming the advert. The director, a grumpy, grizzled man with a heavy Russian accent, screamed for quiet on the set and then screamed, "Action!" Bug opened his mouth, ready to do this so perfectly that the advert would be shot in a single take, when the crowd began to scream.

The Russian turned round with his bullhorn. "Ven I scream it does not mean *you* scream, borscht brains! Oh! OH!"

Bug put his hands on his hips, wondering if he really should start acting up, be the bad boy the tabloids said he was. But he had no opportunity to act up, because something else was acting up. A brown shaggy something was pushing through the crowd, a shaggy thing that looked like a cross between a grizzly and a gerbil. But it was much, much bigger than a grizzly and much, much, much, *much* bigger than any gerbil. It was the size of a bull elephant, this strange and shaggy thing, and it lumbered and lurched along in slow motion.

"Vat?" shouted the director. "Vat is dat? Giant hamster? Argh!" He dropped the bullhorn. The people screamed even louder and then flew, bounced, hopped and ran every which way, followed by the director and the entire camera crew. The only people who stayed put were Bug, who was too surprised to move; Roma, who thought the crowd was yelling for her, and the paparazzi, who wouldn't miss getting photographs of a giant hamster for anything.

"Bug!" yelled Juju Fink, making a break for the limo. "Get the heck out of there!"

But Bug was rooted to the spot. The great shaggy thing padded along on huge feet tipped with half-metre-long claws. Every few metres, it stopped and grabbed a person with an enormous paw, sniffed with its giant pinkish nose, groaned and put the person back on the ground. It was getting closer now, coming right up behind Roma, and Bug could see that its brown fur was splotchy with some kind of bluish-green stuff, and its eyes were large and titled downwards.

It looked sad.

"Bug!" yelled Juju. "Get in the limo!"

The paparazzi backed up but continued to snap pictures as the beast put his pink nose right on top of Roma's head and gave it a great big sniff. Roma shrieked and turned to tell off whatever moron was *ruining her hair* but was struck dumb at the sight of the enormous monster behind her. Unluckily for Roma, Bug wasn't the only one who thought she was pretty. The beast scooped her up with one paw and kept walking, pausing every so often to sniff the top of her head again as if she were some sort of exotic flower.

"Get it off me!" Roma screamed. "It smells!"

The paparazzi kept snapping and Bug kept gaping and the people who hadn't run off started reaching for mobile phones. Several policemen came running after the monster, but stopped when they saw what they were up against.

"What the heck is that?" said one.

"I don't know," said another.

"*Megatherium,*" said a third. "Giant sloth."

The first cop gave the third a look. "It's mega all right. But how do you know what it's called?"

"You might try reading a book once in a while. The museum just got a skeleton of one of these shipped in. Anyway, they were supposed to have died out ten thousand years ago."

"Looks like a big hamster. Doesn't move very fast, does it?"

The third cop got a peevish look on his face. "It's a *sloth*. As in *slow*. See that green stuff on its fur? That's algae. Grows on the fur because the sloth can't clean itself fast enough."

"Well, what do we do? Shoot it?"

"I'm not sure our bullets will pierce its fur and hide."

"You're a big help, Mr I Read So Many Books."

Roma kept screaming about the stinky sloth and its

smelly paws and her ruined dress and her hair and a bunch of other things as the sloth slooooooooowly lumbered past Bug and made its way over to the Empire State Building. It stopped, craning its short, hamster-y neck, and then it started to climb the building.

"It's climbing the building!" one of the cops said.

"No duh," said another. "You're a genius, you know that?"

"We really should try to stop it. Roma Radisson doesn't seem to be too happy."

"That's because it's probably going to eat her."

Bug didn't think Roma was a very nice person, but he certainly didn't want her to be eaten by a giant hamster. The sloth hadn't done anything violent, but who knew what would happen if someone tried to surprise it. It was huge and shaggy and weird, and its tusk-length claws could cut a man to ribbons. (Imagine what they could do to fourteen-year-old boys.) Maybe he should wait until someone called in more police officers, or the army, or the air force?

The sloth continued to climb, seemingly in no real hurry. A few officers in jet packs buzzed by it. The sloth ignored them, moving so slowly that it was almost boring to watch. Almost. The officers in jet packs didn't seem to know what to do either. Roma shrieked at them and told them she would totally sue them if they totally didn't rescue her *right now*.

"You think he's going all the way to the top?" one of the cops on the ground said.

"Oh yeah," said another.

"Huh. This is going to take all year."

Bug spoke up. "Aren't you guys going to do anything?"

The cops looked at him. "Like what?"

"Like go inside the building and try to grab Roma as the sloth passes by a window or something."

"Right," said one of the cops. "And then that thing gnaws our arms off."

"And drops Roma to the ground."

"Besides," another cop added, "we're waiting for our team of experts."

"The police department has giant sloth experts?" Bug wanted to know.

The cops only glared.

Bug looked down at his T-shirt, at the Hero® logo emblazoned on the front of it. What if, he thought, he could help Roma? What if he could save her? Maybe it would stop all those people saying all those nasty things about him in the papers. Maybe they would stop printing those horrible pictures with his eyes crossed or scratching his nose. Maybe they would finally believe that he wasn't like his father. Not even a little bit like him.

"How many floors is the building?" Bug asked.

"One hundred and two," said the cop who'd read all the books. "Looks like the sloth's almost a third of the way up now."

Which meant that the sloth was thirty-three floors up. Which was higher than Bug had ever flown before. Which was higher than *anyone* had ever flown. Which impossible. He was so tired that he wasn't even sure he could fly at all, let alone more than thirty-three floors. Anyway, even if he could fly the thirty-three floors, what would he do once he got there?

Pinkwater flew in dizzying circles around his head. He said, "Munchies!"

"What?" Bug said.

"Feed me!" chirped Pinkwater.

"Are you hungry?"

"Hamster!"

"I don't understand what you're talking about," Bug said.

"Feed me!" Pinkwater spiralled up into the air in the direction of the sloth and then back down.

"Do you mean that the hamster is hungry?"

"Hungry!" replied the bird.

"And that I should feed it?"

"Feed me!"

"What should I—" he began, and then he remembered the M&M'S in his pocket.

Chapter 11

Hero

Before he could think better of it, Bug was running towards the Empire State Building. Behind him, he could hear the cops shouting at him, "Stop! Wait! What do you think you're doing?"

What do you think I think I'm doing? Bug thought as he reached the building and launched himself off the pavement. *I'm the Sweet Man. I'm rescuing the damsel of distress. I'm saving the day. I'm—*

—a total idiot. He was only a few floors up, and already he could feel the drag of the air on his skin, the suck of gravity on his body, trying to pull him down. He groaned and thrust his arms straight up, palms crossed, fingers straight. *Come on, come on. You've been higher than this. Get moving.* Five

floors. Ten. Twelve. Eighteen. Twenty. Twenty-three. Above him, he could see the giant hamster's big, shaggy, algae-covered butt, could see Roma clutched in a fat paw like a doll, but they were still floors away. The pull on Bug's body was strong now, more than strong, it was fierce, it was a thousand hands snatching at him, weighing him down. He could feel himself slowing through the thickening air. He wondered where Pinkwater was, if Pinkwater had followed. He couldn't worry about the bird now; Pinkwater could take care of himself.

Just a little more. A. Little. More. Twenty-five floors. Twenty-six. Twenty-seven. It was hard to breathe. His rib cage ached. Every muscle strained. He felt like he was going to snap, to explode, to burst like an over-inflated balloon. He *was* an over-inflated balloon; how big had his head got that he thought he could do this? Twenty-eight. Twenty-nine. He was nearly on the beast now, right up next to him. Roma, who had been silent with shock, turned her head and saw Bug. She started bucking and screaming, trying to pull at the paw that held her, but the giant sloth took little notice and kept climbing, slowly and methodically as it had before. His arm quivering with the effort, Bug reached into his pocket for the M&M'S and drew them out. The sloth stopped climbing, sniffing the air.

"Yeah, that's chocolate. Bet you never smelled anything

like this," Bug panted. He dangled the sweets by the sloth's nose, and then dipped a little in the air. The sloth paused and then followed, descending a few metres.

"What are you doing?" Roma shrieked. "Are you nuts?"

"No, these are plain," Bug said. Bug descended again, and again the beast followed. Bug's whole being was racked with pain, Roma was screaming something about how stupid he was – he was the stupidest boy to walk the face of the earth, why didn't he just save her already. But Bug did his best to ignore it, to keep dangling the sweets, murmuring to the sloth, luring him down. Up close, the sloth was, he had to admit it, kind of cute, in a weird giant hamster sort of way.

Bug dangled the sweets, descended a few more metres. Dangled, descended. He had never moved so slowly in his life before, never understood the meaning of "a snail's pace", until he found himself twenty-five floors up with a giant methodical hamster and a screaming heiress and aching bones and a heart about to pop.

And then the slow and methodical sloth decided to play against type and do something shocking. Surprise! It opened its paw and let Roma drop.

Roma shrieked and fell. Bug managed, just in time, to catch her by the wrist. She was dead weight; heavier than Georgie, and Georgie was a leadfoot. Bug had never felt anything like it. And she wasn't any calmer for Bug than she had been for the sloth; she bucked and kicked just as hard. If she kept this up, he'd drop her too. And there was no way Roma could fly well enough to stop herself from crashing straight to the ground.

"Stop kicking!" he yelled. "I'm saving you!"

"Well then, save me already!" she shrieked. "Get me down."

Good idea.

He was about to gather her up in his arms and take a dive for the earth, when he saw the helicopters in the distance, heard the thrum of the wings slicing the air. These weren't news copters, they were army green and outfitted with guns. As soon as he flew away from the beast, the copters would move in. And who knew what would happen then?

He knew. He'd seen King Kong. The monkey doesn't make it.

Bug, his arm on fire, his ribs like bands of barbed wire around his chest, looked at the sloth. The sloth looked back at him with sad, pleading eyes set like shiny buttons in his shaggy, reddish fur, sniffing the air with its pinkish nose. What had Pinkwater said? Hungry. It was just hungry, that's all. He couldn't let anything happen to it. Especially when it hadn't done anything except kidnap Roma, sniff her head and take her for a little climb up the Empire State Building. And really was that so bad?

He tightened his grip on Roma's wrist and held out the

bag of M&M'S. "Come on, guy. Come on, Kong."

"What are you doing?" Roma yelled. "Did you actually *name* that stupid, stinky animal?"

"Shut up!" said Bug. "Do you want to make it mad?"

"Do you want to make *me* mad?" Roma spat, but then shut up.

Slowly, slowly, slowly, Bug, Roma and beast descended. Bug dangled the M&M'S, the hamster sniffed, they dropped another few metres. Dangle, sniff, drop. Dangle, sniff, drop. Twenty floors. Eighteen. Fifteen. Twelve. Bug could see people inside the building pasted against the windows, watching their descent. He ignored them as he ignored Roma's occasional protests. Ten. Eight. Six. Five. Four. Three. Two. One.

Finally, he was able to reach down with his burning arm and set Roma gently on her feet. Then he landed himself, falling to one knee, nearly keeling over with pain and exhaustion. But he wasn't quite done, and there was no time for keeling. He put the M&M'S bag to his mouth and ripped it open with his teeth as he waited for the sloth to finish its climb.

And then it did. Bug and sloth stood face to face, each staring at the other. Bug said, "Hey there, Kong. Have an M&M." He tossed a few sweets into the sloth's open mouth. The sloth chewed. And chewed. And chewed. And chewed. And chewed some more. Bug had never seen such thorough chewing. It went on for seconds, then minutes, then centuries. Bug was sure he'd lived and died a dozen times before the sloth, finally, swallowed. Then it sat back on its haunches, its huge paws dangling in the air, and like a great, big, shaggy, algae-covered puppy, barked for more.

Behind Bug, a great burst of applause. The cops clapped. The paparazzi snapped. The crowd said, "Awwwww!"

"Way to go," one of the cops said. The police officers dug around in their pockets and came up with their own bags of snacks and sweets and gum. They vied for a chance to feed the sloth. "Kong!" they said. "Over here, Kong! I've got biscuits! I've got toffee! I've got Kangeroo Kola!"

The crowd chanted, "Kong, Kong, KONG!"

Roma yanked Bug to his feet. "My hero," she announced. She grabbed his face and kissed him. All around, cameras flashed. Bug lamely flapped his arms, but Roma had him in a death grip, and there was nothing he could do except stand there imagining the front page of the tabloids: HEIRESS & HERO, SITTING IN A TREE, K-I-S-S-I-N-G.

A familiar voice – a familiar chirp – rose above the din. "Leaving!"

Bug peeled away from Roma, blinking at the lights from the cameras. "Pinkwater?"

The tiny blue bird was circling off to his left. "Leaving!"

"Are you leaving?"

The bird continued to spiral, further away now.

"Leaving!"

"Pinkwater, where are you going?"

"Leaving!" said Pinkwater, in what Bug could swear was a vaguely exasperated tone.

Bug shook Roma off and limped after the bird.

"Come back!" yelled Roma. "Did I say you could go? Did I say we were finished? Bug!"

Bug was gaining on Pinkwater when he slammed into something, someone, he couldn't see. He fell to the ground. He was surprised to find the pavement so comfortable. Maybe he'd sleep for a while...

"Bug!" he heard someone whisper. "Bug, are you OK?"

He felt hands shaking his shoulders but saw nothing. "Georgie?" he said.

"Shhh!"

"OK," he said, and put his head back down on the ground.

"Wake up!"

"I'm awake."

"Is there somewhere we could go?" the voice whispered. "You need to lie down."

"I am lying down."

A sigh. "Somewhere that isn't the pavement."

"My trailer is right over there."

Georgie helped him to his feet and walked him to his trailer, Pinkwater following close behind. Paparazzi followed too, until a cop told them to find someone else to harass for a while. The cop pointed to Bug's Hero® brand T-shirt. "It fits, kid," he said. "Nice going."

"Thanks," Bug said. He opened the door to the trailer, stepped in and shut the door behind him.

Instantly, Georgie appeared. "You should really lie down. You look terrible."

He opened his mouth, about to say something snarky, but found that the words that came to mind weren't snarky ones, they were the same crazy thoughts he'd had when he'd seen her last, back at his apartment building: Gurl was a *girl*. She was as tall as he was – well, OK, maybe a *little* taller – but it was a good tall, a nice tall. Her silver hair hung thick and loose, the bangs sweeping over her grey eyes in the most disconcerting way. He couldn't believe that he ever thought she looked like a weepy dishwater pasty face. He must have been insane. Bug wanted to say it, say, "Hey! Gurl! You're a girl!" which was a) lame, b) stupid, and c) the kind of thing you can't say to ex-friends who think you're a big loser and just might be taller than you but are still nice enough to help you to your trailer after you've saved a spoiled heiress and a chocolate-eating sloth from certain death.

"What are you staring at?" Georgie said.

He shook his head. "Nothing. I'm tired." He flopped down on the couch and closed his eyes. That was a good plan. Because then he wouldn't see her any more. Something about seeing her made him feel funny and confused. It made him want to yell at her for no reason.

After a minute, she spoke. "You still have Pinkwater."

"Yes. I like him."

For a second, he thought she would say something snotty, but she said, "Good. That's good."

Bug opened one eye and peered at her. What was she doing here? Had she come to lecture him about stealing things? To make nasty comments about "falling in the East River"?

"Look," he said, "that photo shoot by the South Street Seaport? I really was pulled off the dock. By a giant octopus. I wasn't making that up. I saw it. It crawled out of the water and ate all the lunch leftovers. It patted me on the head and then slipped back into the water."

"It patted you on the head?" said Georgie.

"You don't believe me," he said.

"I believe you." She paused a minute. She pushed her hair out of her eyes. "You and Roma seem to be happy. She told me... I saw..." She trailed off, blushing.

He was going to say: "Don't believe everything you see" and "I seriously considered giving her back to the hamster." But he didn't say those things. He said: "Yeah. Well."

"You guys have been going out for a while then."

Again, he wanted to say: "Today was the first time I ever met her. She barged into my trailer and demanded that

I take her to the Red Room. Or the Green Room. Or the Tea Room. Or some kind of room. I don't know. Anyway, she's very bossy. And she yells a lot. Who can take all that yelling?"

But he didn't. He said, "So, why did you come?"

It was Georgie's turn to shrug. "I thought I'd say hi."

"You were *invisible*. You were *leaving*."

"I didn't want to bother you."

"You're not bothering me," he said. "I mean, I'm not doing anything else right now."

Georgie's eyes got wide. "You just rescued Roma Radisson from an enormous rodent."

"Well, besides that."

They both laughed. It was nice.

Then he said something that he didn't expect to say: "Um, can I ask you something?"

"Sure. What?"

"Do you think I need to change my hair?"

"What do you mean?"

"Someone said that it was weird and that I should do something about it."

Georgie crossed her arms. "There's nothing wrong with your hair."

"There isn't?"

"No."

"OK," he said. His hair was all right. It wasn't much, but it was something.

"Bug?"

"Yeah?"

She bit her lip. "Thanks for calling me Georgie. You've never called me by my real name before."

He didn't know what to say to that, so he said, "You're welcome. Thanks for believing me about the octopus."

"Sure," she said.

More silence.

Georgie cleared her throat. "It's easy to believe in a lot of weird things when you've just seen a giant hamster climb up the Empire State Building."

"Yeah."

"And when a bronze dog comes to life, bites someone in the sequins and escapes the art museum."

Bug sat up. "What? Bites someone where?"

"And when you've been visited by a Punk."

"Who was?"

"Oh, and a vampire. Who offered you and your parents eternal life. And a poppy-seed bagel."

Bug groaned and put his hands over his face. "I don't want to hear about any of this, do I?"

"Probably not," Georgie said. "But let me tell you anyway."

Chapter 12

Maybe It's the Fangs

Georgie opened her mouth to speak when someone pounded on the trailer door.

"Bug! Are you in there? We've got news crews! Cameras! It's going to be the story of the century!"

Bug looked at Georgie. "Juju," he whispered. "I don't want to see him. I don't want to see anyone."

"No one will see *you*," Georgie whispered back. She grabbed Bug's hand and made them both disappear. The door flew open and Juju peeked his bald turtle head inside. "Bug?" He stepped into the trailer and poked around. "Bug? Are you in here? Everyone wants to interview you."

Georgie and Bug held their breath. Georgie looked down

and noticed that not everything had disappeared. Her left trainer was plainly visible. She could hardly keep herself from clucking her tongue in annoyance. At least, she thought, it looked like an empty trainer just sitting there on the floor. But what if something else was visible? What if, say, her ears were showing? Or her teeth?

She watched Juju carefully, but he didn't appear to notice the red trainer on the floor. He frowned at Pinkwater, who was perched on top of the mini-fridge. "Hey there, bird. Where's your friend?"

"Lonely," chirped Pinkwater. "Lonely, lonely, lonely."

Juju flipped open his mobile phone and barked into it. "Kid's not here. We're going to his apartment. Stall the five o'clock news shows and start calling the news magazines for tomorrow night. Don't worry, I'm gonna find him. I said, I'll find him." Juju kicked open the trailer door and hopped outside.

Georgie tried to let go of Bug's hand, but Bug held on tight. "Let's just get out of here, OK?" he whispered. Pinkwater flew over and landed on Bug's head, promptly disappearing himself.

The three of them slipped from the trailer, unnoticed by the swirling crowds and news cameras and snappily dressed reporters from every conceivable news channel – all supposedly reporting on the same thing:

"Witnesses say that the monster had climbed nearly a third of the way up the Empire State Building when he was lured down by a quick-thinking Bug Grabowski..."

"The monster was forty-four floors and climbing when Bug Grabowski flew in and rescued Roma Radisson from certain death..."

"Sixty floors up in the air, Sylvester 'Bug' Grabowski used his expert martial arts training to disable what we now know is a giant sloth, thought to be extinct..."

"The sloth appears to enjoy chocolate, peanut butter, butterscotch, pizza, donuts, licorice whips, milkshakes, Cheerios, hoagies..."

"In a bizarre but happy twist on the old King Kong story, today a giant sloth climbed to the very top of the Empire State Building and was saved by none other than Bug Grabowski, the son of the jailed gangster Sweetcheeks Grabowski, and current flame of socialite and heiress Roma Radisson..."

"We are speaking with Roma Radisson right now, the heiress who was rescued by her long-time boyfriend, Bug Grabowski. Can you tell us what happened, Roma?"

"Bug saved my life. That's so fab™!"

At this last, Georgie tripped over her own feet and nearly sent the two of them sprawling to the ground. "Sorry," she whispered. Bug didn't respond. Roma was a jerk and a fake, but at least she wasn't falling all over herself all the time. No wonder he wanted to go out with Roma.

"I have an idea," Bug whispered. "A place they'll never look for us." He pulled on her hand, leading her. She'd held his hand before, but it had never felt so weird and uncomfortable. Her palm was sweaty, and her arm felt way too long for her body, like the arm of an orangutan. She was sure Bug was straining just to reach her hand, which was too embarrassing to think about.

So she didn't. She had become an expert on not thinking about things, anyway. She focused on her steps, on putting one invisible foot in front of the other, on not tripping and not falling. She was so busy not thinking about things that she didn't realise that they were walking straight back to the Empire State Building.

"What are we doing?" she whispered.

"We can't go to my apartment," Bug whispered back. "And this is the last place anyone will think to look. We'll go up to the observation deck."

"What if there are people up there? What if there are cops up there? Don't you think they'll hear us talking?"

"Nah," Bug said. "They'll think it's the wind."

"Are you sure?"

"Georgie, I'm going to fall over if I don't sit down soon."

"OK," said Georgie. "Let's go."

They slipped past the reporters and followed a plain-clothes detective into the building. Several cops got off one of the lifts and Georgie and Bug sneaked in. Bug pressed the button for the observation deck and the two of them waited in silence. But since the Empire State Building has superfast lifts, Georgie only had to wait forty-five seconds before lift doors opened on to the eighty-sixth floor. The two of them walked out on to the deck, which was surrounded on all sides with high bars.

"Cool," Georgie whispered as she looked out over the vast city. The noisy, bustling chaos of the city below seemed quiet and still from way up here, the only sound the eerie whistle of the wind. Though the observation deck was deserted and it seemed safe to reappear, she kept close in case she had to turn them invisible quickly. She tried very hard not to notice that the arm she was so close to was a lot, um, beefier, than it had ever been.

"Beefy!" chirped Pinkwater, making Georgie jump.

It seemed wrong not to try one of the coin-operated binoculars placed all around the observation deck, so Georgie popped some quarters into one of them. Bug and Georgie took turns using it. All around, the buildings rose like enormous stalagmites from the ground and the cars moved like toys on tracks. Bug and Georgie noticed the people trying to fly here and there.

"Hmmpf," Bug sniffed. "They look like fleas."

"Yeah, well, not everyone can fly like a Wing."

"Most people can't fly at all," he said. Then he looked at Georgie in horror. "Oh! Sorry, I meant—"

"Don't worry about it," said Georgie. "Most people can't turn themselves invisible. As a matter of fact, *nobody* else can."

"You win," he said, grinning. "So what were you saying earlier about dogs? And vampires? And bagels?"

They sat down on the ground by the binoculars and Georgie told him how the Punk in the plaid trousers had shown up at her door, how the Punk and Noodle had a hissing contest, and how Agnes had chased the Punk away with a lasso of sausage and a meat fork. Then she told Bug about the trip to the museum, how Giacometti's *Dog* had come to life and bitten "one of her classmates", which made Bug laugh.

"And now for the really weird part," she said.

She could hear Bug snort. "As if the other parts weren't weird enough."

"Weird," chirped Pinkwater.

The night before, Georgie told Bug, she had just begun to fall asleep when she heard an odd knocking at the window. At first, she said, she wasn't scared because she thought it was Bug. But of course it wasn't Bug. A young man hovered outside, a young man pale as death (a young man wearing a perfectly fabulous outfit, a detail she didn't mention to Bug). But she still wasn't scared. Not scared enough. He asked to come in and...

"And?" said Bug.

Noodle howled and Georgie froze, staring at the fabulous man-boy who didn't look so fabulous any more. He looked more like what he was, a vampire. A vampire hanging outside her window, a vampire in a shiny shirt and skinny velvet trousers, scratching the pane with a crooked fingernail, grinning at her with pointy teeth.

But he was outside. It was OK because the vampire was outside and he couldn't come in. The window was closed and she wasn't going to open it.

Except that *he* was opening the window. He was opening the window and putting one skinny, velvet-trousered leg inside her room and she couldn't move. She was frozen. How could he get inside her locked window and how could he open the window without even looking like he was opening it and why couldn't she move? And then she remembered something about vampires, about how vampires can't come inside your house unless you let them and she certainly didn't say he could come in, did she? No, absolutely not, she would never tell a vampire that he could come crawl through her window and come into her room. Never, never, never.

Except. He'd mouthed the words, hadn't he? Hadn't he asked to come in and she'd...

...nodded.

Georgie watched in horror as the vampire pushed the

window open wide and put one leg and the other inside the room. He had both legs and all of his body and his whole, pointy-toothed mouth inside her room and she couldn't move. His wings fell against his body, turning into the smooth silk of a cape.

"Hello," the vampire said, his hair almost as pale as his skin. "My name is Phinneas. Lovely room."

"What?"

"The room. It's very nice."

"Uh, thanks," Georgie said.

The vampire strolled around the bed and computer desk, running a thin, bony finger across the furniture. "Most wealthy people don't have such exquisite taste."

Georgie wasn't sure what to say. "OK."

"I've known hundreds of rich people. Kings. Queens. Models. Film stars."

"Really?"

"The stars are the worst," said the vampire. "You wouldn't believe how many of them have life-sized photographs of themselves all over the place. Tacky. Boring too. Are you boring?"

This, Georgie decided to answer honestly. "Yeah, I think I am."

The vampire sighed. "Too bad." He gestured to Noodle. "Well, that's not something you see everything. Is that a riddle?"

Noodle meowed.

"Well," said the vampire. "At least *she's* not boring.

I always liked cats. Maybe it's the fangs."

He smiled, but Noodle issued a warning growl. Georgie wondered if Noodle was being overcautious. That was the problem with cats. They were always jumping to conclusions. Maybe vampires weren't that bad. This one seemed polite.

For a bloodsucker.

Phinneas the vampire exhaled. "I did come for a reason." The vampire reached up and pulled the chain from his neck on which hung a tiny white square, a folded piece of paper. Georgie opened it and found this:

> *Join us for an evening of fun and art and fun at the grand opening of the Chaos Gallery. See fine works by Mandelbrot, Artist and Chaos King. Food and drinks will not be served so bring your own cheeseballs, Cheeseballs.*

Scrawled along the bottom of the invitation was an address at South Street Seaport and a date and time a week away.

Georgie had no idea what to make of this. "You want me to go to an art opening?"

"Mandelbrot really wants you to be there," said the vampire.

"Who's Mandelbrot?" Georgie asked. "Wait, the Punk?"

Phinneas blinked. "The artist."

"Well, I, um," said Georgie. "I appreciate the invitation, but I think I'm busy that day."

"I don't think you understand," the vampire told Georgie. "He needs you to be there."

"I'm sorry about that, but—"

Phinneas's sigh was now one of exasperation. "I really don't think you understand. He'll get very angry. Crazy angry. He'll get so angry that he might just say to me, Phinneas, since she didn't come to my opening, you should go back to her apartment and have a few bites of this or that. And it's boring, you know, the vampire thing. It gets old. Deadly old. I don't recommend it. Now do you understand?"

Georgie read the invitation again. "You mean to say that if I don't go to your gallery opening, you're going to come back here and bite me? And turn me into one of the undead?"

"No," said the vampire. "What I mean is that we might come back here and bite you. But we won't stop with you. Mandelbrot will have us bite your mum and dad too. Maybe even the kitty. Mandelbrot will take everyone you love away from you. Mandelbrot doesn't like love. He doesn't believe in it. Or maybe he does, but he hates it and wants to bite it out of existence. Who can tell?" Phinneas reached under his cape and pulled out a poppy-seed bagel. He held it out to Georgie. "You want one?"

"No thanks."

"I wouldn't either," the vampire said. "This one's stale." He tossed the bagel over his shoulder. "I'm waiting for your answer."

Georgie said, "I guess if my choices are death or art, I choose art."

"Good," said the vampire. "I'll tell Mandelbrot. He'll be happy." Phinneas looked out of the window at the full moon hanging low in the sky. "It's nice that someone will be happy." Georgie watched as the vampire tucked the poppy-seed bagel back under his cape. He walked slowly to the window, stepped up on to the ledge, and dropped outside. A minute later, he rose up again, a dark comma against a midnight blue sky.

Chapter 13

Old Crow

"Who's this Mandelbrot?" said Bug.

"I know he's a Punk, but I don't know anything else about him," Georgie said. "I was planning on looking it up later to see if I could find out anything else."

"And where are they having that art opening?"

Georgie told Bug the address. "You know," said Bug, "that's right around where that octopus pulled me into the water."

"But what could an octopus have to do with a Punk and a vampire?"

"I had these dreams last night, dreams where someone was knocking on my window saying 'let me in, let me in'."

"Let me in!" chirped Pinkwater.

"Maybe they weren't dreams," said Georgie.

"Maybe they weren't."

Georgie shifted, her back aching from sitting so long. "Didn't The Professor have a skeleton that looked like a giant bat at his place?"

"Yeah," said Bug. "But we didn't believe him when he told us there were vampires around." There was a pause, and then: "Maybe we should go and see him."

Georgie thought about this. "He might have some idea about what I should do. I really don't want to go to Mandelbrot's art opening. And I really don't want to spend eternity eating poppy-seed bagels. Or whatever it is that vampires do."

"And maybe he can tell us about the other stuff," Bug said. "The octopus and the sloth and the statue. Something strange is going on, don't you think?"

"I don't know. Maybe none of it is connected."

"And maybe it's all connected," Bug said. "What about the pen?"

"My dad said that he gave it back to The Professor. And he said it was really dangerous. There's no way The Professor would write anything with it."

"I think we need to go and ask him anyway."

"I think you're right."

"Tomorrow?"

"Tomorrow's good." Georgie stood. "I should get home. My parents will be worried."

"Let's just sit here and rest a few more minutes," Bug said. "I'm still tired."

"That's what you get for being such a hero."

"Hero!" chirped Pinkwater, who decided to leave his perch on Bug's head and neatly darn the sky above them. "Ha!"

"OK," said Bug. "I get the joke. I should have let the sloth have Roma."

"I wasn't laughing," said Georgie.

"Then who was that?"

They turned to see a crow perched on the railing behind them. "Ha!" it called. "Ha! Ha! Ha!"

"I've been seeing a lot of those lately," Georgie said.

Another crow joined the first on the railing. And then a third. And a fourth.

"I see what you mean," Bug said.

A fifth crow perched itself on the railing. Then three more arrived.

"This is starting to freak me out," said Georgie.

Pinkwater darted back and forth in front of the crows. "Hello!" he chirped.

"Ha!" said the crows.

"*Bonjour!*" he chirped.

"Ha!" said the crows.

"Ciao!" said Pinkwater.

"Ha! Ha! Ha!" replied the crows. Four more alighted on the railing. Their eyes were black and beady, and their beaks seemed unnaturally sharp.

"Where's a cat when you need one?" Bug said.

"At home, ordering books from Amazon," said Georgie.

They backed all the way into the door to the building and then slipped through it. As soon as they closed the glass door, they looked back at the railing. The crows were gone.

"What do you think they wanted?" Georgie asked.

"I don't know," said Bug. "Birdseed?"

"Ha!" said Pinkwater.

Georgie made them invisible again and they got in an empty lift. Another forty-five-second ride and they were at the ground floor. After all the hubbub, it was strangely hushed. The cops had moved on to other crimes and the reporters to other news stories. All that was left was a bunch of empty sweet wrappers.

"Litterers!" chirped Pinkwater indignantly.

Because Bug was so worn out from saving Roma from the clutches of the giant sloth, Georgie insisted that they take the subway back to his apartment. The fact that Bug didn't argue proved how tired he was. They walked to the subway station and jumped the turnstiles. (When no one was looking, Georgie left a subway pass sitting on top of the turnstile. Georgie might have to disobey her parents by pulling her ghost routine and running around the city unnoticed, but she would never again commit any crime whatsoever, not even one as small as trying to get on a subway that most people didn't want to use.)

"I don't hear any music this time," Bug said.

"I guess we won't be seeing any gators," Girl whispered back. The last time Bug and Georgie had ridden the subway together, they had been chased by a wild bunch of Punks and then witnessed some musicians capturing one of the large albino alligators that lived in the subway system. This time, Georgie hoped for a less eventful ride.

She got what she wished for. No Punks, no musicians, no gators. Just a pleasant, if sort of bumpy, journey uptown. Bug and Georgie got off the train and walked the few blocks remaining to Bug's building. They stepped in to the lift and Georgie let go of his arm, making them both visible (though Georgie had to check herself to make sure that she'd got the job done thoroughly). Both of them were so exhausted from the events of the day that they didn't notice anyone following them down the hallway once they got out of the lift.

"*Hola!*" chirped Pinkwater.

"Hello!" said a strange voice in reply.

Both Bug and Georgie whipped round, surprised. Behind

them was an older woman carrying a ridiculous number of books and wearing a blue hat with feathers on it, the very same old woman Georgie had seen the last time she was at Bug's building. Her sharp dark eyes flicked from Bug to Georgie and back again, as if sizing them up for a fight.

"Hello again, young woman."

She dug around in her oversized pocketbook and pulled out a crumpled flyer. This she held out to Bug.

"For our book group. I was going to push it under your door, but I'm glad I caught you. We thought you might like to join us. My name is Mrs Vorona."

Bug looked at Georgie then back at the old woman. "I don't really have time to join a book group. Sorry."

"We're reading Washington Irving. *The Legend of Sleepy Hollow*. Scary stuff. That should interest a young man like yourself."

"Yeah, um, it sounds great, but like I said, I'm kind of busy."

"Crow!" chirped Pinkwater.

Mrs Vorona's arm drooped and she stared at the bird on top of Bug's head.

"Old crow!" chirped Pinkwater again.

The woman sucked her shrivelled lips into her face in a gesture of extreme disapproval. She stuffed the flyer back into her purse and marched towards the lift.

"Wait!" said Bug. "I'm sorry. He didn't mean it. He's nuts!"

Pinkwater flapped his wings. "Crow! Crow!"

"Shut up, Pink," Bug said.

"Crow," Pinkwater insisted.

The old woman punched the lift button and vanished inside.

"That's great," said Bug. "We've pretty much covered all the bases. Octopi. Sloths. Statues. Vampires. And now we've insulted an old woman. I think our work here is done."

"I'm sure she's fine," Georgie said. "Pink's just a bird. They don't really know what they're saying."

"Crooooooooow," said Pinkwater, somehow drawing out the word.

Bug rolled his impressively large eyes and put a hand to the top of his head so that Pinkwater could hop to his fingers. "So I'll see you tomorrow?"

"Yeah. Why don't you meet me at my house? My parents would like to see you."

Bug seemed surprised. "They would?"

Georgie was surprised that he was surprised. "Why wouldn't they?"

"No reason," said Bug. They stood awkwardly by Bug's door for a minute. "Well," said Bug. "Good night." He gave her shoulder a friendly punch. "Don't talk to any vampires."

"Very funny," said Georgie, rubbing the spot where he'd punched it.

Georgie left, humming to herself as she rode the lift down to the lobby. Despite the fact that Georgie could be one of the undead in a week, despite the fact that Bug was going out with her mortal enemy, she was absurdly happy that she and Bug were friends again, that they would be visiting The Professor the next day. That they would be visiting The Professor *together*.

She supposed this meant that she was maybe, slightly, insane.

The lift door opened and Georgie stepped out, and into, the old woman with the blue hat, Mrs Vorona. "Excuse me!" said the woman, her eyes narrowing when she saw who had nearly barrelled over her.

"I'm sorry," Georgie said. "I didn't see you."

"Teenagers," said Mrs Vorona, "don't often notice what's right in front of their faces."

Georgie looked past the woman and saw that the doors had opened up on the second floor. "I really am sorry. I thought this was the lobby."

Mrs Vorona considered Georgie with those dark eyes of hers. "Things aren't always what they appear to be, young woman," she said. "You should remember that. You and your friend both need to remember that."

Before Georgie could say, "What do you mean?" or "No kidding!" the old woman took a step back and let the lift doors close like a curtain.

Chapter 14

Mandelbrot

While Georgie was lectured by a cranky old crow in a rumpled suit, the vampires gathered in a stinking loft near the South Street Seaport to watch the Punk paint. Mandelbrot wasn't exactly painting – he was smearing a half-eaten peanut butter and jam sandwich across a canvas. But then, the vampires weren't exactly watching, either – they were busy polishing their fangs or ringing their eyes with vast amounts of the eyeliner they were so fond of, trying not to look too interested in anything. For vampires, looking too interested was worse than death (and they were in a position to know). Vampires never wanted to appear as if they were trying too hard. Vampires were nothing if not cool.

But the Punk *did* interest them. This is why they were gathered around him in a grungy loft that reeked of seawater and fish. The vampires had never known a Punk to come up from the subway before. Because his pupils were perpetually black and dilated, he wore dark sunglasses so that the thin light of dusk streaming through the dirty windows wouldn't pain him. On his skinny frame, he sported a pair of black leather trousers and an artfully torn T-shirt on which was written *Oi*. Worn combat boots completed the outfit. Around the Punk's neck, a live vampire bat hung like a pendant.

"Who's that?" murmured one vampire, gesturing at the bat.

"Roger," said another. "Always had low self-esteem, that one."

In between smearing canvases with random food items, the Punk snacked, napped or read aloud from a large stack of books that he had stolen from the library. Complicated books with crazy names like *Understanding Fractals*, *The Search for Sierpinski's Triangle*, and *Advances in Chaos Theory*. He was especially fascinated with a dusty old volume, leather bound, with no identifying marks on the spine, which he studied far more often than the others. As they were turned, the pages of this volume made strange chattering noises like the clacking of teeth, something that might frighten normal people but had no effect on the vampires, who were not frightened of much except for a well-aimed wooden stake.

In addition to the snacking and the reading, the Punk also enjoyed spinning around in circles to make himself dizzy, muttering to himself in Pig Latin, and smashing things with an old broom handle.

In short, this canvas-smearing, bat-wearing, book-reading, thing-smashing Punk was a small breath of fresh air in an otherwise underwhelming century, something for which the vampires were momentarily, if not eternally, grateful.

While the vampires were enjoying this small sliver of interest that had brightened their dark eternity, Mandelbrot himself was occupied with more quotidian matters. Specifically, his takeover of the art world.

It was true that he came from humble beginnings. Mandelbrot was born at 3:15 in the morning on the R train headed to Queens, just another Sid in a world of Sids and Nancys. His mother took one look at him and said, "Crikey! You're an ugly bugger!" something that Mandelbrot would not have known at all if his various aunts and uncles hadn't found it funny enough to repeat on Mandelbrot's birthday every year.

Like all Punks, Mandelbrot was taught the way of the Punks. He excelled at sneering and posturing, and could make so much noise with a couple of trash can lids and some well-timed screeching that even other Punks couldn't take it. He was a decent handbag-snatcher, a passable beggar, a fabulous breaker-and-enterer, and terrific at frightening small children with his haircuts. But the thing that he did best was tagging. He loved spraying his name in paint over the interiors and exteriors of subway cars, on posters, along tunnel walls. He always took his time with it, considering how differently he could paint each letter. And he thought every single tag was a work of art. Maybe a work of genius.

Until he looked around and saw his own name everywhere.

Sid, Sid, Sid. Everyone was named Sid, so everyone's tag was Sid. It didn't matter that *his* Sid was better than everyone else's Sid, it got all jumbled up with the rest of them and cleaned off the cars and the walls just as quickly. And it was even worse when his clan was rounded up and sent to a Punk preserve in England for a time. More Sids than ever there. They had no art, they had no talent. For a time, Sid abandoned his spray cans for an old guitar, writing songs about hypocrisy and disruption and anarchy, songs designed to enrage everyone who heard them, but instead made other Punks jump around and slam into one another happily. (The slamming he could take, the happy he could not.)

Against his family's wishes, Sid left the warm, safe

subway tunnels, venturing to the surface to visit museums. Picasso! Pollack! He looked at their paintings and thought, "I could do that." He yearned to have art on the walls of the finest museums, have everyone admire him for his talent, his artistry, his unique take on life. And his take on life was that the only order in this world was disorder, the only natural arrangement chaos. His paintings reflected things the way they truly were. Mr Fuss had noticed. All that he needed now was for the world to notice.

Mandelbrot dropped the peanut butter and jam sandwich to the floor and stepped back to study the brown and purple smears he'd left. Frowning, he turned and kicked over one of the many grocery bags strewn about the loft. He picked up a bottle of ketchup and shook it before squirting bright red blobs on to the picture. Then he opened a jar of relish, scooped out a fingerful of the green stuff and threw it at the painting where it landed with a *splat!*

He nodded, satisfied. "Chaotic," he said to no one in particular, "don't you think?"

The vampires shrugged, doing their best to seem indifferent. It didn't matter, as the Punk was indifferent to their indifference.

"Very... er... messy, Sid," Phinneas ventured.

"I told you, my name is Mandelbrot."

One vampire nudged another, whispering: "Suppose

I should mention that 'mandelbrot' is also the name of an almond-flavoured biscuit?"

"Shut up and let the man have his illusions," replied the other vampire. "He's our entertainment. Our little clown."

"I'm an artist," the Punk, Mandelbrot, was saying. "That's what Mr Fuss told me. He said my work was outsider art. And I'm the ultimate outsider. I'm an artist of chaos. No, the *king* of chaos. The Chaos King. And kings don't answer to anyone!"

As if to illustrate this point, Mandelbrot grabbed a broom handle and took some practice swings in the air. He pointed at a large crow that had been cleaning its feathers on the windowsill. "A gathering of crows is called a 'murder'," he said, to himself as much as to anyone. "A murder of crows. *Urder-may rows-cray*. Hey, that gives me an idea." He ran to the window and took a shot at the crow, who flew out of range just in time. Mandelbrot chased it around the room, swinging it as if it were a piñata.

"I wish he wouldn't do that," one of the vampires said mildly. "Crows are good people."

"Some are," sniffed another. "Others are such show-offs. Look at me! I can turn into a crow! I mean, so what? I can turn into a bat. Do you see me doing it all the time? Of course not."

Fortunately for the crow, Mandelbrot's aim was off (especially after he spun around in a circle to make himself dizzy). Giggling madly, he waved the broom handle around until he happened to knock the crow out of the air. The bird fell to the floor, stunned.

"Oops," Mandelbrot said. "Dead birdy."

"Ead-day irdy-bay," said one of the vampires.

Mandelbrot wandered over to the peanut butter-and-ketchup-smeared canvas. He considered his work for a moment, then did a happy dance of glee, or accomplishment, or perhaps insanity.

The vampires began to wonder if maybe things had gone from moderately interesting to silly (and if there's anything that vampires detest, it's silliness). But Mandelbrot stopped dancing almost as soon as he started. He eyed the vampires with a sly smile. "I almost forgot! I have something for you." He rummaged in a paper bag and dipped a hand inside it. "What do you think of this? I personally watched them being boiled." He held out a poppy-seed bagel.

The vampires gasped despite themselves. It was impossible that this pathetic Punk knew about the seeds, how much vampires loved seeds. People knew nothing about vampires. Nothing important. All they ever wanted to talk about were the old rumours: the whole sleeping-in-coffins thing, the bad tuxedoes, the terrible accents: *I vant to suck your blud*. No one cared what the vampires *really* craved, what they *really* needed. It wasn't a coincidence that the vampire puppet on Sesame Street liked numbers. It wasn't a coincidence that Count Dracula was called "The Count". But this man couldn't know that. *Nobody* knew. Not any more.

"So you brought us some breakfast," said the eye-rolling vampire, her voice full of doubt. "How nice. Probably day-old bagels."

"Oh no, these are fresh. I convinced the baker to start his work just a wee bit early, before the sun came up," said Mandelbrot. "Just for you."

Mandelbrot upended the bag and dumped the bagels all over the floor, every one of them covered with thousands of beautiful seeds, just ripe for the counting.

The counting!

For the first time in centuries, the vampires felt understood.

They fell on the bagels, grabbing them, counting the seeds to themselves. *One, two, three, four, five* – Oh, what joy! What ecstasy! – *six, seven, eight, nine, ten* – There's nothing better than a good bagel! – *eleven, twelve, thirteen...*

While the vampires blissfully counted poppy seeds and the Punk grinned in triumph, the stunned crow slowly roused herself from her stupor. She got to her feet and flapped her wings, testing. Her sharp eyes darted around the room, finally settling on the stack of books in the corner, the dusty leather-bound volume on top. The crow's cry – "Ha! Ha! Ha!" – didn't sound the least bit amused. She lifted off the ground and hovered in the air for a moment, laughing her sad, knowing laugh, before she threw herself out of the window and disappeared.

Chapter 15

Running Amuck

On Sunday, Bug woke up with Pinkwater sitting on his nose bonking him in the forehead, and with his phone ringing, Juju Fink on the line.

"Bug, baby! The whole world's looking for you," Juju said.

"Tell the world I'm sleeping," said Bug. "Tell them I moved to Russia. Tell them I died."

"I've lined up the Sunday news magazines and the late-night talk shows," Juju said, as if Bug had never spoken. "I've got interviews with Jack Sawyer, Diane Rodan – she wants both you and Roma there, so I'm talking with Roma's people – Katie Kepley, Peter Smollinger – he'll try to make you look stupid, so you'll have to watch out for him – Richard Pritchard, and—"

"I don't want to go on any shows right now, Juju," Bug interrupted. "Maybe later. Next week or something."

"Bug, this is your career we're talking about."

"Yeah," said Bug, and hung up.

But Juju was right: the whole world was looking for Bug. No sooner had Bug left his building than he was accosted by several dozen reporters, all wanting interviews about the sloth and about Roma Radisson. A crowd of girls had gathered behind a police barricade, nearly all of them wearing T-shirts that said KING KONG with a picture of the giant sloth or I'M A HERO FOR HERO®! with a picture of Bug hovering against an Empire State Building backdrop, or TRUE LOVE FOR EVER AND EVER AND EVER with a picture of Roma kissing Bug. At the sight of Bug, the girls started screaming and the reporters jabbing microphones in his face. He turned and flew back into the building. He had to call for a limo and arrange for a dozen or so bodyguards to push through the crowd and usher him into the car.

When he arrived at the Bloomingtons' building, Deitrich the doorman didn't seem surprised to see him. Deitrich opened the door to the limo, immediately opened an enormous umbrella to obscure Bug's face from anyone who might be watching the building, and greeted Bug with his customary gravity.

"Good morning, young sir."

"Good morning," Bug said. He looked up gratefully at the umbrella. "Thanks."

Deitrich said, "You haven't been giving your budgie any caffeinated beverages, have you?"

"What?" Bug peered under the rim of the umbrella and saw Pinkwater circling maniacally overhead. "No, he's always like that."

"Ah," said Deitrich.

Luckily for Bug, he'd left home too quickly to be followed and no one had thought to have people waiting at the Bloomingtons' building. The Bloomingtons were the only souls who saw him. And the Bloomingtons were *delighted* to see him. More than delighted. Far too delighted.

"Bug!" said Mrs Bloomington, grabbing Bug and kissing him on each cheek. "You look so grown up! A young man now!"

"Bug!" said Mr Bloomington, grabbing Bug's hand and pumping it up and down. "Working out with the weights, I see."

"Mrrrow!" growled Noodle, who wound herself enthusiastically around Bug's shins.

"Hi," said Georgie, waving rather lamely from a few metres away.

"Cat!" Pinkwater chirped, and landed on Noodle's head.

Georgie was sure she was about to watch Noodle make a snack out of Pinkwater, but the cat merely ran a paw over her ear and shoved the bird off her head. Pinkwater was back in an instant. Noodle did it again, and again the bird came back. After the third shove, Noodle adopted a rather resigned expression. "Cat!" chirped Pinkwater. "Purr."

Georgie's mum insisted that Bug join them for lunch and Georgie's dad proceeded to pepper Bug with questions about the episode with King Kong (as the city had dubbed the sloth), Bug's training schedule for various flying races, his opinions on local politics, and his investment portfolio.

"Dad," Georgie said. "He's only fourteen."

"You're never too young to invest wisely," replied Sol, gesturing with a pickle. "I started investing when I was nine years old."

"I—" Bug said.

"I heard something about a sea monster at a photo shoot," said Bunny Bloomington. "And what is this business with Roma Radisson that the reporters keep going on about?" She sipped delicately at her seltzer water.

"Mum!" said Georgie.

"The TV said that you two have been an item for a while," Bunny went on, as Georgie sank lower and lower in her chair.

"Well, I—" said Bug.

"Are you sure she's the right girl for you?"

"I—" said Bug.

"You're a bit young to go steady."

"I—" Bug said.

"Though I remember when I met your father, Georgie. I was twenty-one. He was so handsome. I couldn't resist him."

That's it, Georgie thought. She had to get Bug out of there before the Bloomingtons ran completely amuck. First they would get out the wedding video, and then the honeymoon pictures, and then the fourteen thousand photographs of Georgie, bald and toothless, drooling on a blanket. "OK," Georgie said, leaping up. "We're going now."

"Off so soon?" Bunny said. "Bug isn't even done with his sandwich."

"I—" said Bug.

"He's not hungry," Georgie said, yanking Bug out of his chair. Bug saw the expression on her face and put his sandwich down. "And we want to catch the early show," Georgie added.

"What show is that?" Georgie's mum wanted to know.

Georgie was prepared for this. "The two o'clock showing of the old King Kong. It's playing at the Rialto." She opened her knapsack and Noodle hopped in. The cat turned around in the bag so that her face stuck out the top. Pinkwater perched himself on the top of her head, ignoring Noodle's meows of annoyance. (It seemed that Pinkwater was impervious to signs of annoyance.)

"I thought you didn't care much for black-and-white films," Bunny Bloomington said to Georgie.

"Bug likes them," Georgie told her.

Bunny looked at Bug, who said, "I—"

"Bye!" said Georgie. She kissed her mum and then her dad.

"Remember," said Bunny Bloomington. "The film and straight home, all right?"

"Yes," said Georgie. "Straight home."

"And no outings," she added as Georgie and Bug walked out the door. Only her clasped hands revealed her worry.

"No outings," agreed Georgie, crossing her fingers in the pocket of her new jeans.

Once the door to the Bloomington's penthouse closed, Georgie motioned for Bug to follow her to the stairs. Georgie took deep breaths, trying very hard not to be angry with her parents, who she was sure meant well, even if they were on the verge of embarrassing her to death.

"What did your mum mean, no outings?" whispered Bug once they were in the stairwell.

"No invisibility. She's afraid someone will see us going in or out of sight. She doesn't want anything bad to happen to me."

"Like what my father did to you," said Bug.

Georgie had never apologised for what she'd said back at his apartment and she blushed at the reminder. "Like what *Sweetcheeks* did to me," Georgie said. "He's about as much your father as Hope House for the Homeless and Hopeless was a home."

Bug stared at her for so long that Georgie thought she might melt from anxiety. But then he said, "If we can't be invisible," he said, "we're going to have a heck of a time getting to The Professor's without the planet wondering what we're doing. You wouldn't believe the crowds waiting for me outside my building this morning. And if they see you with me..." He trailed off, blushing.

Georgie bit her lip. The last thing she wanted to do was disobey her parents; she loved them. But then she didn't want to scare them, either, and telling them about the vampires would most certainly scare them, terrify them even, and she couldn't do that. She also couldn't find out what was behind the vampires' invitation, or who Mandelbrot was, or if the sloth, octopus and statue incidents were related if she didn't ask The Professor. And they couldn't get to The Professor unless they were invisible, so...

"Just one more time," she said to Bug. "And only because we have to. We'll take the stairs. The stairwell ends in the garage. We'll sneak out that way. No one will see us coming or going."

Bug peered down over the banister. "How many flights up are we?"

"Thirty," said Georgie.

"That's a lot of steps," Bug said. "I'd fly us down, but I'm still tired from the whole Kong thing."

"One step at a time." She held out her hand and Bug took it. The familiar tingle, the wash of invisibility, came over them both, as well as over Noodle and Pinkwater in Georgie's backpack. Georgie checked to make sure everyone was completely invisible, and then took a step forwards. And missed the first step, barely catching herself on the railing.

"Whoa!" chirped Pinkwater.

"Whoa," said Bug.

"Sorry," Georgie said, cursing her huge, traitorous feet, her stupid clumsy body. She couldn't fly and now she couldn't even *walk*.

"Never mind," Bug said. "I think I can manage this." He lifted them about twenty centimetres in the air and glided them down all thirty flights, dropping them gently at the bottom.

"Thank you," said Georgie.

In reply, Bug squeezed her hand. It was so hard to reconcile the Bug that was squeezing her hand and the Bug that would go out with Roma Radisson, *Dunkleosteous*.

At the door that led to the parking garage, Georgie looked through the small window to see if anyone was around. No one was. Georgie opened the door a crack wide enough to let them through. Though it was a bright sunny day outside, the parking garage was dim and grey, illuminated here and there by a buzzing florescent bulb.

They walked past the cars. One day, there wouldn't be any cars, or at least, cars with wheels. Instead, there would be cars that hovered entirely in the air, propelled by the same kind of energy that allowed humans to fly. At least, that's what Georgie's science teacher believed. Georgie told her father this and Solomon Bloomington had laughed. He told Georgie that her science teacher didn't know anything about the energy that allowed humans to fly. No one but The Professor did. And The Professor, said Solomon, didn't seem too keen on sharing his secrets.

They reached the exit. The exit itself was an iron gate operated by a guard manning a small booth

"Guard," Bug whispered. "What do you want to do?"

She yanked on Bug's arm, pulling him behind the nearest parked car. "Hide here and get ready."

Georgie tiptoed to the booth. Inside, the guard faced away from Georgie, absorbed in a book. She slowly turned the knob. Georgie reached an invisible arm inside the booth and flicked the switch to operate the gate. The guard looked up from his book. "What the...?"

Georgie ran around the parked car and grabbed for Bug's hand, but ended up hitting him in the face by accident.

"Ow!" he said.

"Shhh!" she said.

"Hey!" said the guard, who was now outside the booth,

scanning the garage. "Who's back there? Mrs Hingis? Did you lose your car again?"

Georgie made Bug invisible and the two of them ran through the open gate. But Georgie tripped, and they went tumbling to the ground. Bug instantly reappeared.

"Hey!" yelled the guard, flying towards the gate. "You're not a tenant! Where did you come from? What are you doing?"

Bug scrambled to his feet and ran around the side of the building, an invisible Georgie right behind him. Unfortunately, someone had got word that Bug was visiting the Bloomingtons and there was a sizable crowd of girls gathered there. Screaming, jumping, flying, shrieking girls.

"Bug!" they shrieked as soon as they saw him. "My hero!"

"Bug! I love you!"

"Bug! Dump Roma and marry me!"

Bug frantically looked from left to right, wondering how he might escape; Georgie couldn't make him invisible in front of everyone. But Deitrich the doorman was already on the case. He whistled a piercing whistle and immediately a cab pulled up to the curb. Unfortunately, it wasn't a regular cab; it was a horse-drawn carriage that usually took tourists on leisurely rides around Central Park.

"Beggars can't be choosers," said Deitrich gravely, hustling Bug into the carriage.

"Where to?" said the driver, who was dressed like an

eighteenth-century liveryman, complete with top hat and breeches.

"Can you get me downtown fast?" said Bug.

The driver grinned and snapped the reins. The team of four white horses immediately broke into a swift gallop that nearly propelled Bug from his seat. The horses were going so fast that the motion lifted the carriage off the ground and sent it skidding and bumping on the pavement. Bug sighed with relief when he felt Georgie's invisible hands gripping his arm and heard Noodle's angry yowl as the carriage thundered down Fifth Avenue; at least she had managed to get into the carriage before they'd sped away. All along Fifth Avenue, stunned shoppers paused in midair to gape and cars slammed on their breaks.

"Yiiii-hah!" yelled the driver, cutting off a city bus with a clamour of hooves.

"Look out!" yelled Bug, as the horses bore down on great snarl of cars blocking the intersection ahead.

But the driver snapped the reins again. The horses lowered their heads and charged at the cars. Bug screwed his eyes shut, waiting for the inevitable crash. Then he felt the carriage behind lifted in the air. He opened his eyes to see the horses sailing *over* the cars, dragging the carriage along with them. One car, two cars, three cars, four, six, eight, ten. The leap of the horses seemed to last an eternity. If he didn't know better,

Bug would have thought that the horses were flying.

When the road was clear, the horses landed with a great clattering of hooves and carriage wheels. They kept up this furious pace all the way downtown as Bug directed the driver to The Professor's apartment, tucked beneath a dry cleaning shop.

"Whoa," yelled the driver, pulling up hard on the reins. The horses stopped.

Bug got out of the carriage carefully, as if he didn't trust his legs to hold him up after the wild ride.

"You better get inside," said the driver. "I hear news helicopters. This place will be swarming in a minute or two if me and the girls don't get out of here." The driver tipped his hat towards the horses.

"What do I owe you?" Bug asked. "I mean, what do I owe you and the girls?"

The driver smiled. "Nothing. We owe you. Not often we get to run like that."

One of the horses turned her head and looked at Bug. She was strangely shiny, as if she had been painted. Bug could have sworn that she actually winked at him before the driver once again snapped the reins and the carriage was gone in a blur of hooves.

Georgie waited until they were behind the building before she made herself visible. "I didn't think I'd live through that one," she said.

"Me neither," said Bug. They searched for the familiar KEEP OUT signs that had graced The Professor's door, but the signs had been removed.

"Huh," Bug said. "I think I'm a little sad that he took down all his signs. What do you think that means?"

"I don't know."

They knocked on the door, half expecting to hear what they'd heard the very first time they'd visited The Professor: Go away! Find your fortunes elsewhere! Shoo! But they heard nothing.

"Do you think he went out?" Bug said.

"Out?" said Georgie. "Since when does The Professor go out?"

"He went to your party," Bug said. "The one after Flyfest."

"Yeah, but that was the first time he'd been out in ten years."

"Running amuck," chirped Pinkwater, popping out of Georgie's backpack.

"The Professor's running?" Bug asked.

"Amuck," Pinkwater finished.

"Pink seems to know stuff," Bug told Georgie. "But what does he mean?"

Georgie knocked again. "Professor? It's Georgie Bloomington! Gurl! Hello?"

Still no answer.

"What if something's wrong?" Bug said.

"The Professor can take care of himself," Georgie said, but couldn't help the chill that raced down her back.

"The heck with this," said Bug. *Wham!* He punched the door, then shook his fist in pain.

"Smart," Georgie said.

Bug scowled at her and pulled a paper clip from his pocket, giving Georgie a sheepish look as he unbent it and fit it into the lock. "I always keep a paper clip. Just in case."

In a second, he had the door unlocked. He twisted the knob and pushed. It swung open to reveal a dark staircase. Bug and Georgie glanced at each other and proceeded down the stairs. When they saw what was at the bottom, Georgie gasped, clapping her hands over her mouth.

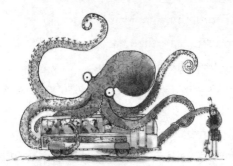

Chapter 16

The Queen Says "Stupid!"

The Professor's apartment was completely different. Gone were the piles of papers, the various hot plates, the old metal filing cabinets, the rows of beer cans, the skeleton of the giant bat, the hundreds of cats. On the bare, dirty tiles sat piles of brown boxes, which men in blue jumpsuits were packing with various items.

"Hello?"

Another man floated from the back room. His wide-set brown eyes were so light they were almost yellow, draped underneath by small pouches of crêpey skin. A high forehead laddered with lines curved into a stiff bristle of hair that fought the heavy gel used to comb it back.

Wayward fronds stuck up here and there.

The man smoothed his hair and stuck his hands in his pockets. "Can I help you?"

Georgie found her voice. "We were looking for The Professor."

"Of course," the man said. "Unfortunately, he's travelling at the moment. He asked that we put his things in storage for him."

"Who are you?" Bug asked bluntly.

"Oh, I'm sorry," the man said in his pleasant, mild voice. "Let me introduce myself. I'm Mr Fuss." He shook each of their hands. "I recognise you," he said to Bug. "You would be Bug Grabowski, yes? I see your name in the papers all the time."

"I hope you don't believe everything you read," grumbled Bug.

"Oh, I don't," said Mr Fuss. "Words are tricky things. And words build into books, which are even trickier." He turned to Georgie. "And you're Georgetta Bloomington. You look just like your mother."

"You know my mother?" Georgie said.

"Only by her beautiful face on the society pages of the *Times*," said Mr Fuss smoothly. "I hope you're adjusting to life outside the orphanage. It must have been a difficult transition for you."

"Yes. I mean, I'm fine, thank you."

"Where is The Professor travelling to?" Bug wanted to know.

"I don't have the particulars," Mr Fuss replied. "All he said was that he was in need of a long holiday. I don't blame him. He's a lot older than he looks. I was always telling him to get more rest."

Bug looked at Mr Fuss warily. "So you were friends with The Professor?"

"Yes. Very good friends." He noted Bug's suspicious expression. "You doubt that The Professor had friends, am I right? I'll admit that he's not the easiest person to get along with, but I assure you we get along very well. He's brilliant. And I'm the sort who admires brilliance." He smiled broadly, and Georgie could see that the first molar behind the left eyetooth was gold.

From the backpack, Noodle meowed loudly. "Where are all the cats?" Georgie asked. "The Professor couldn't have taken them all on holiday."

"We had them shipped to a facility in Brooklyn where they will be well cared for," Mr Fuss said. "But I'm sure you two charming youngsters didn't come here to discuss the cats."

"We had some questions that we thought he could answer."

"Believe it or not, I'm very good at answering questions," said Mr Fuss. "Why don't you give me a try? I've spent lots of time with The Professor. His brilliance might have rubbed off a little." Again with the broad smile, the gleam of the gold tooth.

Bug and Georgie glanced at each other.

"Oh, come on. What do you have to lose?" Mr Fuss perched on the end of one of the boxes.

Georgie wasn't sure if they should trust Mr Fuss. Then again, what would be the harm in telling him about the vampires? If he didn't know anything about vampires he would just laugh at them. And if he did...

Bug decided for them both. "Georgie's having a little vampire problem."

Mr Fuss appeared to be delighted by this. "Really? What do you mean, problem?"

Georgie told him how a Punk named Mandelbrot came to visit, then sent a vampire to threaten to turn her and her family into one of the undead if she didn't attend the opening of an art gallery.

Mr Fuss, who had been watching Pinkwater circle the room maniacally, said, "Who's Mandelbrot?"

"I don't know."

"And you said that whoever this person is, he'll send the vampires to bite you if you don't attend a gallery opening?"

Georgie reached into her back pocket and pulled the invitation out. "Here," she said, handing it to Mr Fuss. He patted his pockets for his reading glasses and put them on. Georgie noticed that the glasses were the designer kind, with small lenses and silver rims.

Mr Fuss removed his glasses and gave Georgie the

invitation. "I don't see much to worry about," he said. "I think the vampires might be playing a joke on you. They love jokes."

"Joke?" said Georgie. "It didn't feel like a joke when they were standing in my room."

"Vampires aren't what people have made them out to be. They're just bored. It makes them mischievous."

"Mischievous!" Georgie said.

"Trust me," said Mr Fuss. "Vampires don't do much but hang around all day and go clubbing at night. They love nightclubs. They're completely harmless."

"What about the blood drinking thing?" said Bug. "That sounds dangerous."

Mr Fuss waved a hand. "Blown all out of proportion because of the fact that you have to be bitten to become a vampire. But they really don't like drinking blood. They can go years without it, you know. A tiny nip of a gerbil now can tide them over for a decade."

"So, should I go to this gallery opening?"

"If I were free, I'd go. It sounds like a lot of fun to me. When will you get another chance to rub elbows with a bunch of vampires?"

Rub elbows? thought Georgie.

Bug said, "What about the giant sloth?"

"What about it?"

"Don't you think it's strange?"

"I don't know about strange," said Mr Fuss. "I just wrote a paper a few months ago about how scientists had been mistaken that *Megatherium* was extinct. Didn't expect to see one wandering around the city, however."

"Or climbing up the Empire State Building," said Bug.

"Or climbing up the Empire State Building," Mr Fuss echoed. "Got a bit of a workout, did you? But you're a strong young man, I suppose you can take it. Did you ever think about trying yoga? I find that it keeps me very limber."

"How do you think a giant sloth got into the city in the first place?" Georgie said.

"I expect someone brought him in to put him in a zoo or in some other type of exhibit and the thing got loose. Just like in King Kong, eh?" Mr Fuss laughed. It was a relaxed, easy laugh that went with Mr Fuss's relaxed, soothing voice and his relaxed posture. Everything about him was relaxed. He was so relaxed he was nearly falling over.

"The sloth is not the only giant thing that's been wandering around the city," said Bug.

"Oh?" said Mr Fuss.

He told The Professor about the giant octopus that had pulled him into the East River while he was doing a photo shoot.

Mr Fuss considered this. "Well, we don't know that much about cephalopods except that that they are very bright. It's possible that a particularly large specimen found its way into the river and decided to have a little fun with you. And perhaps it was looking for a meal."

"But don't you think it's odd that a giant octopus and then a giant sloth show up in the same city at practically the same time?"

Mr Fuss gave a relaxed shrug. "I don't know." He crossed one leg over the other and Georgie noticed his boots. Alligator-skin boots. *Albino* alligator skin.

"There's one more thing that happened," Georgie said, eyeing those boots. She related the story about Giacometti's *Dog* and how it came to life, bit Roma, and ran away. "It's still missing," she said. "I checked with the museum."

"Now, that *is* strange," said Mr Fuss. "I'll have to give that one some thought, perhaps work up a few calculations. Or maybe we'll just wait until The Professor comes back. But I'm not sure that any of these things are things that the two of you need to concern yourselves with."

"Yes, but they seem to want to concern themselves with *us*," said Bug.

Mr Fuss leaned forwards. "Listen, I want you two to pay attention to me. You have good lives now, both of you, very good lives, don't you?"

Georgie and Bug nodded.

"I don't see any good reason for either of you to worry about sloths or any of these other things."

Bug said, "But—"

"I'm simply saying," Mr Fuss interrupted, "that maybe you're looking for danger and for evil plots that aren't there. I know that's how your lives *were*, but I don't think that's what's happening *now*. Just a few strange coincidences. That's all. Just coincidences. And I assure you, there'll be less of those if I have anything to do with it."

Georgie said, "But—"

"Listen to me. Your parents love you. They did everything they could to find you. And you're finally where you belong – with them. Why not enjoy that?"

"But—" said Bug.

"And *you* finally got away from that terrible man, Sweetcheeks. And you found out that in a world full of people who yearn to fly, you're one of the few who can do it exceptionally well. Why not enjoy that?"

Bug and Georgie glanced at each other, unsure of what to think.

"Go to your party," said Mr Fuss. "Have a good time."

Georgie had a funny feeling about Mr Fuss. But then, she couldn't deny what he was saying. All of the weird things that had happened could be just coincidences. The city was a weird place, and a lot of weird things happened in it. Didn't have to mean that all these weird things were about *her*. Actually, that was an arrogant way to think. Like something Roma would think. And the last thing in the world Georgie wanted to be was like Roma.

"Well," said Georgie, "if you really don't think we should worry. Maybe we won't."

At this, Noodle growled, but nobody paid much attention.

"That's the spirit!" said Mr Fuss, standing. "I've enjoyed our little chat immensely, but I'm afraid I do have to get back to packing now."

"OK," said Bug, "but—"

"Bye-bye," Mr Fuss said cheerily and practically shoved them at the door. But before they could leave, Mr Fuss put a hand on Bug's shoulder. "Oh! One more question."

"Yeah?" Bug said.

"The Professor wanted me to make sure that a certain item was in safe hands while he was on vacation, but I can't seem to find it."

"What item?" asked Georgie.

"A pen?" said Mr Fuss. "He said it was around here somewhere."

Georgie felt the flush rising in her cheeks. "We don't know where the pen is."

"No?" said Mr Fuss. He turned to Bug. "I suppose you don't either?"

Bug shook his head. "Nope."

"Too bad," said Mr Fuss, looking from Bug to Georgie with the queerest expression on his face, a *hungry* expression. "Well, thank you both anyway. And have fun at your party." He slammed the door in their faces.

While the men in blue jumpsuits continued packing, Mr Fuss nibbled at a PowerPump! energy bar. It tasted like pulverised wood chips with a couple of mouldy peanuts thrown in, but Mr Fuss ate it anyway. He needed to keep up his strength. He was an important man with an important job. And right now his job was to get all this material back to the lab for analysis.

As he ate, Mr Fuss considered the children. Things were getting out of control, and this annoyed him. And Mr Fuss was afraid he hadn't been subtle, and this annoyed him even more. He prided himself on his subtlety. But the children hadn't trusted him, so of course they weren't about to give him any clues. How he had wished he could have simply throttled the information out of them right then and there. But Mr Fuss could not harm the children, he could not touch a hair on their chinny-chin-chins. His employer would never allow such a thing. It was bad enough that he'd asked about the pen. No, Mr Fuss would have to let his freelancers, Mandelbrot and the vampires, do the dirty work. What an interesting party that art opening would be. As long as the vamps kept their end of the bargain. As long as Mandelbrot entertained them enough.

Oh, the uncertainty of it all! Mr Fuss hated it. Hated that

this city, which should be neat and orderly as a row of windows on a skyscraper, was polluted with magic pens and mad Professors and punky Punks. It galled him that to combat chaos, he had to employ chaos.

It was not natural.

"Hey, boss," said of the blue-suited men.

Mr Fuss crumpled his energy bar wrapper irritably. "What is it?"

"What do you want me to do with this?" The man held out an old rusty coffee can.

"I don't know. Make coffee?"

"Don't think there's coffee in here, boss."

"Fine," said Mr Fuss. "What's in it?"

The man rattled the can. "Sounds like metal."

"Here's an idea. Why don't you open it and take a look?"

"Oh. Right." The blue-suited man opened the can like he was pulling the pin out of a grenade. A mechanical bumblebee darted out.

"Stupid!" it buzzed in its tinny voice. "The Queen says, *stupid*!"

Mr Fuss caught the bee smartly in his hand. "Stupid," he echoed as he threw it to the floor and crushed it under his albino alligator-skin boot.

Chapter 17

Hitting the Books

Bug and Georgie were both so baffled by their visit to Mr Fuss that they forgot about invisibility. They walked down the street, silent, until Bug said, "I don't like it."

"What?" said Georgie.

"Any of it. That guy said he was friends with The Professor. The Professor doesn't have any friends. The Professor doesn't even like people. And if that guy was such good friends with The Professor, and The Professor had asked him to pack up his stuff, why didn't he know where the pen was? And what was that stuff about the vampires not being dangerous?"

"Maybe they aren't."

"That's not how you made them sound," Bug said. "And if

they were harmless, why did Noodle freak out so much? *She* seemed to think they were dangerous."

"Meow," said Noodle, seemingly in agreement.

"Teeth," chirped Pinkwater.

"So," said Bug, "do you think they're club-hopping jokers? Or did you believe them when they said they would bite you and turn you into one of the undead?"

Georgie sighed, thinking of sad vamp with the cool trousers. "I believed them. I think I still believe them."

"What do you want to do?"

Georgie straightened the straps of the backpack. "I think that we have to do things the hard way."

"What's the hard way?" Bug asked.

"I think we should go to the library."

"What's at the library?"

"Books," said Georgie. "And computers and documents. We can start doing some research."

"But research on what? We don't know anything."

"We can start with Mandelbrot. And then we can look up Giacometti, vampires and giant sloths and octopuses... octopi... whatever. Anyway. I'm sure we'll find something that connects them all."

"But what if it's the pen?" said Bug.

"I think The Professor still has it. And I don't think that The Professor would use the pen himself. He knows it's too dangerous. And I don't think he's friends with Mr Fuss; I think he left to get *away* from Mr Fuss. But since we can't ask him what's going on, we'll have to figure it out ourselves."

"OK," Bug said dubiously. "I guess we can try. I don't know what else to do."

They turned the corner and headed for the subway that would take them to the library. At first, people flew, skipped, and bounced all around Bug and Georgie without really seeing them, too busy to focus on any one person. But after walking just a few minutes, Georgie noticed the sideways glances, the stares, mostly directed at Bug, but some looking at her too, some looking at both of them. Georgie grabbed Bug's hand.

"Hey," he said.

"Shhh!" she hissed. "People are looking at us."

Bug's buggy eyes took in the crowds passing by. "I can't go anywhere any more," he said. "It's horrible."

"Yeah, well, we'll worry about your celebrity problems later. We have to get out of the street."

The two of them ducked into a china shop. The shop was small and crowded with shelf after shelf of delicate bone china. In the centre of the shop, a large bull with a gold ring through its nostrils scanned the vast array of teacups and saucers, snorting thoughtfully. The shopkeeper, a bony woman in a cardigan and cat's eye glasses, turned to stare at Georgie and Bug.

"There's a bull in my china shop," she whispered.

"Um, yeah," said Georgie. "Good luck with that."

Georgie turned round and yanked Bug out of the shop. Down the block, a tour group was filing into a souvenir shop tucked between two delis. She pulled Bug over to the group and, once they were inside the store, let go of his hand. As they were too busy poring over postcards of the Statue of Liberty and flipping through T-shirts with King Kong (the sloth version), no one noticed the two extra tourists milling inside the shop.

Georgie bought two baseball caps and a pair of oversized sunglasses. Outside the store, they put on their disguises. Bug, of course, got the sunglasses.

"Why don't you turn us invisible?" Bug whispered.

"We can't take books out or use the computers in the library that way. But we need a disguise. Put the glasses on."

"This is stupid," said Bug. But he put them on.

"Not bad," said Georgie. "With your eyes hidden, no one will be able to tell it's you."

Pinkwater popped out from the backpack. "Eyeballs!" he chirped.

Bug touched Georgie's hair, which she had threaded through the back of the cap in a ponytail. "You should probably tuck this into the cap or something." He seemed to realise what he was doing and pulled back his hand as if burned. "I mean, it's not a regular colour. Most people don't have silver hair."

"Except old ladies," Georgie said.

"I like it," Bug blurted. And then coughed.

"Pretty!" chirped Pinkwater. From deep inside the backpack, Noodle meowed.

Georgie fumbled with her cap, doing the best she could to stuff all her hair into it. *He likes it,* Georgie thought. *What does that mean?* She thought about her orangutan arms, her huge, clumsy feet. *Nothing. It means nothing. He's going out with Roma. The* Dunkleosteus. *The* Velociraptor. *The vampire. That's who he likes.*

When she was finished tucking, she said, "How's this?"

He barely looked at her. "Good."

See? He can't even look. He was just being nice.

"Let's go," said Bug. "But if anyone starts to bug me..."

"You're already bugged."

"Ha-ha. If anyone starts to *bother* me, we're outta there."

"Deal," Georgie said. She glanced behind her. "Noodle?"

One of Noodle's green eyes peered out of the top of the backpack. "You guys need to stay down, OK? We'll try not to take too long."

Noodle meowed in response and pulled her head back into the backpack, settling down for a nap. Bug and Georgie took the subway uptown to the research library. The lions were still and silent as usual, and Georgie wondered if the lion suits were as hot and stuffy as they looked.

Inside the library, it was quiet but for the echo of shoes against the floor, the soft shush of pages turning. Bug stared at the vaulted ceilings, the giant candelabras that held rows of lights.

"Have you ever been here before?" Georgie asked Bug.

"No," said Bug. "Pretty cool. Kinda creepy, though."

"Creepy?"

"Well, it's so quiet. It's like a tomb or something."

"Like you've been to so many tombs," Georgie said.

"Can I help you?" Georgie and Bug turned. Georgie grinned when she saw Hewitt Elder standing in front of them, her head bound in a blue scarf. Hewitt smiled back, but her grin fell when she saw Bug.

"Hi!" Georgie said, too loudly.

"Shhh!" said Hewitt.

"Sorry." Georgie lowered her voice. "It's me, Georgie Bloomington. We met—"

"Yes," Hewitt Elder, staring at Bug. "I remember you. You were with that girl. What's her name? Athens. Paris. Naples."

"Roma," Georgie corrected.

"Whatever," said Hewitt.

"I wasn't with her. I mean, she goes to my school and everything, but we're not friends."

"Congratulations," Hewitt said, with just a little more warmth.

"Did you get my e-mail? I really did like your poems," Georgie added.

Hewitt raised a doubtful eyebrow.

"Really."

Hewitt nodded, a gesture of acknowledgment.

"And Bug did too, didn't you?" she elbowed Bug in the ribs.

"Oh!" Bug said. "Yeah. Sure."

Now Hewitt frowned. "You're Bug Grabowski."

"Yes," Bug said. "But we don't want anyone to know it's me. I've been having some problems being recognised."

"Poor baby," Hewitt said. "That must be terrible."

"It is. I—"

Hewitt cut him off. "Nice sunglasses. Are you two looking for something in particular?"

"We're looking for a bunch of stuff," Georgie said. "But we should probably do one topic at a time."

"Good idea," Hewitt said dryly.

"OK," Georgie said. "How about Mandelbrot?"

"Mandelbrot?" said Hewitt. "You're researching biscuits?"

"What?" said Georgie.

"A mandelbrot is a type of biscuit," Hewitt explained not very patiently.

"This is the name of a person," Georgie said.

"Well, this person was named after a biscuit," Hewitt said. "But I'll look it up for you. Wait here." Hewitt stalked away, her back erect as a queen's.

"She's friendly," said Bug.

"She is, isn't she?" Georgie said.

"No."

"Well, I like her. I think she's the kind of person who will warm up once you get to know them."

Bug shrugged. "OK."

After a few minutes, Hewitt came back. "Not just a biscuit after all," she said. "Turns out it's also the name of a rather famous mathematician. Did some work on chaos theory."

"What's chaos theory?" Bug asked.

Hewitt handed him a book and smiled tightly. "Why don't you read up on it?"

Bug took the book as if it might bite him. "OK."

"The reading room's on the top floor," Hewitt said. "Go up and find some seats. I'll hunt around for something else while you're working. Give me another topic?"

"Sloths," Bug said.

Hewitt scowled. "Not that again. Everyone wants to know about sloths." She stormed away.

"You're right," said Bug. "She's much nicer when you get to know her."

"Shut up," Georgie said.

They took the steps to the top floor reading room. The room was enormous, long as a city block at least, and brightly lit by rows of chandeliers and by the sun streaming through the large windows. Murals of blue skies and fluffy clouds covered the ceiling. Bug and Georgie found some seats near the door so that Hewitt wouldn't have to look too hard for them when she came back. (Georgie didn't want to make Hewitt more irritable than she already was.) They opened the book Hewitt had given them and started reading.

About twenty minutes later, Hewitt returned with some more books. "How's the reading?" she whispered.

Georgie looked up, bleary-eyed. "Hard," she said. "Not sure I understand this chaos theory stuff. This book seems to be saying that everything is random but sometimes isn't. Or it's random in expected ways, which means that's not random. Right?" She shook her head.

If Hewitt understood chaos theory, she chose not to explain it. "Here is some material on sloths," she said, saying the word "sloths" as if it were a curse. "Anything else?"

"Yeah," said Bug. "Vampires. And octopi. Specifically giant octopi." He turned to Georgie. "And what's that guy's name? The guy who made the statues at the museum?"

"Giacometti."

"You want some information on vampires, giant octopi and Giacometti," said Hewitt. "This must be some little book report the two of you are working on."

Georgie felt stupid. "I'm sorry to keep bothering you. You don't have to look for the books for us. I'm sure we could find them ourselves."

"Don't be silly; I'm happy to do it," Hewitt said to Georgie, though she gave Bug another dirty look.

"Yep, that's a nice, nice girl," Bug said.

"Shhh!" said a woman at the next table.

Bug tried to untangle the chaos and Georgie tackled the giant sloths. Soon, Hewitt came back with even more books on vampires and cephalopods and Giacometti. "I prefer poetry myself," she said. "Good luck with whatever it is you're doing."

Georgie and Bug set aside chaos and sloths and read up on cephalopods and Giacometti instead. They found out some fascinating things: giant squid can have eyes thirty centimetres in diameter, the largest octopus ever caught was seven metres from tip to tip and Bug said his octopus was much larger, vampire legends have been found in every culture going back hundreds of years, the mathematician Mandelbrot originally studied cotton prices, giant sloths thrived in the ice ages, and Giacometti's first drawing was of Snow White in a tiny coffin surrounded by the seven dwarfs. But nothing they found explained what was happening in the city, or explained why it seemed to be happening around *them*.

"OK," said Bug. "What do we have: a giant sloth, a giant

octopus, a walking statue, vampires. And what do they have in common? Nothing. Except that none of them are supposed to be alive."

Georgie grabbed Bug's arm. "None of them are supposed to be alive. What if someone is *bringing* them to life?"

"How?"

Georgie's shoulders sagged in defeat. "Except for the pen, I have no idea."

"Hey! Georgie! Over here!" a voice hissed. She turned. Lights flashed, blinding her. She put a hand up to shield her eyes.

"Bug! Over here!" More lights. "Is Georgie Bloomington your new girlfriend? How does it feel to be dating The Richest Girl in the Universe? What's Roma think?"

Two photographers stood by the table taking picture after picture, not caring that they were disturbing Bug, Georgie and everyone else in the reading room.

Hewitt Elder strode briskly over to them. "Stop that! You can't harass patrons here. You need to leave immediately."

"OK, sweetheart," said one of the photographers. "We're going." He kept snapping pictures even as he and the other photographer backed out of the room.

Hewitt stared at Bug and Georgie with an unreadable expression on her face, as if she were furious, but neither Bug nor Georgie could imagine what she was so angry about. It wasn't their fault the photographers had figured out who they were and decided to take pictures. One minute passed, two minutes.

"Can we—" began Georgie.

"Not yet," said Hewitt, in a tone that brooked no argument. "Don't move." She left the room.

Another few minutes passed. Finally, Hewitt returned. She said, "I needed to check that they left the building. Come with me." She motioned Bug and Georgie to follow her. She led them out of the reading room and into a smaller room, which was empty. "This is the Arents Collection room," she told them. She took a red velvet rope and closed off the entrance.

"What's the Arents Collection?" Bug asked.

"Materials on the history of tobacco," said Hewitt. She moved to back corner of the room and pulled out a volume on Cuban cigars.

"What are you—" Georgie said.

The bookcase swung open to reveal a long, dark tunnel.

Chapter 18

Woof

"What's going on?" Bug said.

Hewitt ignored Bug and focused on Georgie. "You know those photographers will be waiting at the front entrance. Probably more than just those two. They won't leave you alone. They'll follow you wherever you try to go."

Bug peeked into the dark tunnel behind the bookcase. "And?"

"This tunnel leads to the storage area in the basement. I can take you under the library and then up to a door at the William Cullen Bryant memorial in the park behind the building. But if we're going, we better go now."

"Come on, Bug," Georgie said, pushing at his back. They

couldn't tell Hewitt that Georgie would make them invisible and no one would see them, so it didn't matter how many photographers were waiting. Besides, Georgie was flattered that Hewitt wanted to help. Also, she wanted to know where the tunnel went. "Let's just get out of here."

Bug hesitated, then nodded. He and Georgie followed Hewitt into the passageway. Affixed on the wall next to the doorway was a small lion's head. Hewitt pressed down on the lion's head and the bookshelf swung back into place behind them, enveloping them in complete darkness. Hewitt turned on a flashlight and pointed it. At the end of the passageway, Georgie saw a spiral staircase. Hewitt moved towards the staircase.

"Be careful," she said. "It's a long way down."

Georgie eyed the wrought-iron steps, the thin railing. The steps themselves were so narrow that she wasn't sure her feet would fit. She wished Bug could fly them down the shaft, but even if he were completely rested, not even the best Wing in the world was able to carry two people, let alone two people and a cat (the bird could fly for himself). Anyway, they would have to walk. Over the thin railing, Georgie could see nothing but blackness. She didn't know how far down the basement was. A few floors? A few *kilometres*?

Hewitt started down the steps, with Georgie in the middle, and Bug at the rear. Georgie was concentrating so hard on *planting* her foot squarely on the steps, *planting* the other foot, *clutching* the railing, her head started to hurt. And the endlessly looping spiral didn't help either; Georgie was getting dizzy. The weight of their bodies made the delicate staircase buck and jerk. Georgie hoped that they weren't too heavy, that the staircase wasn't going to collapse and send them screaming towards their dooms.

"How much further?" she said.

"Not much," said Hewitt. "Watch your step."

"I *am*."

Just then, something crashed into her back. Noodle yowled and Pinkwater burst from her pack, shrieking, "Mayday, Mayday!" Georgie grabbed on to the thin railing and somehow kept herself from pitching forwards. Hewitt swung the flashlight up and behind her. Bug was hanging from the railing, kicking his feet as if he didn't remember he was a Wing. His sunglasses fell from his face and dropped. They heard the faint crash as the glasses smashed to the floor some distance below. He stopped kicking, and pulled himself back on to the staircase.

"Sorry," he mumbled. "I slipped. Still tired from yesterday, I guess."

Georgie nodded. Hewitt sighed. "Come on," she said. "We're about halfway there." She shined the light in Georgie's face, making her wince. "Do you have a cat in that backpack?"

"Yes."

"Cats aren't allowed in the library, you know," Hewitt said. "Just lions." Then she laughed. "Kidding."

"Yeah," Bug muttered. "Funny."

Somehow, they managed to make it down to the basement without anyone plunging to his or her doom, which Georgie thought was quite an accomplishment. Hewitt panned the light around so that Bug and Georgie could see. And what they saw was a cavernous space, double the height of a normal room, packed with floor-to-ceiling bookcases. Georgie could see that some of the books on the shelves were huge, oversized things that would take two people to open. Some of the books were tiny, barely the size of postage stamps.

"Wow," said Georgie. From the backpack, Noodle mewled.

"We keep some of our rarest books down here," said Hewitt. "And some of our most unusual."

"What do you mean, unusual?" Bug wanted to know.

Hewitt began to walk past the shelves of books. "Some of them are very, very old, older than they should be, printed before humans were thought to have written language. Some of them are written in languages that no one can identify. And there are some filled entirely with mathematical equations so complicated that even the most illustrious mathematicians can't figure them out. Others are even more unusual."

"More unusual how?" said Georgie.

Hewitt panned the light over some locked trunks stowed along one wall. "Dangerous. Some of the books were published with inks that poison anyone who touches the pages. Some of the books have contents with the power to drive readers insane. Some of the books have blank pages, but they speak when you open them, whispering to you as if you were the only person in the world, the only person with the ability to understand what they are telling you. Some books are sleeping and can only be awoken by magical means. Some of the books," she said, "can kill."

"Come on," said Bug.

Hewitt Elder spun, shining the light in Bug's eyes. "You don't believe me? I'm not surprised. What else could you expect from the son of a gangster but ignorance?"

Bug scowled and clenched his fists, but he didn't say anything. Pinkwater, who sat on Bug's shoulder, chirped, *"Wham!"*

Hewitt turned the light back to the path in front of them and kept walking. If the library upstairs had been silent, the basement was the very definition of silence. The air was still and heavy, like a held breath. As if somebody, something, was waiting in the dusty stacks. A chill raced down Georgie's spine, and her hair prickled on her scalp. Noodle growled low in her throat, a warning.

Georgie took a deep breath. They were just books, and this was just a basement. Nothing creepy here. No one was poisoning anybody. No one was driving anyone crazy. No one was killing anything. They weren't going to be opening any of the books anyway.

Abruptly, Hewitt stopped and pulled a book from the shelves. She flipped it open and shined the light on the pages. A bit reluctantly, Bug and Georgie gathered close to look. On the pages, there were strange, rough squiggles and round splotches that didn't resemble any alphabet that Georgie had ever seen. They almost looked like... paw prints?

"Listen," Hewitt said, putting her ear close to the book.

Georgie bent her head. *Woof,* she heard. *Woof, woof. Woof?*

Noodle yowled, making Hewitt grin. Her grin, Georgie had to admit, was not a pretty thing. "Dogs, maybe," Hewitt said. "Or perhaps wolves."

Bug frowned. "You can't mean that wolves *wrote* it?"

Hewitt shrugged. "We're not sure. But the kitty doesn't like it, and neither does the lion." She shined her light behind Bug and Georgie. Georgie jumped. Next to them, almost touching them, was a huge stone lion, one of the originals sculpted for the library steps. His eyes bore down on Georgie and she gasped. She felt as if he were staring at her. As if he were alive.

"That's Patience," said Hewitt. "The real Patience. We'll see Fortitude later. The statues are way too valuable to be kept outside. So we keep them down here to guard the books."

"And how do they do that?" Bug said.

Again, Hewitt shrugged. "Nothing has ever been stolen. So however they do it, they do it."

Bug rolled his eyes at Hewitt's deliberate mysteriousness and possible insanity. He patted the stone lion on the head. "Hey, guy," he said. "I bet you'd like a saucer of milk."

Hewitt put the "wolf" book back on the shelf. "I'd watch your fingers if I were you," she said to Bug.

"Yeah," said Bug. "Right."

Hewitt turned and followed the path snaking along the rows of bookcases, the trunks and piles of books on the floor. After a few minutes, they came to the very end of the basement. Here there were no bookshelves or piles, but a bare concrete wall with two heavy iron doors set in the middle of it.

"Hmmm," said Hewitt. "No Fortitude. I wonder where he went."

Bug rolled his eyes again. Hewitt ignored it. She handed him the flashlight and told him to shine it on the iron door on the right. On the door was a wheel like you'd find on the hatch to a submarine. Hewitt gripped the wheel with both hands and turned it. There was a loud clanking sound.

Hewitt opened the door to reveal the ladder behind it.

"You'll have to climb to the surface. When you get to the top, you'll see a round hatch. That hatch opens up into the William Cullen Bryant Memorial. Actually, it opens up into William, himself. You'll be inside the statue. Make sure you close the round hatch. Then, once you're inside the statue, feel around for a panel that should be right at your feet. Slide it open, and you'll be in Bryant Park."

"What do you mean, feel around?" said Bug, clearly irritated with Hewitt now. "Can't we borrow your flashlight?"

"I need it to get back," she said. "Don't worry, you'll be fine. You're practically a superhero."

Hewitt stepped back to allow Georgie and Bug to go through the iron door. Georgie stopped her. "Thank you," she said.

Hewitt's face softened as she looked at Georgie. "You're welcome," she said. "I hope we see each other again."

"Wait," said Bug. "Where's the other door go to?"

Hewitt shook her head. "I don't know. I've never been able to open it." She seemed rather annoyed to have to reveal this. "You better go."

She gestured towards the open right door. Georgie walked through it and gripped the rungs. She started to climb the ladder, hand over hand. As soon as Bug started to climb, they heard the door below them slam shut, and the wheel turning and locking them in. It was pitch black, and Georgie could see nothing – not the rungs, not her own hands. Below her, Bug said, "The heck with this." The next thing Georgie knew, Bug was grabbing her by the arm and lifting her off the ladder and into the air. They flew up five floors until they stopped with a thud.

"Ow!" said Bug.

"What happened?" Georgie asked.

"I found the trapdoor. With my head. Can you open it?"

Georgie reached up and felt around on the ceiling until she found a handle. She pulled the handle, and then pushed at the hatch. It opened with a soft metallic creak. They couldn't fit through the door together, so Bug shoved Georgie through first and himself second. It was still terribly dark, so they made sure all fingers and toes were out of the way before they slammed the hatch shut.

"OK," said Georgie. "Now we have to look for that panel." They dropped to their knees and felt all around them. Since they were inside a hollow statue, the walls were bumpy. It was difficult to find any knobs or hinges or anything else that screamed "escape". Their hands fluttered in the dark, occasionally touching, which was embarrassing and thrilling at the same time. Finally Georgie found it, a thin vertical seam. She scrabbled at it, getting a hold and then yanking sideways. The panel slid open, light streaming in. After their eyes adjusted, Pinkwater flew outside to check to see if the coast was clear.

"Out!" chirped Pinkwater. "Out, now!"

Georgie pulled of her backpack and slid it through the opening. Then she crawled out. Bug followed. Quickly, he turned and shut the panel. The two of them leaned back against the statue of William Cullen Bryant, panting as if they'd just outrun a gang of Punks.

Georgie said, "That was an adventure."

"One word for it," Bug grunted.

"Wasn't it cool to see all those books in the basement?"

"You mean the ones written by wolves? Yeah, that was great."

"Woof!" chirped Pinkwater.

"Hewitt is pretty interesting, isn't she?"

"She's mean," Bug said.

"She's not mean," said Georgie.

"Yes, she is. And she's crazy too."

"She is not. She's my friend."

"Are you sure about that?" Bug said.

"Yes! Why else would she take us through the basement?"

"Because she's a know-it-all. A show-off."

Georgie thought about the regal way Hewitt walked, how

she had put Roma in her place, how she had helped Georgie at the Museum of Natural History and now at the library. "You're wrong," Georgie said firmly.

Bug grunted. "Had enough of the library?" he asked. "'Cause I know I have."

"Yeah," Georgie said. "Let's go." Just in case reporters were still out looking for them, she held out her hand and he took it. Georgie was annoyed about what he'd said about Hewitt, so held on to only one of Bug's fingers.

It was an invisible Bug and Georgie who took the subway uptown to the Bloomingtons' building, slipping past a grave-looking Deitrich the doorman and joining a rather sullen-looking delivery boy in the lift.

Once the delivery boy had got off on the fifth floor, Georgie let go of Bug's little finger. The lift chimed when it hit the top floor of the building. Bug and Georgie got out, slowing when they noticed the three police officers talking outside the open penthouse door. One of them turned to her. "Are you Georgetta Bloomington?"

"Yes. What's going on?" she said.

"I don't know," the officer said. "We were hoping that you could tell us."

Chapter 19

OK, Potato

"What happened? Where are my parents?" said Georgie, shoving past the officers and into the penthouse apartment. Inside, Bunny and Solomon Bloomington sat together on the couch, surrounded by more police officers and several men in dark suits. The television yammered in the background. Agnes put tea and plates of kolachkes – biscuits with jam – on the table. Bunny jumped up when she saw her daughter.

"Georgie! Where have you been? We've been worried sick!"

"At the cinema," Georgie said. "Like I told you."

"No," said Bunny, her face anguished. "We checked the cinema. And then we checked everywhere else we could think of. Why didn't you tell us where you were going?"

Georgie tried to think of a reasonable answer. "It was spur of the moment. We hadn't seen The Professor in a long time, so we thought we'd visit him."

"You decided to go clear across town on the spur of the moment?" Bunny said. "And where did you go after that? It's nearly six o'clock!" Georgie opened her mouth to speak, but it was clear her mother wasn't going to let her. "What is this?" Bunny gestured to the coffee table. Next to Agnes's biscuits was what looked like a miniature black coffin. A dozen tiny black silk roses lay in the box.

"I don't know," Georgie said.

Bunny scooped up the card that came with the box and read it out loud: "For Georgie. I can't wait to see you at my party. OK, Potato. Love and screams, Mandelbrot." She held the card out. "Who is this Mandelbrot? Why is he sending you these horrible flowers? What party is he talking about?"

"I—I—I," Georgie stammered. The policemen looked at her expectantly. The men in suits sipped coffee. Bug shuffled his feet. Pinkwater chirped, "OK Potato."

"Stop that!" Bunny barked at the bird. Pinkwater alighted on Bug's shoulder and flapped his wings.

Solomon spoke up. "We didn't know where you were. And then this thing was delivered. We were terrified. We called the police."

"We just went to see The Professor," Georgie said lamely.

Suddenly the TV blared, *"And now for our entertainment report. Seems that Bug Grabowski is dating not one, but two of the richest girls in the universe. These photos were taken today showing Sylvester 'Bug' Grabowski, winner of last year's Flyfest, getting cozy with none other than Georgetta Bloomington, long-lost daughter of Sol and Bunny Bloomington."* On the screen, a photo of Bug and Georgie at the library. *"Slow down, Bug!"* the newscaster said. *"What's Roma Radisson going to say to this?"*

Solomon looked at Bug. "I think you should go, Sylvester."

"I— yeah," Bug said. He glanced at Georgie. "See you tomorrow?"

Bunny answered for Georgie. "No dear, you won't."

Georgie watched Bug walk out the door, saw him mouth *I'm sorry* before he disappeared. Pinkwater fluttered after him, chirping, "Me too!"

One of the men in suits said, "Sir? Do you still need us?"

"No, I don't think so, Phil. Thanks for coming by so quickly. We're OK now."

The man named Phil gathered up the tiny coffin, flowers and the card. "We'll see if we get some fingerprints off these. Maybe trace the delivery company. I'll let you know what we find."

"That would be great, Phil," said Solomon.

The officers filed out, followed by the men in suits, who thanked Bunny for the coffee before leaving. The door shut, and Georgie was alone with her parents. With her sad and disappointed parents.

Bunny sat on the couch next to her husband. "I don't understand this," she said quietly. "Why did you have to lie to us?"

For a moment, Georgie thought about telling them, telling them that a Punk and a vampire had come, that she had to go to this gallery opening or all of them would become vampires too, that all the strange things happening in the city might be connected, but she couldn't find the words. Even if they believed her, how would they protect her? How would they protect themselves? What if the vampires bit *them*? What would she do without them? She had lost them once; she was determined that it would never happen again.

"Like I said, it was just a spur-of-the-moment decision," Georgie told them. "I didn't mean to scare you. And I don't know what that coffin thing was."

"Are you talking to strangers on the Internet?" Solomon wanted to know.

"No!" said Georgie, horrified.

"Has anyone threatened you?"

Georgie crossed her arms and looked at the floor. "No."

"Did you make yourself invisible at any time today?" Bunny asked.

Georgie didn't, couldn't answer.

Solomon and Bunny Bloomington were silent for a long time, so long that Georgie wondered if they would ever speak again.

Finally, Solomon stood. "We tried very hard to make sure your life was as normal as possible considering what happened to you. To us, to our family all those years ago," said Solomon. "When we got you back, we thought about sending you out only with bodyguards, or keeping cameras on the building at all times. And we did some of that for a while. But then, we realised that we had to try to let you be a normal girl. We had to try to be normal parents. And I guess we are normal parents now." He patted Bunny on the shoulder and then faced his daughter. "You're grounded."

"What?" said Georgie. "But—"

"No buts. You lied to us. And we can't tolerate that. Plus, it seems that some crazy person has focused on you, probably because we have money, but perhaps because they found out what you can do. And we can't tolerate that either. So, you're grounded till further notice. Agnes will escort you to and from school. There will be no visiting Bug, no visiting The Professor, no films, no library, no computer, no nothing until we figure out who sent those flowers and what their intentions are."

Georgie saw his face, saw the determined set of his jaw and her mother's frightened eyes, and knew that there was no talking them out of this. She nodded.

"We love you," he said. "But we're very upset with you. I think you should go to your room and think about this."

Georgie nodded again and slouched off to her room. She almost didn't hear what her father said next: "We need to be able to trust you, Georgie. And now we're not sure we can."

In her new duties as Georgie's personal chaperone, Agnes donned a hockey jersey that hung down to her knees, striped leggings, and high-top Skreechers trainers in bright purple.

"Agnes, you can't wear that," Georgie said.

"Why? What's problem?"

"None of it matches," said Georgie.

Agnes looked down. "Jersey is blue, stripe is blue, trainers blue. Matches good. We go now."

They marched to the Prince School, because Agnes thought marching was great exercise. Georgie trudged after Agnes as if she were being led to the gallows.

"Stop moping," Agnes said.

"I'm not moping," said Georgie.

"Moping," insisted Agnes. "No point. You figure nothing out by moping."

Georgie marched faster to catch up with Agnes. "What do you mean? What do I need to figure out?"

Agnes gave Georgie her signature don't-make-me-get-out-the-horseradish frown. "You know what I talk about."

"What should I do?"

"I told you. Stop moping. Start thinking."

"But I don't know what you—"

"Here now," Agnes announced as she opened the door to the school. "Which room?"

Oh no, thought Georgie. *Please don't come in with me. The Prince School is not the sort of place you can wear jerseys with striped leggings and trainers. This is not the sort of city you can wear jerseys with striped leggings and trainers. This is not the sort of planet you can wear any of those things, ever. I love you, Agnes and I will eat all the horseradish in the universe if you please please please don't come in with me.*

Agnes marched inside like she was leading an army. She glanced at Georgie, one eyebrow raised.

"Room one eighteen," Georgie said, defeated.

Agnes nodded. When they reached the door to room 118, Agnes turned. "Here is pass." Agnes took Georgie by the elbow to steer her into the classroom.

"Wait," Georgie said, looking at the folded pink slip in her hand. "Where did you get this?"

Apparently, Agnes had been told that if Georgie put up any sort of fuss, she could use force. When Agnes ushered Georgie inside, Georgie felt like a five-year-old being dragged into the doctor's office for a shot.

"Georgetta," Agnes said.

The class began snickering, Roma Radisson louder than everyone.

Ms Letturatura peered at Agnes over her glasses. "I know who she is. And you are?"

"An acrobat from the Cirque du Soleil!" yelled Roma.

"I am Agnes," said Agnes.

Ms Letturatura squinted. "Of course," she said. She glanced at Georgie. "Do you have a pass from the office?"

"Um," Georgie said. "Yeah?"

"Good," Ms Letturatura said, snatching the pass out of her hand. She glanced at it, and then gave it back. "Have a seat, Georgetta."

"I come back later," Agnes said. "Which room?"

"Two thirteen," Georgie mumbled.

The class snickered again. Georgie's face burned as she sat down at her desk. Roma, who was sitting diagonally in front of Georgie, turned and smiled at her. "How are you, Georgie? How was the weekend? Do anything fun? I got my fortune told by a woman on the East Side. She told me I would live *for ever*."

"Settle down, class. Today, we're reading William Cullen Bryant's beautiful poem 'New Moon'. London, why don't you start?"

London, who was filing her nails, stopped in mid-file. "What do you want me to do?"

"Read the first stanza of the poem. On page fifty-six."

"Page fifty-six of what?"

"Your textbook!" said Ms. Letturatura.

"Oh!" said London. "I don't have anything like that." She went back to filing her nails.

Ms Letturatura had to go through five students to find a girl with a textbook. One by one, the students read the poem about the moon, and how beautiful it is, and how everyone loves to look at it. Georgie tried to listen, but her mind was on other things, like how she was going to convince her parents that sending Agnes along with her to school every day was a bad, very bad idea, and certainly wasn't going to help her learn to be more trustworthy. She was tempted to become invisible right then and there.

"Georgie!" barked Ms Letturatura.

"What?"

"I said, read! Starting with 'most welcome to the lover's sight'."

Georgie rubbed her forehead and read:

"Most welcome to the lover's sight
Glitters that pure, emerging light;
For prattling poets say,
That sweetest is the lovers' walk,
And tenderest is their murmured talk,
Beneath its gentle ray."

Roma giggled. "This poem could be about me and You-know-who!"

London paused in her admiration of her own fingernails. "What do you mean?"

"This poem's about the moon, right? And something?" said Roma. "We were out last night and we saw the moon. *Duh.*"

"But," said Bethany Tiffany, "I thought that he was going out with..." She paused, looking pointedly at Georgie. "*Her*, too. They said so on TV."

"Don't make me laugh!" said Roma. "Who would go out with her when they could go out with me? It was a total publicity stunt, that's all. His agent put him up to it. Anyway, I could write something so much better than this William Culvert Bubble guy. Maybe I'll get my agent to get me another book contract. Maybe I could write some poetry. Love poetry. That would be so fab™."

"Girls, can we save this conversation for after class?" said Ms Letturatura.

"I think the class is very interested in my book contracts. And they also have a right to know what kind of person Georgie Bloomington is. She's tried to steal *my* boyfriend. Right after I was nearly murdered by a hamster. So *not* fab™."

London had pulled off her shoes and socks and put her feet up on the desk to paint her toenails. "I thought the hamster was cute," she said.

"Thinking is not one of your talents," said Roma. "Giant hamsters are a lot less cute when they're going to eat you for dinner."

London frowned. "I thought it liked M&M'S?"

"You thought, you thought!" said Roma. "Except you don't *think*!"

"Girls!" said Ms Letturatura.

Georgie's head ached and her eyes felt scratchy from lack of sleep. She wanted to yell at Roma, wanted to tell her to shut up, *shut up*, but she couldn't find the energy. She twisted the pink slip Agnes had given her and then smoothed it out on the desk.

1) He not like her, silly.

He who? Bug? And *her* who? Roma? How in the world would Agnes know any of it? But Agnes knew things, lots of things. And Bug was a lot of things – impatient, sarcastic, a little angry sometimes – but he wasn't stupid. Not stupid enough to get mixed up with Roma, not stupid enough to *stay* mixed-up with her.

Her eyes slid to the next thing Agnes had written:

2) The world only seem crazy. There is pattern. You find it if you look hard enough.

Georgie frowned at this, which sounded to her just like chaos theory, and she did *not* understand chaos theory. She skipped to number three.

3) Books are powerful things.

She didn't have time to consider this last one before Bethany Tiffany slid a newspaper clipping on to Georgie's desk. The headline was CAUGHT IN A CLINCH. At first, Georgie thought it was a picture of Bug and Roma embracing, and her stomach withered to the size of raisin. She scanned the article: *"Just hours after Bug Grabowski was photographed with Georgie Bloomington, paparazzi found Roma Radisson out on the town with an unidentified new guy."*

"She doesn't even like him any more," said Bethany. "You can have him. He's a loser."

She doesn't like him any more! He's a loser! Georgie's heart practically burst with relief. Until she noticed that though the face of Roma's new guy was mysteriously blurred in the picture, his clothes were not. He wore a shiny shirt and slim velvet trousers.

Just the outfit a fashion-conscious vampire might wear.

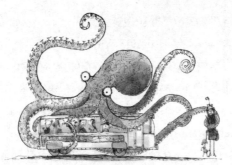

Chapter 20

Hello, Hewitt

Of all the things Hewitt Elder wished could be removed from the public library, the public was at the top of the list. Which was why she made it a habit to visit on Sundays, when the library was officially closed and there were no stupid patrons milling about, pestering her with stupid questions. Hewitt had a special set of keys, a set that she wasn't supposed to have, a set that dangled from a cheap Statue of Liberty key chain. (She'd stolen them from the janitor and had copies made.) She also knew all the alarm codes, even though she wasn't supposed to know them. (She'd found a list in her supervisor's computer.)

Today, after letting herself in and disarming the alarms,

Hewitt was making the usual rounds. She loved floating from room to empty room, gallery to empty gallery, admiring the rows of books undisturbed, the chairs and tables unoccupied. The library held all sorts of marvels – the first edition of *Alice's Adventures in Wonderland* (1866) that belonged to the real Alice, the work of Emerson, Thoreau, Whitman, Twain, Shakespeare, Dickens and Washington Irving (though they'd had to put some of his papers in a locked trunk after someone discovered the secrets that were in them. It was bad enough that he had documented the sleep of Rip Van Winkle and the rides of the Headless Horseman. Good thing everyone believed those things were fiction). And then, of course, were the millions of volumes housed in the basement, volumes secretly studied by only the most prominent scholars and librarians, volumes kept hidden and protected by The Trustees.

Yes, the library housed many wondrous things from the most fabulous to the most dangerous. What it also had: the three volumes of poetry written by Hewitt Elder herself. Twenty-five copies of each, to be precise.

Hewitt wished she could pile up those seventy-five books and burn them on the library steps.

"Go ahead, Hewitt. Tell the nice lady what your poem is called." This was Hewitt's mother talking. She was pushing the seven-year-old Hewitt forwards towards the front desk at the local

library. They were having a poetry contest. The first prize was publication in the library newsletter and a fifty-dollar bond. Little Hewitt didn't know what a bond was, but she did understand fifty dollars.

"My poem is called 'Happy Candy Rainbow Bunnies'," Hewitt told the librarian, shoving her composition across the desk. It had been carefully composed in coloured pencils. "It's inspirational."

"How nice!" cried the librarian. "I can't wait to read it."

"Did you hear that?" said Hewitt's mother on the way out of the building. "She said she couldn't wait to read it! I think you're going to win, Hewitt, I really do. I think you're going to have your own books one day. You're going to be rich!"

"And famous?" said Hewitt. Her mother nodded eagerly. "Of course! Rich and famous! You're my little star!"

This is exactly what Hewitt's mother had said during Hewitt's short flirtation with tap-dancing, derailed by Hewitt's utter lack of balance and coordination. And what she said about Hewitt's attempts at acting, hampered by Hewitt's wooden delivery and lack of facial expressions. And also what she said about Hewitt's singing, which sounded more like the bleating of disgruntled sheep than music.

But Hewitt's mother was the hopeful sort, and never gave up the dream that her daughter was destined to be a star. The kind that she saw every day being interviewed on early morning news shows and late night talk shows, chatting up the hosts with witty yet innocent *repartee. The kind that enchanted audiences the world over.*

Hewitt's mother was not daunted in the least when her daughter didn't win the library's poetry contest. She was inspired. She encouraged her daughter to write more poetry, which she then typed into her computer and printed out herself. She assembled the manuscripts and submitted them to publisher after publisher, receiving rejection after rejection. Finally, after some thirty-five submissions, a bored executive at a small publishing house got the manuscript – and the accompanying head shots of Hewitt – and was instantly struck with the most brilliant idea of her entire career. She was going to publish this nonsense. And then she would book the girl on every talk show, every late show, every news program. And that's exactly what happened. At the age of eight, Hewitt Elder published her first volume of poems. Her second was published at nine. A line of greeting cards followed. Hewitt appeared on talk shows. She was interviewed by news reporters and magazine journalists. She was touted as a prodigy and a genius. Her third volume of poetry made Hewitt a millionaire and an international celebrity.

And then the bottom fell out.

Hewitt turned thirteen, and got sour and grumpy and not the least bit inspirational. Why was the world such an unfair place? she wanted to know. Why was school so boring? Why were adults so boring? Why could some people fly and others couldn't? What was the evolutionary purpose of the pimple? Why did it seem that so many other people who didn't deserve fame and fortune were getting famous and amassing fortunes? She began to write a new book of poems, poems with titles like "Bad Hair Day", "Suing Your Parents for Malpractice" and "The Dumb Girl on TV". Her editor balked. Her agent begged. Her mother – who had bought herself a yacht, a mansion on each coast and a dozen different cars, all with Hewitt's money – demanded. But Hewitt wouldn't budge. After three best-selling books, her publisher pulled the plug. Unless Hewitt wanted to inspire the public with more "lighthearted" verse, she wouldn't get published.

It was just as well, thought Hewitt now. People were too unbearably, unbelievably, unwaveringly idiotic to understand poetry with any sort of deep meaning. No, they just wanted to read "funny" poems about puppies and kitties and rainbows and sunsets. And there were no puppies and kitties and rainbows and sunsets in Hewitt's future.

What *was* in Hewitt's future: *justice.*

Hewitt hummed to herself as she entered the Arents Collection room and pulled the volume on Cuban tobacco products. The secret panel in the wall opened to reveal the staircase beyond. Keeping her flashlight trained on her feet, she crept down the staircase, sure not to lose her footing as that conceited Bug Grabowski had. That people paid *him* to be in advertisements was further proof that the world had gone completely and utterly insane.

Georgetta Bloomington was another story, though. She wasn't like all those other brats. She was humble. She was different. Hewitt thought that given a little time, Georgie Bloomington might even be a friend.

Hewitt finally reached the basement floor. The flashlight cut a wan swathe in the gloom. No lions to be seen. That was interesting. She wondered what they were doing. A person who had never been to the realms underneath the library might think of checking the stacks. Even in a basement this large, how could two enormous stone lions be hard to find? And yet Hewitt knew better. Hewitt knew that one could get lost walking the stacks in the basement of the library. Hewitt knew how quickly one's perspective got skewed. That certain shelves seem to go on and on for ever, impossible as it may seem. That what looked like neat parallel rows turned into a vast maze if you weren't careful, if you didn't know exactly what you were looking for. That a stone lion able to wander about on its own wasn't something you necessarily wanted to find.

Still, thought Hewitt, it was odd that at least one of the lions wasn't guarding the stairwell up to the Arents Collection room. Hewitt wasn't easily made uneasy, but she could feel a tingle in her skin that she didn't quite like.

Something else she didn't like: the clunk-and-scritch sound of stone paws scraping the rough cement floor. Immediately, she swung the flashlight to her right.

"Hello, Hewitt," the man said, over-annunciating the "h" in each word. He appeared like some sort of spectre out of the gloom, riding towards her on the back of Patience, who wasn't looking all that patient. Not a bright idea, but then he wasn't quite as bright as he thought he was.

Crazy. Scary. Unpredictable. But not bright.

"Hello, Mandelbrot," said Hewitt, trying to keep her voice steady. "What brings you to the library?"

Chapter 21

The Book of the Undead

Wham!

Wham!

Wham!

The noise shattered Bug's sleep, startling him so much that he fell out of bed.

"Ow," Bug said, rubbing the elbow he landed on.

Pinkwater darted about in a flurry of flapping wings. "Red alert!" the bird chirped. "Red alert!"

The noise came again. Someone pounding on the door.

"Just a minute," Bug said, hauling himself off the floor. His head was fuzzy from too little sleep and too many crazy dreams. He'd dreamed that Roma had followed him all the way home, calling him stupid and pelting him with M&M'S. He'd dreamed Sol and Bunny Bloomington were grilling him about his "intentions" towards Georgie. He dreamed that the newspapers were packed with stories about what a "bad boy" he was and how very much he was doomed to become a criminal like his father. And then he dreamed that Georgie's vamps came to visit, but these were tiny, all trembling like dark moths against the windowpane. They wanted in, the moths. They had something for him, an invitation to a party. A party he didn't want to miss.

More pounding.

"All right, all right," Bug said. "I'm coming!" He shuffled to the door, not caring about his plaid flannel trousers and King Kong T-shirt. He figured that if someone wanted to see him so badly, they could see him in his jams with his weird hair sticking up. Served them right.

Just as he was opening the door, he had the terrible thought that the paparazzi would be behind it, but it wasn't the paparazzi. It was the old woman with the blue hat. The book club lady. Mrs Vorona.

He was about to open his mouth to tell her as sweetly and politely and in as gentlemanly a manner as he could that he didn't have the time to join a goofy book club run by a bunch of old biddies, but it seemed that Mrs Vorona had other ideas. She reached into Bug's apartment, grabbed him by the T-shirt, and hauled him through the door.

"Hey!" said Bug, as the woman towed him down the hallway towards the lift.

Pinkwater fluttered after them. "Hey!" he chirped.

"Let me lock my door at least!" Bug said.

Mrs Vorona clucked her tongue. "Are you worried someone will steal your suit of armour or the pile of dirty laundry on the floor?" She stabbed at the Down button.

"Ma'am—" Bug began.

"Hush," said the woman. He heard the steel in her voice and hushed, not sure what he should do next. The lift doors opened and Mrs Vorona shoved him inside. She said nothing as she punched the button for the second floor. Even Pinkwater seemed to sense that it would be wise to keep his comments to himself. The three of them were silent as the lift dropped floor after floor until button Number 2 lit up. Bug was unceremoniously yanked from the lift and hauled to the apartment two doors from the lift. Mrs Vorona clanked a knocker shaped like the head of a bird.

The door opened a crack and one rheumy brown eye was visible below the chain. "What's the password?" a creaky voice said.

"Oh, I don't remember," said Mrs Vorona. "It was something about breakfast. Marmalade? Jam? Toast?"

"That's not it," said the voice. "I can't let you in unless you know the password."

"Oh, stop with that nonsense, Imogen, and let us in!" snapped Mrs Vorona.

The door flew open. The one brown eye was paired with another, both of them belonging to a very old woman in a flowered dress and thick, brown orthopaedic shoes. She grinned and nodded at Bug. "Hello there, dear. I'm Mrs Hingis. Imogen Hingis. Call me Imogen."

"Hi," Bug said, before he was shoved into the apartment. A group of maybe a dozen women perched in chairs around an old-fashioned-looking parlour complete with claw-foot furniture and floral wallpaper.

"Sit," said Mrs Vorona, pressing him into a chair.

"Would you like some hot tea, dear?" said Imogen. "We have chamomile, lemon, Earl Grey—"

Mrs Vorona gave Imogen a glare that would have stunned a bull elephant. Imogen gave up and sat on the end of a pink velvet settee. The other women around the room glanced at one another nervously.

"Well," said Mrs Vorona, looking around at the women, and then at Bug. "We're glad that you could make it to a meeting of our little club, Mr Grabowski."

Unless I wanted to beat up an old lady, thought Bug, *it's not like I had much of a choice.*

"So," continued Mrs Vorona. "I'll get right to the point. We need you to do something for us. We want you to infiltrate the vampires and steal a book."

"You want me to *what*?" said Bug.

"Bad news!" chirped Pinkwater.

"Don't pretend you don't know about the vampires, Mr Grabowski. We know that they've visited your friend Georgetta Bloomington and we know that they visited you. Last night, as a matter of fact, there were about fifteen of them at your window, all trying to wake you up so that you would let them inside." Mrs Vorona paused. "You must sleep like a stone."

So he hadn't been dreaming after all. There really were itty-bitty vampires fluttering against the window. But...

"How did you know there were vampires outside my window?"

Mrs Vorona ignored him. "And we also know that if your friend doesn't show up at the party on Saturday night, the vampires will turn her family into bloodsuckers. You too, probably, if they had been able to wake you long enough to threaten you. No matter. They'll probably bite you anyway."

"Thanks for the reassurance," Bug said.

"You're not here so that we can make you feel better," said Mrs Vorona.

"No," he said. "I'm here because you dragged me here.

And you know what? I don't feel like hanging around."
He got up and turned to go.

"I'm not kidding," said Mrs Vorona. "You're in danger.
Your friend is in danger."

Bug spun round. "We've been in danger before."

Mrs Vorona shook her head. "Not this kind of danger."

"And only you guys can help us," Bug said, his voice deep
with sarcasm.

"If you help us first," said Mrs Vorona. "Bring us the book
we're looking for and we can make sure that the vampires
can't harm you."

Bug sat down again. "Who's this Mandelbrot guy?"

"You're going to get the book?" said Mrs Vorona.

"I'm thinking about it," Bug told her. "But first,
Mandelbrot. Who is he?"

"A Punk," said Imogen. "They live in the subway systems.
Usually live in the subway systems. We don't know why this
one decided to come to the surface. But then, if I had a
choice I wouldn't want to live in the subway systems either.
Can you imagine the dirt? And the smell of all those fumes?
And the noise! Why, I—"

"Imogen!" Mrs Vorona said.

"What?" said Imogen. "I was only explaining to the boy.
I don't know why you're in such a mood today." Imogen
shook her head at Bug. "She's not normally so cranky."

"I'm not cranky!" shouted Mrs Vorona.

"What's a Punk doing with a bunch of vampires?" Bug asked.

"We don't know that, either," said Imogen.

"Well, what *do* you know?" Bug said.

"You're a cheeky young man, aren't you?" Imogen said. "Are you sure you don't want any tea? It might calm your nerves."

"Imogen, please!" Mrs Vorona said again, this time more wearily.

Imogen reached over and patted Mrs Vorona's hand. "Stop beating around the bush, dear," she said, "and tell the boy what he needs to know." The other women in the group nodded.

Mrs Vorona sighed. "It's called *The Book of the Undead*. It contains a series of incantations that can animate the unanimated."

"Huh?" said Bug.

"It can bring things to life," Imogen explained.

"Hamster!" chirped Pinkwater.

"Yes," said Mrs Vorona. "The museum of natural history had a skeleton of a giant sloth shipped in. And then whoever's in possession of the book brought it back to life."

"But why would someone want to bring a sloth back to life?" Bug said. "It's not even scary. It eats sweets. What's the point?"

Mrs Vorona shrugged. "We don't know. And we don't

care. All we know is that we have to get that book back. There's no telling what Mandelbrot will do next."

"How do you know Mandelbrot has the book?"

Mrs Vorona brushed at her wool sleeves as if she were brushing away cat hair or lint, but there was no lint on her clothes that Bug could see. "We're a book club."

"Yeah. And?"

"That means we're very, very interested in books, dear," Imogen said. "There isn't a book we're not aware of."

"There's a large storage facility beneath the library, one that houses many, many more books than the library itself," said Mrs Vorona. She leaned forwards. "Some of those books are dangerous. Some of them—"

"Can kill," finished Bug. "I know about the basement of the library. And I've heard this stuff before."

Mrs Vorona glanced at him curiously, but didn't ask him to explain. "In any case, I saw something very odd when I was down in the basement. Mandelbrot came to visit. I was hidden some distance away, so I couldn't quite hear what was going on, but I think he was threatening the library volunteer. The volunteer handed over what looked like a leather book. I got suspicious, so I decided to follow Mandelbrot. And I found him, a whole band of vampires, and the book. I'm sure it was *The Book of the Undead*. But I couldn't get it back. I was... um... outnumbered." She sighed heavily, as if the weight of the world rested on her shoulders. "He calls himself The Chaos King. And that's what I think he's interested in: total chaos. Who knows what that madman is planning to unleash on the city? This is our home. We need to get that book back. Besides," Mrs Vorona continued, "it's all our fault that the book is so dangerous."

"Why? What do you mean?"

Mrs Vorona didn't answer. She got up and went to a rolltop desk in the corner. From the top drawer, she withdrew a shining silver pen, a pen that looked like it was from another time, perhaps, or from another world, a pen like no other. "Do you know what this is?"

Bug swallowed hard. "I think I do."

"This belonged to a man you know, a man called The Professor. He dropped it late one night about six months ago, and Imogen picked it up."

Imogen grinned. "I like shiny things so much!"

Mrs Vorona shot Imogen a look. "She didn't know it was a special pen, though. None of us did."

"Until I wrote the note," said Imogen.

"What note?" Bug asked.

"This note." Imogen Hingis pulled a scrap of paper from her pocket. On it, in rich blue ink, was written: *Wake up!*

"I don't get it," said Bug. "What does it mean?"

"I always write myself a schedule for the day and my

schedule always begins with the words "Wake up", as in wake up, make breakfast, get dressed, etc. But I couldn't find a pen. So, I used the fancy one I'd found. As soon as I wrote the words I knew something was wrong. I felt it. I'd woken something up. I just didn't know what."

"Until we saw the news reports of your run-in with the octopus. And the sloth. And your friend Georgetta Bloomington's little problem with a certain Giacometti statue. We knew it was *The Book of the Undead*. Another one of The Professor's little inventions."

"The Professor!" said Bug. "We tried to find him and we couldn't. He's missing."

"And we fear the worst," said Mrs Vorona. "So we have to get that book back ourselves. And we need your help."

"Why don't you all go to the party?" Bug asked. "Why don't you call the police or something?"

"First of all, the vampires know what, I mean, *who* I am. And if I call the police to tell them that Mandelbrot has a book that can bring things to life, how hard do you think they'll laugh at us? No, you must do it. You have to go to the party anyway. You must get that book back."

"Why me?"

"Because you're already invited to the party," Mrs Vorona said. "You're a Wing. The best the city has ever seen. And because you're the son of Sweetcheeks Grabowski and—"

"So?" said Bug. "So what? What's that got to do with anything?"

"Well," Mrs Vorona said, "we just thought you might know a way to get things that other people don't want you to have, that's all. We're not implying anything."

"Sure you are," said Bug. "You think I'm some sort of gangster because my father is."

"Dear," Imogen said kindly, "we just need to get that book back. And maybe you need to get that book back as well. It won't stop the reporters from saying all sorts of terrible things about you, but it might stop you from suspecting that they could be right."

"And what about us? Me and Georgie?" said Bug. "While we're keeping the city safe, how will you make sure *we're* safe?"

"With the book, we can render the vampires harmless."

"How?"

"By bringing them to life again, silly," said Imogen. "They won't be vampires any more. They'll be just like you and me. Only paler, of course."

He might not be able to get the book back himself, but he was sure he could get it back with Georgie's help. That is, if Georgie wasn't grounded for the rest of her life. A life that wouldn't be very long if Georgie didn't show up at Mandelbrot's party.

Bug thought of something else. "What did that library volunteer look like?"

"Her name is Hewitt Elder. You might have heard of her, she's—"

"I know who she is," Bug said. "I wonder how Mandelbrot knows her."

"Maybe he doesn't, dear," Imogen said. "Maybe she was in the wrong place at the wrong time."

"Maybe," said Bug.

"So," said Mrs Vorona. "You'll do it? You'll get the book?"

"Yes," Bug said. "I think so."

"Good," Mrs Vorona said, the relief visible on her face. "Very good."

Bug stood to leave. Imogen hobbled with him to the door. "We're very glad that you could come by. And that you agreed to help us."

"Well, if I don't help you, there's a chance that the vampires might come after me."

"There is that," Imogen replied. She opened the door to let him out. "Oh, and dear?"

Bug turned. "Yeah?"

"You might want to do something with your hair. It's a little weird."

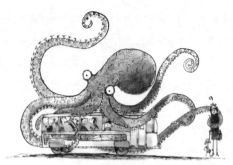

Chapter 22

Like You, Like You

Georgie pushed Agnes's fat-laden food around her plate, trying to think of something to say and the right way to say it.

Mum, Roma Radisson's boyfriend is just a little too old for her. Hundreds of years too old.

OK, Dad. I didn't want to say anything, but Roma Radisson's hanging out with Dracula.

"Did you say something, Georgie?" Bunny Bloomington said.

"Uh, no," said Georgie. "Nothing."

Her parents glanced at each other meaningfully. Since Georgie had come home late from the library and found the penthouse full of cops, her parents had been glancing at each other meaningfully. Except, being a person who had only had parents for six months, Georgie had no idea what the glances actually meant. Maybe other kids who had spent their whole lives living with the same people understood what those people were doing when they glanced at one another over Polish sausage and scalloped potatoes with sour cream. But Georgie didn't know. And she was afraid to ask, afraid that if she tried to explain everything now – the visiting vampires, the giant sloth, the world beneath the public library, all of it – she would sound crazy. Or desperate. Or desperately crazy.

So she said nothing. She pushed her potatoes around her plate until her parents took pity on her and told her to help Agnes with the washing up.

In the kitchen, she and Agnes filled the dishwasher and scrubbed the pots and the pans. Finally Georgie said, "Why haven't you told my parents anything?"

"Because *you* should tell parents," Agnes said.

"I can't," said Georgie. "They'll try to save me."

"Maybe you should let them?"

Georgie dried a large pot. "You *are* my Personal Assistant, aren't you? That's why you haven't told my parents. That's why you hint at things but you never tell me the whole story."

"You think I know whole story?"

"I think you know everything," said Georgie.

"Nobody knows everything," Agnes told her. "We each do

our part in world and that's all. Just one part. And you need to be more careful doing yours."

"I have to keep my parents safe, Agnes."

Agnes sighed. "You need boy with you."

"Well, he's not here, is he?"

Agnes pointed at Georgie's heart. "He's right there."

Georgie flushed. "I'm going to my room now."

"Yes," said Agnes. "But remember one thing."

"What?"

"You can't disappear because things are hard."

After the cleaning was done, Georgie went to her room with Noodle. She sat on her bed, marvelling at the state of the world, a world that her parents didn't seem to be fully aware of. It was a world filled with vampires and giant sloths and giant octopi and lumpy statues that leaped off their bases to bite people in the sequins. It was a world filled with Roma Radissons and Mr Fusses and a mysterious wacko named Mandelbrot.

She was sitting on her bed, petting Noodle, wishing that the cat would purr and all the mixed-up, desperately crazy thoughts would go away. And then Noodle did start to purr, and Georgie felt herself relax. But she didn't relax the way she used to. She didn't *fall into* the purr the way she used to. She didn't think of strange riddles and her head didn't clear.

Now, what was up with that? Suddenly, Georgie was angry. So angry she didn't know what to do. It wasn't fair that things changed so quickly. First she was invisible to the world, and then she really *was* invisible, and then she wasn't supposed to be invisible, and now her power didn't work right all the time, and she had to worry about her feet showing or her nose showing or whatever. First, she didn't have parents, then she did have parents – amazing and wonderful parents – and now she couldn't tell her amazing and wonderful parents anything. She had no friends, then she found Bug, and now she wasn't allowed to see him. Shouldn't a person be allowed to get used to things before they change? It wasn't right!

A scratching at the window caught her attention. "Oh no. Not again!" she said. But she was still angry at the unfairness of it all, so she lifted Noodle off her lap and marched to the window with the intent of telling off whichever vampire happened to be hanging there, no matter how cool that vampire's outfit was. But there were no vampires at the window. Bug hovered outside, waving, Pinkwater fluttering beside him.

Georgie held up a finger, telling him to wait a minute. She ran to her bedroom door and propped a chair against the knob so that her parents wouldn't be able to come in. She ran back to the window and opened it.

"Surprise!" chirped Pinkwater.

"Shhh!" Georgie said. "My parents will hear you."

"Oops!" chirped Pinkwater, more quietly. He flew over to the bed and perched on the tip of Noodle's tail. Irritated, Noodle lashed it. "Whee!" said Pinkwater, as if he were on an amusement park ride.

"Nice to see the kids getting along," Bug whispered, and Georgie stifled a laugh.

Bug sat at Georgie's desk, whirling the chair around to face her. "You're still grounded?"

"Yeah."

"Till when?"

"I don't know. The twenty-third century?"

"That bad, huh?"

Georgie shrugged.

"Well, at least you have parents to ground you. That's more than I have."

Georgie opened her mouth to say something, but then what was there to say? They both knew what it felt like to be alone in the universe.

"I've got a lot to tell you," Bug said. "Remember that book club woman?"

"The grumpy one with the funny hat?"

"Yeah. Well, she woke me up yesterday and practically dragged me to one of her meetings. You won't believe what she asked me to do."

"She wanted you to read something."

"No, she wanted me to *steal* something. A book. Get this: a book that can bring things to life."

Georgie snapped to attention, suddenly remembering what Agnes had written on the note: *"Books are powerful things"* "Wait, what book? What are you talking about?"

Bug explained that the book club ladies figured out Mandelbrot had a book called *The Book of the Undead*, and that he was the one who was causing the odd things that were happening and that these book club ladies were the ones who had awakened the book because they, not The Professor, had the pen.

Georgie's mouth dropped open as she worked to untangle his story. "But why would this Mandelbrot guy bring all these weird things to life? What's the point?"

"That's what I said. But maybe there isn't any point. Maybe he's just a crazy Punk doing crazy Punk things. The book club ladies are scared that he'll bring something even more terrible and dangerous to life and destroy the city in the process. They want me to go to Mandelbrot's party and get the book back from him. I have to do it. But I can't do it alone."

Georgie sighed. She saw the determined look on his face. And if he felt like he had to save the world, then she would have to save the world, too, because nobody could save the world all by himself. They would have to go to Mandelbrot's party not only to stop the vampires from going after Georgie's parents, but to stop Mandelbrot from doing whatever it was that Mandelbrot planned to do.

"OK," Georgie said. "How do you want to work this?"

Georgie endured the next couple of days as best she could, with Agnes taking her back and forth to school, with Roma taunting her, with her parents eyeing her as if she were some completely different girl, someone they weren't expecting and were not sure they wanted to keep around.

On Friday night, Georgie complained of a headache and a stomach-ache and went to bed early. She stayed in bed most of Saturday as well, doing her best to appear sluggish and ill, but not so sluggish and ill that a doctor would be required. After telling her parents she was turning in for the night, she did what any self-respecting girl who needed to sneak out and save the city would do: she arranged pillows underneath her blankets to look as if she was still there. She told Noodle that Noodle would have to stay home for this particular adventure.

"*Rrrrow!*" Noodle growled in response.

"I need you to watch my parents, OK? If anyone – anything – comes to the window, you make sure you get Agnes. Protect them, Noodle. I need you to."

Bug showed up a few minutes later. Georgie opened the window, and he held out his hand to help her through. If she had to describe the feeling of stepping out of that window with nothing to hold her up but Bug, she would have said that it felt like being cradled by a cloud; the very air seemed to thicken around her, setting her in place like a cherry in a cup of gelatin. But she didn't have time to dwell on how it felt to step out of her window. They had places to go. Books to steal. Vamps to con. Punks to punk.

Bug took off. Georgie looked down to see Deitrich the doorman peering gravely up at them, watching as they hurled away from the penthouse. With Pinkwater dancing a few metres above them, Bug blew by skyscrapers and over rooftops. The wind pulled at Georgie's hair and whistled through her teeth as they flew. The lights of the city blazed all around them, giving everything a fuzzy golden halo and making the flight seem all the more impossible, all the more magical. Georgie was tempted to tell Bug to forget about the Punk and the vampires and about the pen and The Professor and about the book, tempted to tell him to keep going until he couldn't go any more. But then the kind, worried faces of the Bloomingtons rose up in her mind, and she knew there was no escaping what they had to do. When they reached the lower end of the island, Bug came in for a landing, setting them gently down on their feet.

"Wow," said Georgie, after he let go of her hand. "You've got really good."

Bug smiled. "Yeah?"

"You know you have," she said, "so stop with the modest stuff."

"I'm a modest guy."

"Sure," Georgie told him. "I'll remind you that you said that the next time you tell me about one of your photo shoots."

"Shut up," he said, knocking her with his shoulder. Her stomach fluttered in her gut, but she couldn't be sure whether it was because of Bug or because they were about to attend a party thrown by a lunatic Punk and his battalion of bloodsucking minions.

They found the address they were looking for. The two of them stood in front of an old building that stank of seawater and fish, staring up at the lights in the windows.

"Are you ready for this?" Bug asked her.

"No," said Georgie. "Are you?"

"Nope."

"Nope!" chirped Pinkwater.

"Great," Georgie said. "Let's go."

"Wait," Bug said.

Georgie turned. "What?"

"This could be dangerous," he said.

"I know."

"I mean, really dangerous.

Georgie nodded. "I know."

"It's just that I..." He trailed off.

"You what?"

Bug stared at the sidewalk and mumbled something.

"What?" Georgie said.

Bug looked up. "I like you."

"Oh," said Georgie, not sure exactly what he meant by this. There were so many possibilities. *I like you like a friend. I like you like a cousin. I like you like a sister. I like you, but not as much as I'd like you if you weren't three metres tall with delusions-of-grandeur hair and that weird tripping-over-yourself problem.*

I like you, but I don't like you like you.

But Bug was standing there staring at her with his enormous eyes. Pinkwater chirped. Georgie had to say something. She said, "Thanks."

As usual, it was not the right thing to say. Bug sighed. "What I'm trying to say is, I was never going out with Roma Radisson. I let you think that because... well, I don't know why. I don't like her. I like you. I *like* you like you. Do you know what I mean?"

Now Georgie felt so awkward that she had no idea what to do. She wanted to jump up and down. She wanted to moult out of her own skin and leave the drying husk on the sidewalk. She wanted to disappear. And then she wanted to smack him upside the head for his incredibly bad timing. They were about to confront a crazy Punk who had named himself after an almond biscuit. She didn't need to be worried about how bad her hair looked or whether she should have worn lip gloss or maybe slouch a little so that she didn't look so ridiculously huge.

Bug seemed to read her mind. "I just wanted you to know, that's all. In case anything happens."

"Nothing's going to happen," she blurted, practically shouting. How dare he say something like that? How dare he make her worry more than she already was worrying? She repeated herself: "Nothing's going to happen."

He smiled. "OK."

They approached the doorless doorway. All around the jamb and the windows, the blue paint was chipped and faded. They kicked through old soda cans, newspapers and empty take-out containers in the entranceway, broken bottles on the stairs.

"This is a nice place," said Bug, and Georgie could hear the tightness in his voice, the same sort of tightness that she could feel in her muscles as they walked up the three flights of stairs to the "gallery".

On the third floor, the landscape changed. Gone were the newspapers, the cans and the bottles. The walls gleamed with fresh white paint and the floors shone with wax. A sign marked the right door.

THE CHAOS GALLERY:
A New Perspective in Art

"Right." Georgie reached out, twisted the doorknob, and pushed open the door.

Chapter 23

Art Appreciation

The first thing they noticed: the place was packed.

The second thing they noticed: it was a veritable who's who of the rich and famous.

Correction: the place was a veritable who's who of the *children* of the rich and famous. To whit:

Nathan Johnson Jr, son of three-time Flyfest winner Nathan Johnson. Because he was a leadfoot, Nathan Jr couldn't follow in his father's flight path, so he was recording a rap CD. The CD featured songs about Nathan's life as a young gangsta (though he'd spent all of his sixteen years in a brownstone on the Upper East Side with a chef, a valet, a butler, a personal trainer, a driver and a guy who came once a week to polish the chandeliers in the bathroom).

James Todd Sean, son of director/producer Sean Todd James. James's dad regularly cast him in bit parts in his films, where he tortured the rest of the cast with his incomprehensible improvisation and bad breath.

Isabella Sophia Radicchio, the daughter of real-estate tycoon Leonardo Radicchio. Isabella sold her own line of pet carriers, Tiny Totes, designed to tote wealthy teens' miniature parrots around. Isabella was developing a TV sitcom for her own bird, Boo Boo. The show was called "Boo Boo's Boo-boos".

"What are all these people doing here?" said Georgie.

"I have no idea."

"Hey," Georgie whispered to Bug. "Do you think they know they're hanging out with vamps?"

"Even if they did, I don't think they'd care," Bug said. And there they were – pale-skinned, black-garbed, black-hearted demons – lurking in the corners of the room, their faces pasted with the most exquisitely bored expressions that Georgie had ever seen. If you didn't look too closely, you wouldn't know they were vampires. You would have thought they were a bunch of disgruntled Goth kids at a square dance.

"Never mind them," said Georgie. "Look at this 'art'."

Numerous canvases covered the walls on all sides. Georgie got close to the nearest canvas, a piece entitled

Roly-poly Fish Heads. There was nothing fishy about it, but there were pickle slices affixed to the surface of the canvas with some sort of yellowish goo that Georgie couldn't identify. The whole thing had a peculiar smell.

"Do you like it?" a voice said behind her.

Georgie turned and stared. Behind her stood Mandelbrot. He was tall and thin and pale like the vampires, but with the wolfish, pupil-less dark eyes of a Punk. He wore black leather trousers, combat boots, and a yellow T-shirt that said THE CHAOS KING. Two rolls of duct tape served as bracelets. On his head was what looked like an Indian headdress, complete with dangling beads and dyed feathers.

"I said, do you like it?"

"Oh! Yes!" said Georgie. "A lot."

"Good," said the man. "Remember me? I'm Mandelbrot. The Chaos King. You can call me Mandelbrot. Or Chaos. Or King."

"OK, um, Mr King."

"Ing-kay," said the man.

"Excuse me?"

"Ing-kay. Pig Latin," said Chaos / King / Mandelbrot / Whoever. Mandelbrot slapped Bug on the back hard enough to make the boy lurch forwards and Pinkwater go flying. "And you must be Master Grabowski."

"None other," Bug said, reaching around his neck to rub

his shoulder blade. Pinkwater flapped his wings and squawked as he settled back down on Bug's shoulder. Bug reached into his pocket and pulled out a couple of seeds to feed the bird, calm him down.

"Good, good," Mandelbrot said. "You're rich too. You're all rich. And that's so nice. The world needs rich kids." He broke out in a twist, which Bug and Georgie watched in shocked silence.

"Something cool better happen here," said Isabella, "or I'm taking Boo Boo home." She held up a teeny pink Tiny Tote with the name "Boo Boo" in diamonds across the side. Something inside squawked irritably.

"You are about to do something really cool," Mandelbrot said. "The most important thing you will ever do in your lives."

"Yo, what that, Dawg?" said Nathan Jr (or Natty Bumpo, if you wanted to use his rap star name).

"You," Mandelbrot said, "are about to become art patrons."

"What?" said James Todd Sean. "What's a patron?"

"So that I can continue to make my art, you are all going to give me money. Lots of money. You're each going to buy at least one painting. Maybe two or three or four or five. Cash is appreciated, but I also take personal cheques."

There was a silence in the gallery for a moment before Isabella Sophia Radicchio spoke up. "And why would we give you money? Why would we buy any of this?"

"HELLO! Because your parents will hate it!"

There was a collective sigh among the crowd and a few high fives. The rich and famous kids loved the idea. Everyone started opening wallets and purses.

Georgie couldn't believe it. Surely Mandelbrot wasn't so crazy that he would threaten the lives of her parents for this?

Just then Mandelbrot started doing his own version of an Indian war chant, whooping and circling around the room.

OK, maybe he was crazy enough for anything.

"I guess Mr Fuss was right," Bug said. "You can't take these guys too seriously."

Georgie shook her head. "Well, we still have to find that book, so let's start looking."

Bug and Georgie split up and made a show of looking at every painting in the room as the gallery filled up even more. None of the guests knew what to make of Mandelbrot and his Indian headdress, and they seemed to be disappointed that there was no caviar or sushi available, and that there were no photographers to take their pictures. They did think the vampires were cool, though, and asked them lots of questions about eternal life, and what parties were like in the seventeenth and eighteenth centuries. They wrote Mandelbrot large cheques and stuffed them, plus wads of cash, in the collection can he set up in the middle of the gallery.

"Hey!" a voice rang out. "What is Georgetta Bloomington doing here?"

Roma Radisson. Well. What would a party for the rich and famous be without The Second Richest Girl in the Universe?

Roma was wearing a yellow gown that appeared to have spent a bit of time in a food processor. Vast shreds of gauzy fabric tumbled over her shoulders and down her legs. In her red hair sat a jewelled crown. On her feet were jewelled shoes. In her hand was a jewelled mobile phone. She had little jewels pasted on her cheeks. She looked like an overwrought parade float.

"I mean it, Phinneas," Roma said to the vampire at her side. "I want to know what Georgie Bloomington is doing here and I want to know NOW."

"Relax, Roma," the vampire said in a bored tone. Georgie recognised him instantly. It was the vampire that had first come to her window, the one with the fabulous velvet trousers. Tonight he was wearing fabulous suede trousers. Georgie decided that it probably wasn't a great time to nudge Bug and point out the fabulousness of the trousers and suggest that he, Bug, might think about getting some fabulous trousers of his very own.

"And what's HE doing here?" Roma shrieked, pointing at Bug.

Phinneas put both hands over his ears and walked to the other side of the room. Roma stamped her foot. London England and Bethany Tiffany, who were also in the gallery, tried hard to calm Roma down. London offered her a piece of Juicy Mint Bubble Fresh gum.

"What is that going to do?" said Roma.

"Blowing bubbles always cheers me up," London said.

"Your head is a bubble," Roma snapped. The three girls marched past Georgie, Bethany Tifffany bumping Georgie with her shoulder.

"Sorry," she said automatically.

"You're always bumping into people and you're always saying you're sorry," said Georgie.

Bethany Tiffany crossed her arms and glared. Roma barked, "Phinneas! What are you doing all the way over there? Come back and stand by me."

Mandelbrot yelled, "Did any of you cheeseballs bring any cheeseballs?"

"What kind of host makes you bring your own snacks?" said Roma. "And anyway, I don't eat *snacks*. I eat caviar. Why don't you send out some of your people to get me some caviar." This did not seem to be a request.

Mandelbrot nudged Bug and hooked at thumb at Roma. "Oi, oi, high maintenance, that one."

Bug nodded.

"But rich. Almost as rich as your girlfriend Georgetta Blooooooomington," he said, drawing out the "oo" until he sounded like a baying dog.

Bug flushed at the word "girlfriend" but said nothing. There was a desk in the corner of the large space, a desk piled with books. Bug pointed to the paintings that hung near it. "I want to take a look at some of those," he said.

"Look away!" sang Mandelbrot.

"Uh, thanks," said Bug.

A few minutes later, Bug found Georgie standing in front of a painting called *Hugs and Kisses*. He whispered in her ear: "That's got to be the worst painting I've ever seen."

"I know," she said. "Good thing that's not what we're here for. Did you see the pile of books on the desk in the corner?"

"I did better than that," said Bug. He lifted his T-shirt a couple of centimetres and showed her the leather-bound book that he'd tucked into the waistband of his jeans.

"Are you sure that's the book?"

"None of the other ones were bound in leather. And the rest of them all had titles about fractions or something. This is the only one that looked old enough."

"OK," said Georgie. "Now all we have to do is get out of here."

"Do you think Mandelbrot will care if we leave?"

"I don't know," Georgie said. "Maybe we should buy a painting first. Though I'm not sure if this guy even uses paint," Georgie said. "As a matter of fact, I'm positive he doesn't."

"OK," said Bug. "Why don't we circle the room one more time until we get to the painting closest to the door. We'll pretend to look at it for a while and when we can, we'll duck into the hallway. You make us disappear, and I'll get us back uptown."

Georgie took a deep breath. "You think my parents will know that I was gone?"

"Probably."

"Yeah," said Georgie. "And then I'll be grounded till the twenty-fourth century."

"It will be worth it," Bug said.

"Easy for you to say."

Pinkwater, who had been quiet for so long that Georgie and Bug forgot he was there, chirped, "Don't look now."

They looked. Standing in the doorway was Hewitt Elder in a long orange caftan and a matching head scarf and messenger bag. Her eyes were glittering, and she seemed to be extremely happy about something. Georgie wondered if maybe she got another poetry book published.

"Hello, Hewitt," Mandelbrot boomed.

"What's SHE doing here?" Roma shrieked. "I thought I was the honoured guest! I don't hang out with book geeks. And Phinneas, weren't you going to get me some caviar?"

Phinneas had had enough. He grabbed Roma's arm and sank his fangs into her wrist.

"Hey! HEY!" she yelled. "Ow! That hurts! Ow! Ow!" Phinneas released her arm and walked away, leaving Roma dazed and drained (literally).

Mandelbrot fell to the floor giggling. "You know what you just did?"

"I bit her," Phinneas said sullenly.

"You didn't just bite her, you turned her into one of the undead, you idiot! You just made sure you'll have to spend the next four centuries listening to her whine. That. Is. So. Funny. I. Can't. Breathe." He curled into a ball, wheezing with laughter.

"What do you mean, undead?" Roma wanted to know, which made Mandelbrot laugh even harder. Already, Roma's fangs were starting to show. Some of the other vampires glared at Phinneas, clearly not thrilled that Roma would be around a lot longer than they'd expected her to be. The other rich kids started to look a bit nervous.

"Roma's a vampire," said Georgie in near disbelief. Somehow, it seemed rather appropriate.

"We should try to get out of here while they're all distracted," Bug murmured.

"OK," Georgie said. The two of them began to drift through the crowd counter-clockwise, stopping at different paintings to "admire" them before moving on to the next one. No one glanced in their direction; no one seemed to notice what they were doing. They made it all the way around the gallery and slipped into the hallway easily. Georgie took Bug's hand and turned them invisible, though she had a bit of trouble. Her right hand didn't want to cooperate and stubbornly stayed visible for a few awkward minutes.

Finally, they completely disappeared. As quietly as they could, they crept down the stairs, slipping past the stray vamps hanging out in the stairwell. They were almost out the door when someone clamped a hand on Georgie's shoulder.

Phinneas the vampire smiled sadly with red, red lips. "Going somewhere?"

Chapter 24

Hangman

Phinneas sighed. "Yes, I can see you. I can see you both. I've walked the earth for a thousand years and I know your type. You're a Wall. But that's not going to help you here."

Bug squeezed Georgie's hand and she squeezed back. He gathered himself and then yanked on Phinneas's arm as hard as he possibly could.

Phinneas sighed again. "That's not going to help you either."

Mandelbrot appeared on the landing, the rest of the vamps and rich kids piling up behind him like water behind a hair clog. "Don't tell me that someone is trying to leave my party." He was holding a baseball bat and he pointed it at Phinneas and his captives.

James Todd Sean said, "No one's there, dude."

"Yes, there is," said Phinneas. "Two of them."

"If Phinneas says someone is there, then someone is there," Mandelbrot said.

"Whatever, dude. We're out of here," said James Todd Sean.

"Thank you for your money," said Mandelbrot. "Money, money, money. It makes the world go round. It makes the head go round. It makes the Mandelbrot go round." Mandelbrot spun in a circle as the rich kids filed past him, down the stairs, and out the front of the building. Bug kicked at Phinneas but could not break his hold. It was like kicking at a statue.

Hewitt popped up behind Mandelbrot. "Why's everyone leaving?"

"Because they gave me money, that's why. All I wanted was their money." He gestured down to Phinneas with the bat. "But I'm not letting these two leave, because they didn't ask my permission and they didn't give me money. Why didn't they give me any money? Also, a friend of mine wanted me to ask them a few questions. I figure I owe him that much."

Hewitt peered at Phinneas. "I see one vampire. There's no one else there."

"Yes, there is," Phinneas said indignantly. "Vampires have

excellent eyesight. And we use sonar. There are two people standing here, a boy and a girl."

"A boy and a girl who did not give me any money," said Mandelbrot. "A boy and a girl who stole my book."

Bug felt himself go cold. He'd been seen! He'd been caught!

Mandelbrot seemed to read his mind. "You can't punk a Punk," he said.

"Besides," Phinneas said. "You're not a very good thief. Not like your dad at all."

"You got that right," Bug muttered.

"Who?" said Hewitt. "Who isn't like their father?"

Though Bug and Georgie were holding on to each other as tightly as they could, Phinneas pulled them apart as easily as tearing a piece of wet newspaper. Because he was no longer touching Georgie, Bug appeared. And since Bug was already visible, and since the vamps could see her anyway, Georgie popped into view.

Hewitt gasped. "I don't understand," she said.

"Who said you had to understand everything?" Mandelbrot told her. "Who said you had to understand *anything*? And who invited you here anyway?"

"What do you mean?" said Hewitt. "You invited me. We had a deal."

I knew it! thought Bug. *I knew there was something weird about her!* He felt like punching something. And then he did punch something, Phinneas, right in the rib cage. *Wham!*

Phinneas didn't even blink.

Mandelbrot shrugged. "I changed my mind. Go away."

"But I gave you the book!" Hewitt said.

"So?" Mandelbrot said. "If I were you, I would have given me books too. That doesn't mean you can crash my parties whenever you want to. That doesn't make us friends. You're not the boss of me. Nobody is the boss of me." Mandelbrot hopped down the steps, the feathers on his headdress flying. He held out his hand. Bug didn't see any other choice. He pulled the book out from under his shirt and gave it to Mandelbrot.

"Now for my question. Uh... what was it again?"

Phinneas exhaled heavily. "You're supposed to ask them if they have any information about the pen."

"Right!" said Mandelbrot. "So, you kids. Do either of you guys have any idea where the pen is?"

"We don't know anything about any pen," Bug said quickly. Too quickly.

"Really?" said Mandelbrot. "Not sure I buy that one. So, I'll ask again. Do you guys know where the pen is? It's a really special pen, and my friend really wants it." He laughed. "Though I'm not sure I'll give it to him. Why should he have it? Why can't I have it? "

"I said, we don't know where it is," Bug repeated.

"Oi, oi, oi!" Mandelbrot said. "We've got a sassy one, here, boys." Mandelbrot picked up one of the long feathers trailing off his headdress and tickled Bug's nose with it.

"We don't know anything," Georgie said. "Really, we don't. We just heard there was a cool book here and we thought maybe we could take it. We used to take things and—"

Mandelbrot interrupted. "I say we play a game. Phinneas, let's take the kids outside." He swung the baseball bat menacingly.

"OK," said Phinneas. He dragged Georgie and Bug out the door of the building. Bug couldn't believe how unbelievably strong Phinneas was for someone so pale and skinny. (And, um, dead.) Phinneas barely seemed to be making any effort at all, and yet nothing Bug did made the vamp relax his grip – he and Georgie might as well have been newborn chickadees in the clutches of a gorilla. Pinkwater zoomed around their heads chirping, "Unhand them, you fiend!" which had little effect but to make Phinneas smirk fiendishly and Mandelbrot erupt in fiendish giggles.

Bug wished Georgie had brought Noodle. Maybe Noodle could have grown fourteen times her real size and used the vampires as chew toys. But all they had was Pinkwater, and Pinkwater zooming around sounding like something out of a superhero comic book wasn't going to deter any fiend from doing fiendish things. It would probably *encourage* fiendishness.

Speaking of fiendishness: all the vamps followed Phinneas, Georgie and Bug as they moved in the direction of the East River. What were they going to do? Drown them? Bite them? Drown them and then bite them?

Hewitt Elder, who had also followed the group outside, said, "Why don't you let Georgie Bloomington go? She's The Richest Girl in the Universe and I'm sure—"

"Boring!" Mandelbrot announced. "I don't want to talk about boring things. I don't want to talk full stop. I want to play some games. How about Hangman?" Mandelbrot danced a jig in front of Georgie and Bug. "You guys know Hangman?"

That doesn't sound good, thought Bug.

Mandelbrot thrust the bat up like a warrior charging into battle. "To the Brooklyn Bridge!"

Before Bug had time to think about it, Phinneas launched himself into the air, dragging Bug and Georgie along with him. Bug could hear Hewitt yelling below. "Wait! I can't fly like that! Wait! Someone take me!"

Mandelbrot, who was getting a piggyback ride from one of the vamps, waved at her. Hewitt got smaller and smaller, a bright orange splotch on the glazed city street.

The vamps flew even higher, lurching and pitching so hard that Bug thought he might be sick. Bug remembered The Professor telling him and Georgie long ago that vampires could only fly in bat form, but the only bat-like part of Phinneas was the pair of large leathery black wings that beat thunderously at the air. Pinkwater, who had been struggling to keep up, got further and further behind until Bug couldn't see him any more. Bug thrashed and kicked, hoping it might throw the vamp off balance, but Phinneas merely crushed the breath from his lungs with one squeeze of his iron arm. The wind lashed Bug's face and drew tears from his eyes, blurring his vision, but not enough that he couldn't see the Brooklyn Bridge snaking out underneath them, its thick cables like yarn on an enormous loom.

The vamps made a bumpy, shuddering descent and landed on the bridge's wooden pedestrian walkway. People in passing cars stared curiously out their windows as they passed. Bug could only imagine what they were saying to one another: *Honey, did you see that? That guy had wings. Actual wings!*

"So this is what we're going to do," said Mandelbrot, climbing off the back of a vamp with blond hair. He dropped the baseball bat, pulled Georgie away from Phinneas, spun her round, and marched her to the edge of the bridge. He lifted her arms over her head and made her grip the cables that formed the structure of the bridge. "We'll put Georgetta Bloomington over here. Then, I'm going to think of a phrase or a saying or some random words. You, Bug Boy, will have to try to guess what I'm thinking of letter by letter.

Every time you guess the letter wrong, we'll move Georgie up a little higher. Maybe even a lot higher. Till she's hanging from the cables. Like Hangman. You get me?"

Even though he knew it was futile, Bug tried to yank away from Phinneas, who was behind Bug with his iron hands locked on Bug's elbows. "Look, I'm sorry I took your book, but it wasn't Georgie's fault. It was all my idea."

Mandelbrot made a sound like a buzzer.

"And didn't you say you wanted money?" Georgie said. "We have a lot of it. If you could take us to a bank, we could get some."

Mandelbrot made another buzzing sound. "The other kids gave me plenty of money. And besides, if I need more, I'll just get it from your parents."

"What do you mean?" Georgie said.

"Plan B. After I have Phinneas bite them, I'll take their money."

"What if he doesn't want to bite them?"

"Oh, he will," Mandelbrot said.

Georgie twisted her neck to look at Phinneas. "Do you always listen to everything he says?"

Phinneas shrugged. "We had another boss originally, but this one gives us fresh bagels. Plus, it's something to do."

At this, Georgie tried to run away, but one of the vamps scooped her up and put her back where Mandelbrot had positioned her.

Mandelbrot whipped round, headdress feathers flying. "So! Bug! I'm thinking of a phrase. It's really easy! And hard! And chaotic!" His wolfish eyes twinkled evilly. "Unless you want to tell me where that very special pen is, pick a letter."

Bug closed his own eyes. It had seemed so easy – lift a measly book from an art gallery, what could go wrong? And now it was all wrong. This was insane. Perfectly insane. But he had to play along, at least for a little while, till he could figure out how to get Georgie away from these stupid vampires.

"The pen's hidden," Bug said, opening his eyes. "In my apartment."

"Phin? He telling the truth?"

Phinneas stared into Bug's eyes. "No," he said.

"It's in Georgie's apartment."

"Lying," said Phinneas.

"I'm waiting," said Mandelbrot. "I don't like to wait."

Bug's eyes flew open. How was he supposed to guess this? It could be anything. "Usually in Hangman you get categories," Bug said. "Like you're thinking of a film or book title or whatever."

Mandelbrot thrust his face into Bug's, his pupil-less eyes like black holes. "Haven't you figured out that there's nothing 'usual' about The Chaos King? Pick. A. Letter."

Bug's brain worked frantically. What were the most common letters in the alphabet? E? S? T? "T," he said.

Mandelbrot smiled. "Nope." One of the vamps moved towards Georgie. He took her by the wrists and moved her hands a few centimetres to the right, forcing her to grip the twisting metal cable. Even though she was tall, she had to stretch to reach it.

"Pick another letter," Mandelbrot said.

"S," Bug said.

"Oops!" said Mandelbrot. He jerked his head and the vampire moved Georgie up another few centimetres. Now her toes were barely scraping the wooden planks of the walkway.

"Another," Mandelbrot said.

Bug began to sweat. Maybe Mandelbrot was thinking of his name? "M," he said.

"Yes!" said Mandelbrot. "Oh, wait a second." He made a show of counting on his fingers. "No, I thought there was an 'M', but there isn't. Bad news for little Georgie Bloomington."

The vamp moved Georgie over another foot. She was hanging completely, the cable biting into her fingers.

"Don't let go," Mandelbrot told Georgie. "Or you lose the game."

"Yeah?" said Georgie, kicking her legs. "What happens if we lose?"

To answer her question, Mandelbrot made loud chomping noises. Then he turned back to Bug. "Another guess?"

Maybe they should allow themselves to be bitten, thought

Bug. Then they would be as strong as the other vampires. They could take the book from Mandelbrot and bring it to the book club. Then Mrs Vorona could bring them back to life.

But what if they didn't bite them? What if the vampires did something worse? Bug didn't think it was wise to take a bunch of vamps and their loopy Punk leader at their word. Maybe he should just tell them the old women had the pen. They might be able to get to them before the vamps did. But maybe not.

Bug's forehead started to sweat. So much for playing along. There must be something he could do. Something to distract them just long enough for him to get in the air. He knew if he could just get in the air, he could outfly these guys, could get them away.

"Guess!" Mandelbrot bellowed. "Guess! Guess! Guess!"

Guess. He had to guess. OK, not Mandelbrot, but what about Chaos King? "E," Bug said.

"E! That would be a NO! Move her on up, boys!"

The vamp lifted Georgie's hands from the cable and moved her even higher on the bridge. Georgie winced as her hands closed around the cable. She was about three metres from the ground.

"Hang on, Georgie," Bug called.

"Yes, hang on, Georgie!" Mandelbrot mimicked.

Bug nearly growled in frustration.

"Guess again," Mandelbrot said.

"This is stupid; I don't want to guess," said Bug. "Why don't you—"

"You don't want to guess? Move her higher. Much higher." The vamps plucked Georgie off the wire and flew her higher, much higher, much too high, so high that if she fell...

"No!" said Bug. "Just tell me what you want and I'll—"

Mandelbrot jumped up and down. "I! WANT! YOU! TO! GUESS!"

Bug's brain raced even harder. He strained against Phinneas. V for vampire? "V!" he said.

Mandelbrot's up-and-down motion turned into funky disco step. "Noooooope! Higher, boys!"

The vampires moved Georgie yet again. "Bug, I can't hold on much longer."

"Yes, you can!" said Bug. Mandelbrot twirled in circles, and Bug's brain raced just as fast. What if Mandelbrot wasn't thinking of any word or phrase? What if he wasn't thinking of anything? What if he was just toying with them?

Phinneas's grip on his elbows was still tight, but not as tight as it had been. How do you ward off a vampire? Silver bullets? No, that was for werewolves. And it didn't matter anyway, because he didn't have any silver bullets or silver rings or silver anything. He had no wooden stakes or garlic, either. All he had was a pocket full of birdseed. And what could you do with a pocket full of birdseed?

He looked up and saw the crows before anyone else did and suddenly he knew what you could do with a pocket full of birdseed.

You could throw it.

Georgie had to bite her lip to keep from screaming at the pain in her fingers and palms and knew she could not hold on. She tried to cheat a little, pulling her feet up to rest them on the cables, but when the vampires saw her, they flew up to kick her feet down.

She looked down at Bug and Mandelbrot. Bug, who had been struggling with Phinneas the whole time he was playing Mandelbrot's "game", had stopped struggling. *He's planning something*, she thought. *He's going to try something.* She hoped he would try it fast, because she was going to fall soon and she really really really didn't want to fall. She didn't know how high up she was, but she knew it was too high to drop without breaking bones she didn't want broken.

She tried to keep images of plummeting on to the ground or into the river out of her head. Georgie thought of her parents and wished she had left them a note that would have let them know what she was doing and why. But then what could she have written? *Dear Mum and Dad, There is a Punk who is bringing dead things back to life with a magic book. So Bug and I are going to steal the book and take it to these old ladies who have a book club (they have the magic pen, too, but that's beside the point). They'll use the book against the Punk's army of vampires – oh, wait, did I mention the vampires? – so that they won't bite you or me or Bug or any of the rest of us and turn us into the walking dead or use the book to unleash some giant sloths or octopi on us. (Wait, did I mention the giant octopus)? And—*

Someone below shouted, "Hey! Crows!" Georgie looked up to see a dozen crows circling overhead.

A dozen crows and one bright blue budgie.

"Pinkwater!" Georgie said.

The crows attacked. Each one picked a vamp and went after him with beak and claws while Pinkwater took a dive towards Bug and Phinneas. "Feed me!" he chirped. "Feed me!"

Phinneas took one hand off Bug to swat at the budgie, so he didn't notice when Bug dug around in his pocket, pulled out a handful of something and tossed it in Phinneas's face. For a moment, Phinneas appeared stunned. Then he and the rest of the vamps fell to their knees on the wooden walkway. Georgie could hear them counting, "One, two, three, four, five..."

Bug took off, headed for Georgie. Mandelbrot leaped up, quick as a cat, and grabbed Bug around the legs. "Stop counting!" he yelled at the vamps, struggling to hang on to Bug.

"Six, seven, eight, nine, ten..."

"I said STOP THAT!" Mandelbrot yelled. "We're playing HANGMAN!"

"Eleven, twelve, thirteen, fourteen..."

Bug thrashed in Mandelbrot's arms.

"Argh!" Mandelbrot grunted. "Help me, you cheeseballs!"

Frantic footsteps echoed on the wooden slats. Roma lurched in her high, jewelled heels, half walking, half-flying with her huge, awkward leathery wings.

"Bethany and London wouldn't let me bite them!" she shrieked. "I said that we could be friends for ever and ever, but they just ran away. So *not* fab™. You guys have to be my friends now. And you can't just LEAVE without me like that. It makes me really really mad and you so don't want to get me mad. Who here wants a steak? I need a steak. What are you doing with Bug Grabowski? Why is everyone crawling around on the ground? Ooh! Are those seeds?"

Bug kicked away from a distracted Mandelbrot and was at Georgie's side in a few seconds. As Bug curled his arm around her waist, Georgie saw Mandelbrot pick up the baseball bat. He ran to Roma. "After them!"

"What?"

"Them! If we catch them, you can bite them!"

Roma turned and saw Bug and Georgie. "Oh! Cool!" She grabbed Mandelbrot by the scruff of the neck like a puppy and took off.

"Hurry, Bug!" Georgie said. "They're coming!"

Bug shot straight up and away from the bridge. Even

though they hadn't escaped yet, even though Roma and Mandelbrot were careening after them, she felt so light flying with Bug. Flying with Phinneas the vampire had hurt. A vamp's flying power remained his own – a vamp didn't share. When she flew with Bug, she could feel Bug's strength flowing into her muscles, understood that she was borrowing his buoyancy, the same way he borrowed her invisibility when she touched him.

She turned and saw Roma and Mandelbrot closing the distance. "Bug," Georgie yelled. "They're gaining on us."

"I know," he said.

"Fly faster!"

"I know!"

For a newly-formed vampire with newly-formed wings, Roma was speedy. But she was also clumsy. Her wings pumped the air so hard that she bobbed up and down like a yo-yo. Mandelbrot waved his bat, but every time he got close enough to take a swing, Roma bobbed them out of range again.

"Faster!" Mandelbrot screamed, and Roma drew up alongside Bug.

Bug banked hard towards the bright lights of the city just as Roma bounced left. Mandelbrot swung his bat and...

Georgie was falling, falling, falling. A strange sound filled her ears, a low and mournful howl, but she didn't know if she was the one howling. The water of the East River gaped like a mouth below her, like a great black hungry mouth, and Georgie crashed right into it.

Chapter 25

The Temple of Dendur

Cold. At first all she felt was cold. And then the pain set in, the ache of bones and flesh and skin that had been hung from a bridge and dropped into a wall of water. Where was Bug? she wondered. Did he fall too? Did he get away? Was he OK? She drifted, her lungs like stones in her chest, her limbs useless as a doll's. She was going to die here in this black and stinking river. She was going to die and her parents would never know what happened to her. She was going to die and she would never see them again and—

—something grabbed her leg.

Something huge and strong and monstrous. It grabbed her leg – *twirled itself* around her leg – and then she was moving. Moving so fast that it felt like she was being dragged by a jet. Still, she couldn't breathe and she was close to blacking out completely when whatever it was pulled her to the surface. She coughed and coughed, sucking back sweet mouthfuls of air. But the monstrous thing still had her by the leg and was towing her so swiftly that she couldn't see what she was towed *by* or where she was being towed *to*. Her back burned where she skidded on the surface of the water.

At last, they slowed down. Another monstrous something twirled itself around her waist and she was lifted high into the air and laid with the utmost gentleness on the rocky shore of the river. It was then that she saw what had towed her to the shore: the biggest octopus that a person had ever seen, the biggest that was ever imagined. Its large eyes peeked up in front of a limp bluish-grey mantle, eyes that seemed old and kind and wise. As she watched, the octopus laid a limp Bug next to her on the rocky shore. With the tip of a single metres-long tentacle, it ruffled Bug's hair. Then it reeled in its limbs and disappeared in a froth of bubbles.

Georgie rolled to her knees, coughing. "Bug," she said. She shook his shoulder. "Bug. Wake up."

She leaned in. Bug's eyes were closed and his skin was pasty. "Bug!" She shook him harder. He didn't move. Had he been hit with Mandelbrot's bat? Had he been hurt by the fall to the water?

"Bug!" she yelled. "Bug!"

Shivering and terrified, she pressed her ear to his chest. And heard nothing.

She sat back on her heels, staring. No, it couldn't be. No, no, no. It wasn't possible. She pressed her ear to his chest again, sure that she was wrong. She had to be wrong.

She listened, her whole body straining to hear a beat.

Still nothing.

"Bug," she whispered. "You have to wake up, OK? Please? Please, please, please wake up." She remembered what he said before they went into the gallery, how he wanted to tell her that he liked her in case something should happen. She remembered how she said nothing could happen, how she'd insisted on it, but never told him how she felt, never said, "I like you, too." And now he would never ever know.

Something thick and awful gathered in her throat and she thought she might choke or explode or crack completely in half. She didn't know what to do. She was frozen. So when someone came scrambling down the rocky shore, she didn't even turn. She didn't care who it was. What did it matter who it was?

"Georgie." Someone was shaking *her* shoulder.

"Georgie!"

More shaking.

"Georgie, they're coming. We have to get out of here."

Who was shaking her? Who was coming?

"Georgie, listen to me!" Hewitt Elder grabbed both Georgie's shoulders. "They're coming! We have to get away from here." Hewitt pointed into the air where a cloud of vampires blackened the already dark sky. "We need to leave right now."

"Bug..." Georgie said.

Hewitt shook her head. "He's gone. You're not. We have to go." She hauled Georgie to her feet.

"I can't leave him," said Georgie.

"Yes you can. We'll get some people to come for him later. Come on."

Georgie shook her head. But her heart wasn't in it. Her heart wasn't in anything.

Hewitt scoured the sky frantically. "Georgie, think of your parents! Think of what will happen to them if they lose you!"

This got her feet to move a little. Hewitt did the rest, half dragging her, half flying her up the riverbank towards the highway that raced around the edge of the city. "We'll have to catch a cab," said Hewitt.

Georgie nodded dully. Bug, she thought. *Bug*.

Somehow Hewitt managed to get a taxi to pull over, much to the irritation of the other drivers on the road. She shoved Georgie in the cab and gave the cabbie an address that Georgie didn't recognise.

"Hey!" said the cabbie. "Don't let her drip all over my cab."

"Shut up and drive," Hewitt said in her customary haughty tone. "As fast as you possibly can."

He shut up and drove. Horns blared behind them and the cabbie made monkey faces in the rearview mirror. To Georgie it seemed they drove for hours, hours in which she reminded herself how she didn't tell her parents what she was doing and how she didn't bring Noodle who might have saved them from the vampires and how she never told Bug how much she cared for him and how she was a useless, worthless, horrible person who got people hurt and got people killed and that there was nothing anyone could do to fix it. She could hardly breathe. She could hardly remember what they went to the gallery for. What was so important that—

Georgie stiffened. "Stop the car!"

"What?" said the cabbie. "Here?"

"No, the next block," Hewitt told him.

"That's what I thought," he said. Muttering to himself: "Crazy people dripping all over my cab. I just cleaned this cab."

"Hewitt," Georgie said. "We have to go back. We have to get the book. You have to help me."

"Don't worry, I'll help you," Hewitt said. "Let's go."

Hewitt threw some money at the cabbie and they climbed from the cab. Georgie frowned. "The Metropolitan Museum of Art? What are we doing here?"

"You were all supposed to come, but that's OK. It doesn't matter. You're the most important anyway."

"What?" said Georgie. She couldn't understand anything Hewitt was saying. All she knew was that Mandelbrot had a book that could bring things to life. Maybe it could bring Bug back to life. She had to get that book. She didn't care how. "Hewitt, that book that you gave Mandelbrot. It has the power to bring things to life. It could save Bug. We have to find Mandelbrot."

Hewitt grabbed Georgie's arm and led her up the steps towards the doors of the museum, taking the steps two at a time with the peculiar hopping of people who couldn't fly so well. "Mandelbrot doesn't have the book," she said.

Georgie stopped walking. "What?"

"I said, he doesn't have the book. I have the book."

"You?" said Georgie. *"You?"*

"I'll explain when we're inside."

"Wait—"

"You want the book, right?"

"Yes!"

"Well, I smuggled it out of the library and hid it here. It will only take a minute to get it. Come on." The museum was dark, but the front door opened easily. Georgie gave Hewitt a puzzled look. Hewitt shrugged. "Someone left it open for me."

Inside the museum, their footsteps echoed in the dim and

cavernous entranceway. Hewitt turned right and headed towards the galleries containing the Egyptian Art. It was as quiet as a tomb, which was fitting, as the Egyptian galleries contained so many coffins and mummies and artefacts found buried with kings and queens. Georgie swallowed hard and hurried to keep up with Hewitt. Finally, they entered an enormous room with floor-to-ceiling windows along one side. Directly in front of them was: a dark pool of water guarded by two seated statues. Behind the pool, a stone temple.

"Here we are," said Hewitt. "The Temple of Dendur."

"OK," Georgie said. "Where's the book?"

"In the Temple," Hewitt said. "I hid it there because I was afraid someone else would take it from the library."

"Who?"

"Anybody. Everybody. Don't you think that everyone in the city would want to get hold of a book that can animate things?"

"I guess." Georgie's mind was elsewhere: how quickly they could back to the banks of the East River. "Is there a phone somewhere in here? Maybe we can call my parents to let them know I'm OK. And then we can tell them where Bug is. I don't want the vampires to get him. I don't want anyone else to find him."

"What do you care, anyway?" Hewitt said.

Georgie frowned. "What do you mean?"

Hewitt didn't answer. She moved past the still waters of the pool and up on to the large platform on which the Temple sat. Dendur, according to the plaques positioned around the buildings, was the only Egyptian temple in the western hemisphere. It was reassembled in the Metropolitan as it had appeared on the banks of the Nile.

Hewitt stepped inside the Temple and Georgie followed. "What did you mean by that?" Georgie said. "Why wouldn't I care about Bug?"

Again, Hewitt didn't respond. She felt along the left wall of the interior of the Temple until she hit a loose stone. She was able to shove it to the side just enough to fish her fingers in the gap. From the gap she withdrew a thin leather book so fragile and yellowed that it could have been as old as the Temple itself. "Here it is," said Hewitt. "Now this is a book of poetry! I bet you want to know how it works."

"All I need to know is that it does work," Georgie said. "Let's get back to the Brooklyn Bridge. You can tell me about it on the way."

Hewitt stepped out of the Temple. "I found it in the basement of the library, of course. I'd got lost in the stacks. You wouldn't believe how easy it is to get lost in those stacks. They seem to go on for ever. I don't know why I picked it up but I did. And I started reading the poetry – well, incantations really – out loud. And guess what happened?"

Now that Georgie was facing away from the Temple, she noticed the six granite thrones lining that same wall. Empty thrones. As if whoever had been sitting in them had just run out to get a drink or a piece of pizza.

"Can you guess?" Hewitt was saying. She sounded odd, excited, enthusiastic in a way that she had never sounded before. But then, Georgie had only met Hewitt a few times. Who knew how she sounded?

"Let's go, Hewitt. We have to get back to Bug."

Hewitt laughed as if Georgie hadn't spoken. "The chair I was sitting on actually started to dance, if you can believe that. I thought it was just one of the strange things that happens in the library. So many odd things happen in the library. But then I realised what had really happened. The poem I'd read enchanted the chair. It was probably used to animate Patience and Fortitude, the marble lions, though I don't know who did that or when. I figured out that when you read the incantations, whatever you touch comes to life. I was sitting on the chair, so—"

Georgie didn't care about Patience or about Fortitude or about chairs dancing around the library. "Hewitt!" she said. "Bug is dead!"

Hewitt clutched the book to her chest. "So?" she said sullenly. "We don't need him."

Georgie's mouth dropped open. "What?"

"Him! Who does he think he is anyway? He's the son of a

criminal. And those others. They're even worse."

Georgie took a step back. "What others?"

"You saw them. Roma Radisson and all those other twits at the gallery. All of them rich and famous. In the magazines and on TV all the time. But what have they ever done? Nothing! They don't deserve all that attention. They don't deserve all that money. Why do people follow them around taking their pictures? I'm the famous poet! Me!"

Georgie took another step back.

"And that stupid Mandelbrot. You think he's an artist? I gave him all kinds of books about art and he's still hopeless. He paints with food products! He's obsessed with chaos! What an idiot! Too stupid to even serve his purpose."

"And what was his purpose?" Georgie said, trying to keep Hewitt talking. Clearly she was nuts. Clearly Georgie had to get the book from her. But how to do it?

"He was supposed to get you to give him information about the pen. But when he couldn't force you to do that by himself, his employer gave him to the vamps for entertainment, figuring that *they* would deal with you."

"Employer? Who's his employer?"

"His employer never imagined that Mandelbrot would come to the library," said Hewitt as if Georgie hadn't spoken. "Never thought Mandelbrot would be so dumb as to tell someone else about the plan. Did you know that vampires are obsessed with counting? That when they see seeds they simply must stop and count them? Eastern Europeans used to put piles of millet or poppy seeds in graves. There's a book about it. I gave it to Mandelbrot so that he could control the vamps instead of the other way around. That book was amazing. When you opened it, it chattered. It sounded like clacking teeth. Or fangs."

Hewitt smiled then. "The ironic thing is that I wouldn't have known how to use *The Book of the Undead* to reanimate things if I hadn't got the idea from Mandelbrot. Anyway, he was supposed to get all you rich kids to the gallery opening. Just like I told him, those stupid kids thought Mandelbrot and his vampires were cool and gave him all the money that he wanted to support his 'art'. That Punk loved the idea of having patrons. Isn't that hilarious? A Punk who wanted patrons?" Her face darkened. "But he was supposed to bring everyone here to the museum afterwards. That was going to be *my* party."

"And what were we going to do at your party?" Georgie asked carefully, her eyes still trained on the book.

"See, I was going about everything all wrong. I was trying to tackle my problems one at a time. I heard that Bug Grabowski was having a photo shoot at the Seaport. I heard that the American Museum of Natural History had the remains of a giant octopus in their labs."

"That's why you were at the museum?" said Georgie.

"I snuck into the labs, brought the octopus to life, and

flushed it down a toilet. I bet you didn't know that something that big could squeeze down that small, but they can. Anyway, the thing swam through the sewers, out into the East River and over to the seaport, and pulled Bug into the water. Priceless!"

"Pretty funny," Georgie said bitterly.

"Then you told me that your class was coming to the art museum – including that twit Roma Radisson."

"You animated the dog," said Georgie.

"Yes, but it seems that whatever you animate remains true to its nature. So, the octopus wasn't really aggressive and the dog wasn't, either. Even the sloth was a big problem. Who knew they liked chocolate? But the biggest problem was that none of these things made Roma or Bug any less famous. If anything, it made them more famous. More! It's insane!"

You're insane, thought Georgie.

"So, I figured that instead of trying to deal with all these undeserving people one at a time, I would deal with them all at once. Here, in the museum. See, I figure that if this book can animate what's dead, then it can probably de-animate what isn't dead. And I can't think of better people to de-animate than Roma Radisson and her band of useless paparazzi pinups."

"You were going to kill us?" Georgie said, aghast.

"Oh no!" said Hewitt. "Not you! You aren't like them. You

have more money than all of them combined, but you have an appreciation for real art. Maybe because you grew up in an orphanage, you weren't spoiled like the rest of them. You wanted to read my poetry." Hewitt appeared almost shy. "Did you really like it? My poetry, I mean."

"Uh, yeah," Georgie said. "I loved it." Georgie had to get that book from her and get out of here as fast as she could. Her eyes flicked left and right, trying to calculate the fastest route out of the Temple of Dendur.

"And it turns out that you're even more special," Hewitt said. "You're a Wall. I couldn't believe it when I saw you at the gallery. I mean, when I didn't see you. Do you know that there are shelves and shelves of books about Walls in the library? Tell me, have you started walking through them yet?"

"Walking through what?" said Georgie.

Hewitt smiled. "Walls, silly."

Walking through walls? "Not yet," said Georgie.

"Georgie?" said Hewitt.

"Yeah?"

"I don't think you really liked my poetry."

"Oh, I did! I did," Georgie protested. "Really! There was that one about the... uh... the..."

"You're still thinking about Bug Grabowski. I can tell. You keep looking at the door as if you're about to run away."

"Why would I want to run away?"

"Oh, because of them."

Georgie felt a queer sort of itch in her gut. "Because of who?"

"Them," Hewitt repeated.

Right behind Georgie, a strange scraping following. The sound of stone on stone. Slowly Georgie turned, barely able to look but unable to stop herself. Standing in a line were six statues, each made of dark granite. But these statues were breathing. Solid granite chests rose and fell; cold granite breath chilled Georgie's crawling skin. Their bodies were the bodies of lithe young women, but their faces were those of lionesses. In one hand, they each held an ankh. The symbol of life.

"Georgie, I'd like to introduce Sakhmet, Goddess of Chaos." Hewitt chuckled. "Times six."

Chapter 26

Goddess Worship

Georgie vanished.

"I figured that would happen," said Hewitt. "But what I didn't figure was that I'd still be able to see your left foot."

Oh. No.

"Get her!" Hewitt yelled.

Georgie lunged, snatching the book out of Hewitt's hands, and then ducked just as one of the Sakhmets swung a stone fist. Georgie sidestepped Hewitt and ran past the Temple towards the back entrance, the whole time thinking *I am the wall and the ground and the air I am the wall and the ground and the air.* Thudding stone footsteps followed her. Could they see her? She didn't know, and didn't stop to find out. She jumped through the doorway and found herself in the American wing. Paintings and sculpture blurred as she sped past. Her lungs were already aching from her trip through the East River; now they were on fire. She tried to visualise the layout of the museum, but nothing looked familiar and everything looked familiar and she didn't know which way to go. She heard a loud crashing and whirled round to see two of the six Sakhmets charging through the gallery, several sculptures in pieces on the ground in their wake. There was a doorway on Georgie's left and she ran through it, ending up in the Arms and Armour gallery. A parade of armoured figures was posed in marching position in the centre of the room. Around the perimeter, suits of armour were displayed in glass cases, along with swords and guns and weapons of all kinds. If she thought it would do any good, she'd try to smash one of the cases and steal a rifle or even a cannon, but what harm could they do to walking goddesses made of granite?

The goddesses! Where were the goddesses?

Georgie froze, looking around wildly. She listened for the scratch of stone feet. Instead, she heard Hewitt calling from somewhere in the next gallery.

"Georgie," she said. "Don't think you have any power just because you have the book. I brought the goddesses to life, so I'm the one they're going to listen to, not you. They're hunting you because I told them to. The Egyptians revered cats. Worshipped them. Lionesses, too, because they were such excellent hunters. They might not be able to see you – though who knows what a goddess can see? – but they'll be able to hear and smell you. You won't know that they're behind you until you feel their cold breath on the back of your neck."

Georgie backed up against a wall, eyes darting left and right.

"I want my book back," Hewitt said.

I want Bug back, Georgie thought, gritting her teeth. She crept to the end of the gallery and slipped into the next: European Sculpture and Decorative Arts. She moved past cases full of china to large, roped-off displays of seventeenth century parlours complete with hypnotising wallpaper, enormous chandeliers and fussy furniture, all of it stripped from "country" houses in England and France. Georgie stepped over the nearest red velvet rope, catching her foot and causing the hook to chime against its mooring in the wall. Wincing, Georgie dived behind a large chair. She peeked over the arm just in time to see one of the Sakhmets enter the gallery. Her stone feet barely made a sound as she walked down the hallway holding the ankh like a club. At the display where Georgie had hidden, she stopped, nearly stopping Georgie's heart in the process. The Sakhmet's blank, expressionless face and lidless eyes scanned the parlour, settling on the chair Georgie crouched behind. Georgie willed herself to be still, more still than a stone statue that was *really* a stone statue and not some freakish animated handmaiden of chaos chasing innocent girls around museums for kicks. Georgie held her breath as the lion goddess tested the air with her wide lion nose, hoping that she was too far away for the goddess to sniff her out. Finally, the Sakhmet turned and stalked down the hallway. Georgie waited a few more anxious minutes and then crept out of the display, crawling under the velvet rope this time.

Exit, she thought. *Where the heck is the exit?*

She glanced up. Hanging from the ceiling was a red exit sign. She followed it, but it merely led her into another gallery with the same sort of room displays as the first. She doubled back, hoping to find a way out, but all she found were more fussy rooms filled with more fussy furniture. She couldn't tell if the rooms were different from the first she'd seen, if the red or pink or powder blue furniture in front of her was the same red or pink or powder blue furniture she'd just been looking at. She ran this way and then that way, sure that she was to be trapped for ever in a haze of clawed feet and massive gold tassels. Maybe she was going in circles, which was why the low scratch of stone feet seemed to be coming from every direction.

Or maybe the Sakhmets were closing in.

Maybe they were right behind her.

She ducked through a doorway she was almost positive that she hadn't ducked through before and almost laughed with relief when she saw that she had reached the Modern Art wing. Surely there was a way out here. She passed the Picassos and the Giacomettis and everything in between, making a huge loop around the displays, only to realise that there were just two exits in and out of the Modern Art wing and neither of them led outside the building.

Nearly crying with frustration, Georgie again turned around. Her heart thudded against her abused rib cage. Her ruined hands burned as they tightened around the book in her arms. She wished Bug were with her, wished it so hard and so deeply that she was sure she could bring him back to life all on her own if only she could escape the museum and get to him.

Scratching noises sounded to her left. Georgie shot right, running straight into a large stairwell. The stairwell! The stairwell that could be seen from the museum's entrance! Another right turn brought her into the atrium. She ran past the visitors' booth and stopped short. Guarding the doors were three goddesses, each of them prowling back and forth, arms spread wide, ensuring that no one, not even an invisible girl, would get past them.

Georgie whipped round.

And stared right into the face of another Sakhmet.

The stone goddess growled, sounding like two rocks

being scraped together. She raised her ankh high and brought it down hard. Georgie jumped sideways but not fast enough. The stone ankh thumped against Georgie's shoulder, sending bright bolts of pain down her left arm. Biting her lip to keep from screaming, she ran for the nearest doorway, hoping that this too wasn't blocked by the other Sakhmets. She didn't even know where she was running to, she didn't even register the items on display all around her until she lurched into a large room.

She was back at the Temple of Dendur.

Trapped.

Scratchy footsteps sounded behind her. She had no choice but to move forwards and hope that she could reach the doorway at the far end of the room before she was caught. Georgie careened wildly past the still pool of water gleaming in front of the Temple. And tripped over her own feet.

The book went flying, instantly appearing as soon as it left her hands.

Georgie fell into the water, the splashing sound reverberating off the walls of the gallery. Coughing and choking, she sat up in the shallow pool. All around her, Goddesses of Chaos loomed. Hewitt Elder scooped up the book from the ground.

"Thank you for bringing this back," she said. And then she said, "Ladies? Do what you must."

The Sakhmets closed in and Georgie closed her eyes.

"Meow."

Georgie's eyes flew open.

Noodle! But how...?

The little grey cat trotted into the room. The Sakhmets shrank back.

"What are you doing?" yelled Hewitt. "It's just a cat!"

But Noodle was not just a cat; as the Egyptians well knew and as we have forgotten, *no* cat is just a cat. When Noodle meowed, it sounded like the cracking of thunder, the splitting of sky. The Sakhmets fell to their knees before her, pressing their lion faces against the floor.

"No," Hewitt whispered.

"Yes," said Georgie. She climbed from the pool.

Hewitt's eyes followed the wet footsteps Georgie left on the floor. She clutched her precious library book of death and rebirth to her chest. "It's mine," she said. "You can't take it from me."

Georgie grabbed the book out of her hands. "Watch me."

Hewitt wrung her now-empty hands. "That's not the only book that can do powerful things," she said. "There are so many books in the library. So many. Don't you want to know who you are? Don't you want to know what you can do? There are books in the library that can teach you. I can get them for you. We can be friends."

"Friends?" said Georgie. "No, we're not going to be

friends! Why did you do this? Why did you cause all this chaos? Because nobody wanted to read your stupid poetry any more? Because nobody was paying attention to you? Because someone made more money? Because someone was more popular?"

"Oh, what do you know?" said Hewitt, her eyes flashing, no longer trying to plead with Georgie. "You've never done anything but get kidnapped by some lunatic. You don't know what it's like to live in a world where the crooked son of a gangster gets more attention than you do."

Georgie thought of Bug lying cold and alone on the banks of the East River and fury pulsed in her veins. She raised the leather book and smacked Hewitt right in the face. *Wham!* Hewitt fell back on her bum, her hand on her cheek.

"That," Georgie said, popping into view, "was for Bug." She turned her back on Hewitt. "Hey, Noodle,"

"Rrrow," Noodle replied.

"Not like I really have to ask this, but do you think you have things under control here for a while?"

The little cat yawned.

Georgie nodded. "I'll take that as a yes."

The cabbie wouldn't let Georgie in the car until she showed him several wadded bills that she found in the pocket of her jeans. Still, he wasn't happy about driving her.

"Whaddya do?" the cabbie barked, taking in her wet clothes and bedraggled hair. "Fall in the East River?"

Georgie was in no mood to make up a story. "Yes, actually, I did."

The cabbie rolled his eyes. "Uh-huh. So, where to?"

He rolled his eyes even harder when she told him and wouldn't agree to stop on the side of the highway near the Brooklyn Bridge until she showed him two more wet and crumpled bills. Large bills.

"I know I should ask you where you got all this money, kid," he said. "But I ain't gonna ask you. You'll probably tell me that your rich daddy gave it to you."

"Something like that," Georgie said. She climbed out of the cab, her arm and shoulder screaming where the Sakhmet's ankh had hit her. She wondered vaguely if something was broken. But she didn't care. She scrambled down the rocks of the shore, nimble as a mountain goat (not that she noticed this). She kept thinking: What if someone moved him? What if Bug is gone? How would she ever find him?

But Bug was just where she'd left him.

Except he wasn't alone.

"Give me one good reason why I can't bite him," said Roma.

"OK," Phinneas replied. "He's dead."

"Yeah, so are you!" Roma said. Crows circled her and she swatted at them.

Phinneas tossed his hair from his brow. "There is a difference, you know."

Roma stomped her foot. "I don't care! I want to bite him!"

It was then that Phinneas saw Georgie. "Hey, look who's here." Georgie wasn't sure if she was imagining things or not, but Phinneas seemed to be thrilled to see Georgie standing there. (As thrilled as a vampire could be, anyway.) "You made it," he said.

Roma smiled at Georgie in triumph. "If I can't bite him, I'm going to bite her." She charged at Georgie. But before she could reach her, a bluish-grey tentacle popped from the water, grabbed Roma's ankle, and tripped her.

Roma kicked and screamed. "Will you stop doing that?!"

"Every time we try to get near the body, the octopus smacks us with a tentacle," Phinneas explained to Georgie. "Mandelbrot got bored, so he left us to guard the body just in case you survived the fall. And here you are. We're supposed to bite you. But I don't think the octopus is going to let us do that, either. Haven't seen anything like that before. Kind of interesting."

"Interesting!" shrieked Roma, getting to her feet. "That's not interesting! It's horrible! It's a slimy, awful, disgusting, totally gross—"

Another tentacle reared up and smacked Roma upside

the head, removing her long red wig in the process. Roma shrieked and tried to grab it, but the octopus held it just out of her reach. Her short dishwater-blond hair was so thin her scalp showed through.

Phinneas ignored Roma. "What do you have there?" he said, gesturing to the book that Georgie held.

Georgie thought fast. "A schoolbook."

Phinneas frowned. "That's not a schoolbook. I've seen that book before, that's..." He trailed off, an astonished expression dropping over his perennially bored countenance.

"What?" said Roma. "What is it?"

"Nothing," Phinneas said. "Stupid mortal stuff, that's all."

Georgie watched Phinneas carefully. "So you don't mind if I read it to Bug?"

Phinneas's eyes seemed to glow with some vampirish semblance of excitement. "No, I don't think I'd mind that at all. I think I'd like to see that. I think that would be very interesting."

"Very interesting," said Roma. "You don't think anything is very interesting. You didn't even think *I* was very interesting, though I'm the most interesting person in the universe. I have my own line of deodorants!"

"Of course you do," said Phinneas.

He followed Georgie as she sat next to Bug. She hated to

see Bug like this, smeared with dirt and weird East River slime, pale and...

Quickly, she opened the yellowed pages of the book and started to read:

"Every day is like a flower
Waiting for the rain
Needing life's sustaining force
To bloom and bloom again.
And you are like the water
That falls upon the earth
That nourishes this garden
And gives each day its worth."

She frowned. What the heck was this? She kept reading. *"'May your dreams come true, today and every day, and your wishes, too, as you go along life's way.'"*

Another page: *"'Roses are red, violets are blue . . . .'"*

"This is like a bunch of bad greeting cards!" Georgie said.

"Well," said Phinneas. "Seems you've been tricked."

"Georgie's been tricked!" Roma sang. "That's so fab™!"

Georgie frantically flipped the pages of the book looking for the incantations, but all she found were reams of bad poetry. No, she thought. No, no, no! It couldn't be! "This has to work," she said. "It just has to. Maybe you have to read these stupid things in a special order or something. Maybe there's a pattern."

All of a sudden, she thought of what Agnes had written in her last note, the thing that Georgie didn't understand. *"The world only seems crazy. There is pattern. You find it if you look hard enough."*

"Connections. Patterns," she said.

"What do you mean?"

"I don't know what I mean!" Georgie wailed. "Just something somebody told me."

"Oh," said Phinneas, his voice tinged with disappointment. "I hope you can figure it out. Otherwise, your friend will stay dead."

"Ead-day," said Roma.

Ead-day. Georgie stared at Roma. "What did you just say?"

"Pig Latin," Phinneas said. "She picked that up from Mandelbrot. He's always going on in pig Latin."

Georgie flashed on what Hewitt had said in the museum: *"I wouldn't have known how to use* The Book of the Undead *to reanimate things if I hadn't got the idea from Mandelbrot."*

"That's it!" said Georgie.

"What's it?" Phinneas asked.

"I know what to do," she said. She laid one hand on Bug's chest.

To her surprise, Phinneas laid his own cold hand on top of hers. When she glanced at him questioningly, he flicked his eyes towards Roma, who was throwing rocks at the giant octopus (which the octopus casually batted away). He said: "Let's just say that this death thing is not so fab."

Georgie began to read, the pig Latin tripping off her tongue like the most ancient of chants: *"Very-ey a-day s-iay ike-lay a lower-fay, aiting-way or-fay he-tay, ain-ray, eeding-nay, ife's-lay, ustaining-say, orce-fay, o-tay, loom-bay nd-ay loom-bay gain-ay."*

After she read the first two poems, Bug's fingers began to twitch. After five, his legs began to jerk. Phinneas covered Georgie's hand with his own as Bug suddenly gasped, his lungs filling with air. When she reached the last word of the very last poem, Bug's enormous blue eyes fluttered and opened. He blinked at Georgie, opening his mouth to speak. His first words could have been anything: Where am I? What happened? What's going on?

Instead, he said, "It's you," in a tone close to wonder.

Georgie closed the book and smiled. "Who else would it be?"

Chapter 27

Chaos

Bug and Georgie only had a few moments to enjoy Bug's rebirth before the arrival of the police helicopters, the squad cars, the fire trucks, the ambulances, the federal agents, the news reporters, the camera crews, the paparazzi, Solomon and Bunny Bloomington, Harvey "Juju" Fink, and a bunch of old ladies who claimed they were a book club. They all converged on that scrubby, rocky scrap of the East River shore, everyone talking at once. Questions were asked, answers demanded, photos snapped, clues investigated, rivers dredged, news stories filmed, threats levelled, tears shed. But even with all of this activity, nobody seemed to know exactly what had happened to Bug Grabowski and Georgetta Bloomington.

And most of them never would.

What was clear was that something terrible *had* happened to them and that something had involved vicious and shadowy characters filled with dangerous ideas. With that in mind, Bug and Georgie were whisked off to a private hospital to be checked out by medical professionals. The oddly pale young man who had been found with them was also taken to a hospital. This young man claimed to remember nothing about his life except for his name, which he claimed was Phinneas. He told reporters that he wished Georgie and Bug the best and hoped to get a job working with children one day, perhaps as a history teacher.

Another cause of speculation: the mysterious disappearance of Roma Radisson. In the weeks following the East River Incident, as the press was calling it, Roma was often spotted frequenting the hottest late night clubs, but no one – not her parents, not the police – could confirm this, and no one could actually find her. When questioned about Roma, her friends London England and Bethany Tiffany spouted a story so outrageous that their parents sent them to boarding schools in Switzerland to cure them of their obvious delinquency.

Mandelbrot, however, was found and charged with the kidnapping and assault of Georgetta Rose Aster Bloomington and Sylvester "Bug" Grabowski. After his arrest, the value of his artwork skyrocketed, a piece called *Anarchy Rocks* commanding a quarter of a million dollars at auction.

Also interesting was the appearance of former child prodigy Hewitt Elder at One Police Plaza. In her possession was a Giacometti sculpture that had been stolen from the Metropolitan Museum of Art some weeks before, a statue called *Dog*. She claimed to have been brought to the station by half a dozen "Goddesses of Chaos" commanded by a small grey cat, but the police could not locate said goddesses or said cat. Though Hewitt was charged with the theft of the statue, she was declared mentally unfit for trial and sent to a facility in Idaho for treatment. "Tragically," said the newspapers, "the prognosis isn't good."

As for Bug and Georgie, Georgie was treated for a cracked shoulder bone and Bug was treated for a concussion from a blow to the head. Bug and Georgie had told them enough about what happened that the Bloomingtons could have Mandelbrot arrested, but they suspected that more sinister forces were at work. Even more disturbing: they had tried to visit The Professor for some answers, but his apartment was empty.

So, all three Bloomingtons gathered around Bug's bed in the private hospital. With them were Noodle and Pinkwater, both of whom had played their parts in this strange story. But the whole story had yet to be put together, and the Bloomingtons wanted every detail.

"You have to tell us again what happened," Bunny said.

"And that means *everything* that happened," said Sol. "From the very beginning. And don't leave anything out. We promise we won't be angry. Or at least, we'll try not to be."

"First, though, I brought you these." Bunny set a vase full of freesia plucked fresh from Solomon's desk drawer and carpeting on Bug's bedside table. Bug inhaled deeply of the now-fragrant air as if the mere act of breathing was a gift. Which, Georgie supposed, it was.

"And then there's this," said Georgie, handing Bug a copy of the newspaper. She pointed to the lead article.

GIANT OCTOPUS GOES ON RESTAURANT RAMPAGE;

EVADES CAPTURE IN EAST RIVER

Diners in a South Street Seaport eatery got the shock of a lifetime yesterday evening when a giant octopus pulled itself out of the East River and went on a rampage.

"It stole my lobster!" a distraught female diner told reporters.

"It ate my clams casino. And my scampi!" another said.

A man reported that the monster "tickled" him under the chin, though there were no witnesses to this particular incident.

Before animal control units and scientists from area aquariums could be dispatched, the octopus escaped back into the East River. This morning, a squad of police divers and local fisherman went into the river to see if the monster could be photographed. The police released the following statement:

"At 6 a.m., city police divers and several scientists dived into the waters next to South Street Seaport. We did locate the creature and attempted to photograph it, immobilise it, and bring it to the surface for further study. The octopus grabbed one of our officers, flipped him over a tentacle, and spanked him. Then it spat clouds of ink at us before disappearing. Needless to say, we didn't capture the animal. But we did get some cool photos."

Experts at the American Museum of Natural History say that cephalopods are bright and playful, and antics such as these are not out of the ordinary. What is out of the ordinary is the immense size of the animal, which had limbs reported to be seven metres in length, making it more than thirteen metres from tip to tip. The existence of the monster smashes all previous theories of the bulk of giant octopi as well as their habitat.

The sighting of this spectacular creature also calls to mind the assertions of Bug "Sylvester" Grabowski, who had claimed to have been pulled off a dock by a sea monster at the very same port a month ago.

"Maybe," said the chief of police, "that boy was telling the truth after all."

"Maybe I was telling the truth," said Bug. "I guess that's a start."

"Speaking of starting," Solomon said, "this whole thing started with the octopus. What happened then?"

Bug and Georgie took turns telling the story. The octopus, the vampires, the statue, the sloth, Mandelbrot, the book club ladies and how all of them connected in a seemingly random but nonetheless powerful pattern. When Bug reached the part about Georgie hanging from the Brooklyn Bridge, Bunny Bloomington cried out and hugged her daughter. When Georgie told of Bug's death on the shores of the East River, Bunny just cried. Both Solomon and Bunny held their breath as Georgie related the details of the chase through the Metropolitan Museum of Art and the blank horror of the Sakhmets.

"Noodle saved me," said Georgie. "She found me just like

she found me in the alley that first time back when I lived in the orphanage, didn't you, Noodle?"

Noodle meowed in agreement, looking very satisfied with herself, the way any cat would.

"And Pinkwater found us," said Bunny Bloomington. "He rang the doorbell! I have no idea how he figured out how to do that. And then he zoomed around the apartment chirping 'Mayday!' and 'Danger!' We had no idea what he was talking about."

Solomon said, "But Agnes did. She told us to follow the bird and save 'good Polish boy with good Polish name'."

"Good boy!" chirped Pinkwater. He bonked Bug in the cheek.

"Dad, Agnes knows things," said Georgie. "She really does. She's been like some kind of fairy godmother. You know, if fairy godmothers really existed." Georgie cleared her throat. "I think she's been watching out for me."

"Yes," Solomon replied. "For which I am very thankful." He leaned forwards. "Georgie, I know we haven't been your parents for very long. And maybe we didn't think about how hard it might be for you to adjust to having us around. Maybe we've been a little too overprotective. But you understand now why we're overprotective."

Georgie said, "I was afraid that the vampires would get you. I wanted to save you."

"It's not your job to keep us safe," said Solomon. "It's our job to keep *you* safe. But we can only do that if you're honest with us." He looked at Bug. "You are special. And because of that, people are going to notice you and not always for the right reasons. You have to talk to us. You have to keep telling us what is going on with you, even if we annoy you sometimes, even if you'd rather not. Do you promise to try?"

"Yes," said Georgie. "I promise."

"And that goes for you too, Bug. As a matter of fact, I think that it might be a good idea for you to move into our building. There's a vacancy now that Mrs Hingis has moved out."

"Mrs Hingis?" Bug said. "*Imogen* Hingis?"

"Yes," said Solomon. "How did you know?"

Bug looked at Georgie. "She was one of the book club ladies. She was there with Mrs Vorona. The women who asked me to steal the book for them."

"Old crow!" chirped Pinkwater.

"Oh!" said Mrs Bloomington, flushing angrily. "If I ever see that dotty Mrs Hingis again, I will give her a piece of my mind. What was she thinking, putting the two of you in such danger. Why, I ought to call the police right now!"

Pinkwater helpfully made siren noises. Noodle joined in with some strangled meowing.

Solomon put his arm around his wife. "It's OK," he said. "It's all over now. It's all over."

"Almost over," said a voice.

They all turned. And stared. In the doorway stood The Professor. He was soaking wet, his coat dripping on the floor, his grassy hair sparkling with droplets. The Answer Hand had a ribbon of seaweed wound around its fingers that it was struggling to remove.

"Professor!" said Georgie. "What happened to you?"

"Same thing that happened to you, I think," The Professor said gruffly, pulling the seaweed from the wriggling hand. "I fell into the East River. I managed to find a piece of driftwood to cling to for a while. I imagine you didn't know there was a tiny island the size of a studio apartment off the coast of the city? Neither did I. Anyway, after a while I was eventually rescued by a rather large—"

"Octopus," Bug finished. "But did you fall into the East River in the first place? Did the octopus pull you in?"

"No," The Professor said. "It's a long story. Let's just say a rather unsavoury character chased me into the storm drain right before high tide. I preferred drowning in the East River to having a conversation with Mr Fuss. He's a little too accident-prone for my taste. Who knows what he would have done?"

"Wait!" said Georgie. "Did you say Mr Fuss?"

"Yes. Why?"

"We met him! At your apartment! He was packing up all your stuff."

"Really?" said The Professor. "Interesting. I'll have to talk to him about that."

"I thought you didn't want to have a conversation with him," said Bug.

"Well, sometimes we all have to do things we'd rather not. Besides, I'll be meeting him at a safe place. No storm drains this time."

"Where?" Georgie asked.

"Trust me. I'll be fine."

Georgie bit her lip. "You should know that some old ladies have your pen. *The* pen."

Told you, signed The Answer Hand.

"Yes," The Professor said. "I know that. I've already spoken with them about that."

"And I have your book," Georgie said. She searched in her backpack and handed the leather-bound volume to the old man.

"Haven't seen this in a long time," said The Professor. "Thank you."

"I hope you keep a better eye on the book than you did the pen," Bug said.

"Sylvester!" Bunny Bloomington said. "That wasn't a very nice thing to say."

"But it's a true thing," said The Professor. "I promise not to let this get into the wrong hands."

"Good," said Bug, yawning widely. "Because I'm getting pretty tired of saving the city all the time."

Bunny took a deep breath of the air that smelled of freesia, of spring, of everything. She smiled at Bug and then at Georgie. "It's OK now, isn't it? Everything's OK."

A nurse walked into the room carrying a lunch tray, almost dropping it when she saw the menagerie in front of her. "What do you think you're doing?" she said. "There are no animals allowed in this hospital! And you're only supposed to have two visitors at any one time!" She set the tray in front of Bug and wagged her finger at him. "You're lucky to be alive!"

"Yes," said Georgie, slipping her hand into Bug's. "Yes, we are."

The Chapter After the Last

Fussy

The pavement glistened as Mrs Vorona brushed the rain off the shoulders of her black coat and rapped softly on the library doors. It was midnight, warm enough for condensation to fog the glass and obscure the face of the man who opened the door.

"Hello, Mrs Vorona," said the man.

"Good evening, Mr Fuss," she replied.

"Lovely night. I always love rain in the springtime."

"Hmmm," Mrs Vorona said. That she didn't care much for Mr Fuss was obvious in the expression of distaste and disapproval she wore. Not that Mr Fuss was interested in anyone's approval.

The two didn't bother with any more pleasantries. Mr Fuss led the way upstairs to the Arents Collection room. He pulled the volume on Cuban cigars and opened the secret passageway to the library's basement vault. They chose to walk down the spiral staircase – Mr Fuss because he enjoyed walking, Mrs Vorona because she would have to change forms to fly and she didn't want to drop what she was carrying.

They reached the basement. The stroll past the numerous shelves was slow and mostly silent, except for the soft, distant scrape of stone paws against concrete floor.

"Patience and Fortitude making the rounds," Mr Fuss murmured.

"I know," Mrs Vorona replied a bit too forcefully.

Mr Fuss merely smiled.

After a time, Mr Fuss and Mrs Vorona found themselves at the very end of the library's basement vault, at the wall in which two heavy metal doors were set. Ignoring the door on the right, Mr Fuss grabbed the round handle of the door on the left and wrenched it open with one strong yank. Inside hung an ornate, wrought-iron lift.

"Almost looks like a birdcage, doesn't it?" said Mr Fuss.

Mrs Vorona shot him a glare before opening the door of the lift and stepping inside. Mr Fuss joined her. He pressed a red button next to the door. The lift lurched and then began its slow descent. One minute, two minutes, three minutes passed. Mrs Vorona could hear the eerie howls of the subway cars careening through nearby tunnels.

The lift stopped. Mr Fuss unfastened the gate. Mrs Vorona stepped out into a vast cavern that appeared to have been chipped by hand out of the grey bedrock under the city. Underfoot lay a mosaic of tiles in shades of blue, grey and green. All around the cavern, medieval-looking wood and iron doors concealed storage rooms, labs and other areas about which Mrs Vorona could only guess. In the centre of the room was a still pool. A very tall man in a pin-striped suit stood beside the pool, feeding the koi – the large goldfish – who lived in it.

"Mr Knickerbocker," said Mr Fuss. "Mrs Vorona is here."

The man turned. He was grey as a grave. "Mrs Vorona. Good of you to come all the way down to see me."

"Of course," Mrs Vorona said.

"I think you have something for me."

"Yes, I do." Mrs Vorona reached into her black coat and pulled out the silver pen. This she handed to the man called Mr Knickerbocker. Behind Mrs Vorona, Mr Fuss frowned.

Mr Knickerbocker admired the pen. "You've witnessed its use?

"I've seen the result."

Mr Knickerbocker said, "Thank you for bringing it to us. We wouldn't want it to get into the wrong hands again."

"Then perhaps you might consider destroying it,"

Mrs Vorona said. "It's too dangerous. Far too dangerous."

Mr Knickerbocker tipped his head. "I'll take that under advisement."

Mrs Vorona gave a curt nod. "I'll show myself out."

"Mrs Vorona, we at the library really do appreciate your work."

Mrs Vorona gave a curt nod.

"One more thing."

Mrs Vorona looked back over her shoulder.

"I think you should let Mr Fuss take you." Mr Knickerbocker hesitated, picking his words carefully. "Let's just say that Patience and Fortitude aren't the only guardians here at the library."

Mr Fuss held the front door open for Mrs Vorona. "Thanks so much for stopping by," he said in his relaxed and mild voice.

Mrs Vorona rolled her eyes and pushed past him. She was only outside for a moment before her body seemed to collapse in on itself, shrinking and morphing into the sleek black body of a crow. Mr Fuss watched without surprise as the crow launched itself into the air as if it couldn't get away fast enough.

After Mrs Vorona had gone, Mr Fuss's relaxed expression morphed into one of rage and confusion. He stormed back into the Arent Collection room, down the wrought-iron staircase and through the storage basement. The pen! The whole time the crows had had the pen? How was it possible? He stopped to kick one of the walls. Then he kicked it again. Patience, who was watching from the gloom, licked her lips. But then Mr Fuss stopped kicking the wall and made his way back to where his employer waited at the koi pond, his countenance back to its regular state of bland fussiness.

"There should be an easier way to get here," said Mr Fuss fussily.

"If there were an easier way to get here, I'd have way too many visitors. And you know how I feel about visitors," Mr Knickerbocker said.

"I remember what happened to the last one," said Mr Fuss. He looked pointedly at the koi pond.

Deitrich Knickerbocker said nothing, silently watching his fish nibble at the flakes floating on the surface of the pond. Then he said: "You're losing your touch, Mr Fuss."

"Excuse me?" said Mr Fuss.

"Your touch. Your control. Your organisational skills, whatever you want to call them. You made a mess of things. I could call *you* The Chaos King."

Mr Fuss drew himself up to his considerable height. "I'm sure I don't know what you mean."

"No? I'm talking about a certain someone washed out into the East River."

"That," he said, "was entirely an accident."

"That accident happened to be my brother."

"It wasn't my fault that he ran through the storm drain at high tide," Mr Fuss whined.

Mr Knickerbocker shook his head. "You weren't even aware that he didn't have the pen."

"He refused to answer any of my questions! He ran away!"

"And what about the Punk? And the vampires?"

Mr Fuss's already cold blood ran colder. "Who?"

"The funniest part of it is that you had no idea you'd been double-crossed by your own people," Deitrich Knickerbocker said. "Or that they'd double-crossed each other. Mandelbrot went to see Hewitt Elder at the library. At first, he just wanted to be a famous artist, and then he decided if the pen was so special he should have it for himself. She, on the other hand, had other plans."

"I don't understand," Mr Fuss said.

"Hewitt Elder had *The Book of the Undead*. She was the one who used it to bring all those things to life."

"I don't know about any of this," said Mr Fuss.

"I *told* you not to go near the children. I *told* you they were not to be harmed. I even took a part-time position as a doorman to keep watch over Georgie Bloomington. Just in case you forgot your place and chaos ensued."

"I don't know what you're talking about," Mr Fuss said stiffly.

Mr Knickerbocker sighed. "There's a lot you don't know."

Out of the koi pond, a bluish-grey tentacle poked up through the water. Mr Fuss stared at it. "You don't want to do this," he stammered.

"Do what?" said Mr Knickerbocker.

The tentacle shot out of the water, grabbed Mr Fuss by the ankle, hung him upside down, and shook him. Out of his pocket fell his day planner. Mr Knickerbocker picked it up and began leafing through it as Mr Fuss was pulled into the koi pond. There was some violent thrashing and splashing. Then the water was still again.

Mr Knickerbocker was still leafing through the day planner when he felt a presence behind him. "Hello Professor," he said, before turning around.

"Deitrich," the man said. He was a small man with grass for hair. He held a mounted hand on a marble slab. An army of cats slinked around his legs.

"You found your cats, I see," Mr Knickerbocker said.

"They found me."

Mr Knickerbocker nodded. "As usual. You haven't changed. Except for the hair."

The Professor stared up at the other man's iron-grey head. "I could say the same for you." He reached down and let The Answer Hand pet one of the cats. "You should be more careful about the people you hire."

"I know," said Mr Knickerbocker. "I'm sorry. Once, he was the best."

"The best *what*?"

Mr Knickerbocker closed the day planner. "I was only trying to keep some things contained. Make sure that all of the truly dangerous stuff was safe in the library. It's my job. You know that."

"My brother, the ever-important Library Director."

"This city is crazy enough as it is," Deitrich said. "And you know you have a tendency to lose things. Remember that time we were kids? And you made that wireless telephone? Whatever happened to that?"

"I don't know. I dropped it somewhere," The Professor muttered.

"Uh-huh. You know that someone found it and now almost everyone has one. And then the pen. And the book!"

"I have the book right here," said The Professor, who patted his front pocket.

"That's not the point. You can't just go around inventing things and then throwing them to the wind."

The Professor considered this. "Why not?"

His brother took a step back. "What do you mean, why not? Because it will cause absolute chaos, that's why!"

"Deitrich," said The Professor. "With or without me, this city *is* absolute chaos. Where else can you find Dominicans,

Africans, models, Mongolians, hamsters and hipsters all living in the same place?"

"What are you talking about?"

"Think about it! It's absurd! It's absurd to live vertically in high-rises like beehives. It's absurd to cram into trains underground and hop like fleas above it. A place where you might not be an international celebrity but you could have a cup of coffee right next to one. It's impossible not to meet interesting people here. I know because I spent years trying to stay away from all of them, but I met them anyway."

Deitrich Knickerbocker's mouth dropped open. "What happened to you?"

The Answer Hand signed: *Do you have a fever?*

The Professor smiled, the first time in a long time, perhaps the first time in a hundred years. "I spent a lot of time stranded on a little island just off the coast of the city, a tiny island with nothing but some scrub brush and a few rocks. I learned something important there."

"What?"

"Roast lizard tastes a bit like chicken."

"And?"

"The city is chaos. *Life* is chaos. And isn't that what makes it beautiful?"

Deitrich Knickerbocker didn't speak for two full minutes, his mouth a round O of shock. Then his grave expression gave way to a smile, then to a chuckle, then to a great rolling burst of laughter. "You know, you might be right," he said, tossing the day planner into the koi pond. "You just might be right."

Don't miss the previous adventures
of Bug and Gurl (sorry, Georgie) in

The Invisible Girl

LAURA RUBY

The first book of the enchanting
Wall and the Wing stories.

"What the heck..." Bug began. "You can turn yourself invisible."
"Yes."
"You just turned me invisible, too."
Gurl bit her lip. "Yes."

Ever wanted to turn yourself invisible?

Gurl can, but life's still tough: Mrs Terwiliger is threatening to
starve her cat, rat men are chasing her in the street – and who is
that weird boy Bug who says he can fly? Join her as she struggles
to make sense of her new talent on a wild ride through a
magical New York City, where no one can stay invisible for ever...